CHASING EXES

MIKE

PUBLISHING PARTNERS

Publishing Partners
Port Townsend, WA

Copyright 2021 Mike Neun

Library of Congress Control Number: 2021907503

ISBN 978-1-944887-66-7
eBook ISBN 978-1-7369183-1-9

INTRODUCTION

This is a work of fiction, which means everything is made up. There is no Jitters coffee shop in Ketchum, Idaho. I saw that name forty years ago and loved it, so I put it in. I put motels anywhere I wanted, gave them any name I felt like, made towns bigger or smaller to suit my purposes, and there is no Chaipon's Siam Restaurant in Boise, Idaho. I also made up casinos that don't exist and I've never been to Déjà Vu Showgirls club in Las Vegas. For all I know it's a flower shop. If any of this comes true it's a ridiculous coincidence, not evidence of the second coming of Nostradamus. The characters are drawn out of thin air and I reveled in the God-like power to invent all their actions. In short, this is a cheerful, post-pandemic fantasy. I like to break new ground.

ACKNOWLEDGMENTS

Huge thanks to Todd Sawyer, a Seattle writer/comedian now living in Chiangmai who taught me the ultimate secret—writing doesn't matter, re-writing does. Doug Moeller and Marcia Breece got my first book published when I was content to give it away. Obviously, we made millions. Mike Williams, a Seattle/Chiangmai friend who sailed around the world and wrote a fine book about it, helped edit. My wife, Jintana, and her Thai family have given me the best years of my life. My brother, Tim, gave me encouragement plus years of astoundingly funny emails. He has a book on Amazon called, "Ear to Ear". It is terrific. My sister, Nancy, overcame addiction and is one of the strongest people I know. Her life story would make a great movie. I'll stop here, knowing there are tons of people who have made my life better. Thank you all.

CHAPTER 1

Protection.

She needed protection.

Kirsten Haugen sat by her picture window and realized she was afraid to walk the streets of Seattle. Businesses were boarded up, unemployment hovered at thirty percent and the city still suffered fallout from the surprise third wave of the pandemic. Seattle, once an intelligent, beautiful city, had become dangerous. Kirsten was a young, single woman. It was not a good combination.

This had been her dream apartment—two bedrooms, a cozy kitchen, and a living room with sliding glass doors to a balcony with a beautiful view of Lake Washington, the floating bridge and Mercer Island in the distance. Now it had become an upscale prison, in lockdown.

The buzzer rang, announcing the grocery delivery. She grabbed a sharp kitchen knife and put it in her purse, then took the elevator down to the lobby of Sherwood Apartments. Outside the glass door, now reinforced with steel bars, she could see the delivery van and the big, teen-aged kid waiting on the front steps with boxes of groceries. He held up the correct order form and she took out her keys and unlocked the locks. She opened the door and reached into her purse as he carried the boxes inside. He was over six feet tall, in jeans and a long-sleeved shirt with the store logo on it.

"Want me to take them up?" he asked.

"That won't be necessary," she said.

"It'll just take a minute."

"No." she said firmly. "I'll do it."

"No problem, I'm just trying to do good work. My family depends on this."

Kirsten smiled warily.

"I understand, but it's better if you stay down here."

She released the knife she'd been gripping, took money out of her wallet and paid him. Then she gave him a bigger tip than she'd planned.

"Thank you," he said.

He turned and left. She made sure the door was firmly locked and shoved the boxes over to the elevator. She admitted to herself that she'd been nervous, maybe even scared. Damn it.

Fear was new to her. She'd been a college athlete, a pole vaulter and basketball player. She was no shrinking violet, yet the upheavals in society had everyone on edge. When the elevator came, she shoved the boxes inside and rode up three floors. The doors opened and there stood Tommy, her next door neighbor. She looked down. He was a small man.

"Hi, Tommy," she said.

"Hi."

"Going down?"

"Yeah, but I'm in no hurry. Need some help?"

"That would be great. Thank you."

Five months they'd been neighbors and It may well have been their longest conversation. She pushed the stop button. They shoved the boxes out and carried them to her door. She opened it and they carried the boxes in and set them on her counter.

"Thank you," said Kirsten. "Want some coffee?"

"No thanks," he said, and backed hastily out the door. Kirsten loved the fact that he was no threat but she wished she could at least talk to him. Since she'd gotten divorced and lost her job a lot of her friends had faded away. It was hard to make new ones these days.

She put away the groceries. She longed to go for a run along the lake, but that wasn't wise. There were too many desperate people out there. She'd come to hate her treadmill, but it was the only option so she put up a movie and ran for thirty minutes. She'd do yoga and lift weights that evening. It gave her structure and she liked staying in shape. She was living on her savings and looking for work. Any work. She figured she could last another six months if she existed on ramen noodles and pop tarts.

CHAPTER 2

Next door, Tommy Price, back from checking for mail, sat in front of his computer on a three-hundred-dollar office chair he'd bought before the crash. His feet dangled off the floor. Tommy was five feet, five inches tall.

He cursed himself for not accepting Kirsten's offer of coffee, but that was too painful to contemplate. Him? Talk casually with the hottest woman he'd ever known? Not a chance.

Only in Seattle could a black woman be named Kirsten Haugen. Her skin was the color of chocolate, but with that name her dad had to be Norwegian. She was tall—at least five-ten—athletic, and stunningly good looking. Tommy, on the other hand, was small, skinny, pale, with blue eyes and brown hair. She was major league gorgeous, he was Class-D utility infielder handsome. He fantasized, and that was it.

He logged on using a complicated password he changed frequently. He worked for Google, using the hacking skills he'd perfected as a kid to help patch up software and keep everything running. He was hours into his programming when the door buzzer buzzed. What the hell? He never had visitors.

He looked through the peep hole. It was Kirsten,

and she held up a bottle of wine. Tommy was stunned. He opened the door.

"Hi Neighbor," she said. "I'm bored and we've never talked. Do you drink wine?"

"Yes," he stammered, "I drink wine."

He stood there.

"Should I open it here in the hall?" she asked, smiling.

"No! No, come on inside. I'll get some glasses."

He hustled to the kitchen while she wandered into his living room. It was much the same as hers, with big windows and a glass door to the balcony. The sofa and matching easy chair looked far more expensive than hers, done in soft leather, with a heavy, cut-glass coffee table between them. Computer magazines were laid out neatly. His shelves had lots of books—science fiction, mysteries, technology texts—no surprises there. Tommy came back with a corkscrew and two wine glasses, trying desperately to stay calm.

"It's not a great wine," said Kirsten, "but it's the best I could afford."

"No problem. I'm not a connoisseur."

He struggled a bit with the corkscrew but managed to get the cork out and pour the wine. They clinked glasses and sipped, then sat down, with him in the easy chair, her on the sofa. She was wearing jeans, a UW sweatshirt and running shoes, and her hair was getting close to a full afro. Going to a salon was dangerous these days.

"How long have we been neighbors?" she asked.

"I moved in five months ago and you were here already."

"Yeah, five months. And how many conversations have we had?"

"You mean other than 'Hello, how are you?'"

"Yeah."

"None?"

"Right. So I was sitting in my apartment with no one to talk to and I thought it was time we got to know each other. Is that okay with you?"

"Sure. But I should warn you, conversation is not my strong point."

"Don't worry. We can drink, relax, and you don't have to talk if you don't want to."

"Okay."

"But first, you have to ask the question."

"What question?"

"The one I always get asked. How did a black girl get named Kirsten?"

Tommy laughed.

"That never crossed my mind."

"Bullshit."

Tommy laughed again.

"So, how did a black girl get named Kirsten?"

"I'm mixed race. Norwegian dad, black mom."

He'd guessed right.

"Okay, your turn," he said. I bet you're dying to ask how a middle-class white guy got named 'Tommy.'"

She smiled.

"That has bothered me for months."

"I know. It baffles everyone. 'John' was taken."

She laughed. The wine was a godsend.

"I hope I didn't catch you at a bad time," she said.

"No, I was just doing some work, but I can do that anytime. Working from home gives me a lot of freedom."

"What kind of work?"

"I work for Google. Mostly trying to keep things up and running. The Internet's pretty sketchy these days. Then too, there are a lot of hackers out there running scams and trying to break past firewalls."

"Wow. You must be hell on wheels with computers."

"I'm pretty good," he admitted. "What about you? Are you working from home too?"

"No," she said sadly. "I lost my job."

"Damn. That's too bad. What were you doing?"

"Financial stuff. I was an analyst at a brokerage house. I looked for trends, studied world markets, that sort of thing."

"Wow. So you're an economist?"

"Yeah. That was my major at the university."

"Where'd you go to school?"

"The University of Washington here in Seattle. I had a basketball scholarship."

"No kidding. You must've been really good."

"I was a decent college player but not good enough for the pros. So I got a job with my Econ degree."

Tommy couldn't think of anything to say. There was a pause. Surprisingly, it didn't feel awkward.

"Where did you go to school?" she asked.

"Stanford. Computer science. I ended up in Palo Alto at the Google campus. I liked it there, but I got mugged one night."

"Mugged? Were you hurt?"

"No, luckily it was just a robbery, but other people had worse experiences, so I decided to come back to Seattle and work from home."

"Well, nice to finally meet you, Tommy."

"Can I ask you something?"

"Sure," she said.

"Why are you here? I know we're neighbors, but you'd be surprised how seldom a beautiful woman with a bottle of wine knocks on my door. Are you selling something? Have you found Jesus?"

She laughed delightedly.

"No, I'm not selling anything and I'm not religious. The truth is, I've been stuck in that apartment for weeks, afraid to go out and I'm desperate to talk to a real person. FaceTime just doesn't cut it."

"That's a relief. Some of the beautiful women who knock on my door try to sell me stuff."

"That happens often?"

"All the time. It's the old beautiful-woman-salesperson gambit."

"A well-known ploy."

"Luckily I don't fall for cheap tactics like that."

"What a man. Shall we come back to reality now?"

"Okay, but my fantasy world is a lot more exciting."

"How did you end up at Sherwood Apartments?"

"I lived here before," said Tommy, "for about a year. I worked in a startup here in town and loved it, so I came back. How about you?"

"When I was at the university I had friends who lived here. It was a great place and I swore someday I'd get an apartment. I never dreamed it would be during the plague years."

"Life is weird, isn't it?"

"Yeah. And if it weren't for the financial crash, this would be perfect. It's on the lake, beautiful view, pool down below, a nice dock, wild parties..."

"It was fun in the old days," said Tommy.

"Yeah."

"I guess it's as good a place as any to ride out the storm."

"It should be," she said, "but I have problems inside the building too," she said.

"Really? Someone bothering you? Want me to go beat the crap out of them?"

She smiled. The vision of Tommy in a brawl didn't really compute.

"That won't be necessary. Nothing has happened so far and I hope it works out."

"Want to talk about it?"

"Not now. Maybe later, over another bottle of wine."

Tommy liked that possibility.

"You think the pandemic is finally over?" she asked.

"It looks like it." said Tommy, "The second vaccine is working on the mutant strain, but the economy is trashed. That third wave put the nail in the coffin. Are you surviving okay?"

"Not really. No job opportunities out there."

"I hope something turns up. Some company must need a good analyst."

"I sure hope so. I see we've finished the bottle," she said.

"I'm sorry, I drink fast when I'm nervous."

"Are you still nervous?" she asked.

"A bit. I also think I'm borderline drunk. Am I slurring my words?"

"Not yet. I've enjoyed this."

"Next time I'll supply the wine. Thank you for coming over, it really brightened up my evening. I hadn't realized how much I missed talking to someone."

"Thank you too. I was getting depressed. And thank you for being a gentleman. Some guys would've tried to make more out of this."

"I find that hard to believe. Guys put moves on you?"

"It has happened."

"Well shame on them. How crude."

"I'm glad you didn't. It could've screwed up a really nice evening."

"Hey, just talking this long is a giant step for me."

"Well, don't be too humble. I had a good time and we should do it again."

"I'd like that."

He walked her to her door and said good night.

Back in his apartment, if Tommy had known how to dance he would've. Instead, he just smiled hugely, shook his head in wonder, and went back to work.

CHAPTER 3

Tommy found the little girl.

Sometimes he went down to the lobby to check for mail, and sometimes there actually was some. The post office delivered on random days, and he never knew when he'd get lucky.

He looked out the reinforced front door and there, huddled in the doorway, was a small figure. He walked over and took a careful look up and down the street. It could be a trap. Gangs would try anything to get into buildings and he was very careful.

It was a girl, very dirty, maybe eleven or twelve years old, wearing ratty old jeans, a ripped hoodie over a thin tee shirt, and shivering in the morning cold. He knew he shouldn't do it. There were thousands of kids out there, urchins, wandering the streets and trying to help them was like sticking your finger in a dam. Just then she looked up, with big brown eyes, and he moved involuntarily to unlock the locks. He finally got the door open.

"Hello," he said, again checking the road and the parking lots on either side of the building.

She said nothing, just stared at him.

"Are you hungry?"

She nodded.

"Come inside and I'll get you something to eat."

She mutely got up and came inside. He carefully locked the locks.

"Come with me," he said, and she followed him to the elevator. Her skin was brown, her face pinched, her hair matted and dirty. He looked down and saw she was wearing ragged Converse All Stars with holes in them. No laces. No socks. They rode up to the third floor and he walked her to his apartment, unlocked the door and led her into his living room. She stood there, taking it all in. Then she took his hand and led him into the bedroom, turned, and started to take off her clothes.

"No!" he said, panicked, "No! Stop. I don't want that."

What sort of hell was this? She raised her eyes and looked at him steadily.

"Come with me," he said.

He led her out of his apartment and down the hall. He knocked on Kirsten's door. He saw her eye looking at him through the peephole.

"Are you alone?" she called.

"I have a child with me."

She unlocked the locks, opened the door, and then looked at him and down at the little girl.

"Who is she?"

"I have no idea. She was in the front doorway, cold. I brought her up to my apartment to give her something to eat and she thought I wanted sex. I need help. She needs help."

"What do you want from me?" asked Kirsten.

"Can you clean her up? You can use my shower and

I have clothes she can wear. They'll be too big but they're better than what she's got. I'll cook something."

"You have enough food?"

"Sure. Are you hungry? I can fix breakfast for all of us."

Kirsten thought about it. Then she looked down at the skinny girl, who hadn't made a sound. Could she talk? The girl was very, very dirty and hugging herself.

"Okay," said Kirsten. "Do you have soap?"

"Don't you?"

"Yes, but I'm being very careful with my money and soap is expensive."

"We can take her to my place. You can use my soap and give her a shower. There's shampoo there too."

Shampoo. Kirsten had quit using shampoo, trying to save money. She was tempted to climb into the shower with the little girl, then laughed to herself. How desperate was she?

"Let me get my keys," she said.

Kirsten closed her apartment and locked the locks. Then she followed Tommy and the little girl into his.

Tommy showed them to the bathroom and went to get clothes. He had a small pair of low-rise briefs that he figured was better than whatever the little girl had. He found a pair of jeans, a belt, a tee-shirt and a sweatshirt. It would be safer if she didn't look girly. Shoes were a problem because his were too big, but he grabbed a pair of Adidas. He walked to the bathroom, knocked, and handed everything in. Then he went to the kitchen and started cooking breakfast.

He had six eggs left. It was time for a grocery delivery. He scrambled the eggs and made toast and coffee. He took his time, figuring the girl's cleanup could be a long process and he didn't want the food to get cold.

Thirty minutes later, Kirsten and the girl walked into the kitchen. The girl bolted to the table and started stuffing down food. She was obviously starving. Kirsten sat down and tried to take her time, but this was the best breakfast she'd seen in days and it was all she could do not to wolf it down too. Tommy realized he hadn't cooked enough, so he mixed up some pancake batter and poured it into the frying pan. In a couple of minutes he put a stack on the table, along with syrup. The girl watched every move. Tommy put two pancakes on her plate and she drowned them in syrup. Then she made them disappear.

When they were done, Tommy and Kirsten sat back, drinking coffee. The girl still hadn't said a word. She was very thin, swallowed up in his jeans and sweatshirt, and the shoes were too big but better than the All Stars. She had brown hair and brown eyes, and Tommy guessed she was mixed race, but he couldn't tell what. Part Filipino? Mexican? Black? He had no idea. She wasn't a beautiful child. Her teeth needed work. They were discolored and the two front ones were crooked. Kirsten had pulled the hair back into a pony tail and Tommy noticed the girl's ears were big. She was cute, he decided. Not beautiful but cute. Then again most kids were cute.

"Do you have a name?" asked Kirsten.

The little girl nodded.

"What is it?"

The girl just stared at her. Then she got up, walked over to the sofa, lay down and immediately fell asleep. Obviously she was full of food, warm, and totally worn out. Tommy went to the bedroom and got a blanket and pillow. He slipped the pillow under her head and covered her.

They returned to their coffee.

"I found a new toothbrush in your bathroom and gave it to her," Kirsten said, "I hope that's okay."

"Certainly. I'm guessing it's been a long time between brushings."

"And we used a lot of soap and shampoo. She was really dirty."

"No problem. I have more."

"Do you have a plan?" she asked.

"Nope. None. I just felt terrible seeing her in the doorway like that."

"Can you afford to keep her?"

"I suppose. I've still got the job. But I could get arrested. People see a grown man with a girl who isn't his..."

"Not good."

"There could be other problems. She's a street kid, so I assume she has learned to steal, lie, cheat, be violent, anything to get by. I'm a computer geek. I'm not equipped to deal with that."

"I see what you mean, and she could know bad people. If she tips them off that you've got all this stuff up here you might be looking at home invasion."

"I know. I may have made a huge mistake. If I let her go, there's no telling who she could tell and I'd be in danger. If I let her stay, she could steal me blind and run off. I may have bitten off more than I can chew."

The girl woke up that afternoon and they made sandwiches. She ate, and promptly went back to sleep, obviously still exhausted. They offered her Tommy's spare bed, but she wanted to stay in the room with them and sleep on the sofa. She made this known through gestures, and still hadn't said a word.

Tommy and Kirsten spent a lazy day watching TV and talking. That evening Kirsten and Tommy cooked pasta. Again Kirsten tried to speak to the girl.

"What's your name, sweetie?"

No answer. She just stared at Kirsten.

"How old are you?"

Again, nothing.

"Can you make any sounds at all? Can you sing?"

Kirsten softly started singing. "The itsy bitsy spider..."

The little girl smiled but said nothing so they continued eating. After dinner they sat on the sofa, the girl between them, and watched a couple old episodes of Cheers.

"I'm getting tired," said Kirsten. "Do you mind if I go to bed early?"

"No problem," said Tommy. "I might stay up awhile and do some work. Can she sleep at your place? Just tonight? If she sleeps here I'll look like a pedophile."

"I guess so, but we have to think this out."

Kirsten got up, took the girl's hand and walked to the door. The girl panicked and stopped. She didn't want to leave.

"We'll be just next door sweetie," said Kirsten, "and we can come back to Tommy's in the morning."

The girl held back. It was clear she wanted the three of them to stay in Tommy's apartment.

"I've got the spare bedroom," said Tommy. "You could stay here tonight and she could sleep with you. I'm sure she's scared."

"Okay," said Kirsten, "but just tonight. Tomorrow we have to sort this out."

She knelt down to the girl.

"Honey, I'm going to get my toothbrush and stuff. I'll be right back, okay?"

The girl nodded solemnly.

Five minutes later Kirsten was back, and she led the girl to the bathroom. She took a shower, with the girl sitting on the toilet seat watching every move. Kirsten looked at the shampoo, and couldn't resist. She poured a big dollop on her hand and reveled as she rubbed the suds into her hair. Luxury. And there was conditioner! What kind of guy has conditioner? She used some. Glorious. Had any woman ever traded sex for shampoo and conditioner? She was tempted.

After showering, she brushed her teeth and put on lotion. Then Kirsten gave the girl another shower, washed her hair thoroughly, and dried her off. She brushed out the girl's hair, which had been a tangled mess that morning and only now was showing signs of life. She gave her the lotion and the girl imitated Kirsten's moves, rubbing it into her arms, legs and body.

Her body had bruises, and Kirsten could only hope it was from the rough and tumble of the streets and not something worse. She'd brought back a tee shirt for the girl to wear to bed, but she wanted to put her new clothes back on. She obviously loved her jeans and sweatshirt, baggy as they were. The two of them left the bathroom, said good night to Tommy, and walked to the guest bedroom. They climbed under the covers and slept, hugging each other.

Tommy, back at his computer, brought up a website of missing children. He narrowed it down to Seattle and there were still hundreds of them. Families had fallen apart, liquor and drug use was off the charts, and the homeless were everywhere. He searched the pictures, but found no match.

CHAPTER 4

The next morning Tommy made waffles, toast, and cut up oranges and bananas. He again realized he needed to order groceries. They ate, and he poured more coffee for Kirsten and himself. They sat awhile.

"Are you okay?" he asked.

"I'm good for about six more months if I avoid luxuries, like actual food. I have to admit I'm getting tired of noodles. If nothing changes I'm going to be in big trouble."

They sipped coffee. Kirsten looked at the girl.

"How old do you think she is?" she asked.

"At first I thought maybe ten or eleven, but she's malnourished. What do you think? Twelve?"

"I guess so, but I haven't been around kids that much. What are you going to do with her?" she asked.

"I haven't the faintest idea. Do you want a little girl?"

She laughed.

"That'll bring my financial expectancy down to about two months."

"Yeah. Not a good solution."

Tommy paused.

"We could join forces," he said quietly.

"Really?"

"I'm not making a move here," he said, "really I'm not."

Kirsten smiled.

"Okay."

"I have the extra bedroom. You could give up your apartment and save rent. We can both watch her, make sure she doesn't cause trouble, and give her a chance at life."

Kirsten thought about that. It was out of the blue but it sure was tempting. She was so tired of being alone, and financially it would be a godsend. On the other hand, she'd gone through a messy, angry divorce and wanted no part of a new relationship.

"You sure you're not making a move?"

"You're joking."

"No, I'm serious. I'm just recovering from a divorce and I'm not up for complications."

"I'm not making a move."

"What if I meet the man of my dreams and bring him home?"

"No problem. You've got your own bedroom and the girl can sleep on the sofa. But I'm not making him breakfast. I have to draw the line somewhere."

She laughed.

"What if a woman comes on to you? Anyone with a job is a major stud on the dating scene."

"I found that out on Tinder. There are a lot of gold diggers out there."

"I could be one."

"I don't think so. You could have your pick of men. You don't need me."

MIKE NEUN

Kirsten never thought of herself as beautiful. She certainly wasn't a high fashion model—too athletic, her features too strong, and her dark hair way too unruly. Then too there was the racial thing, which could get tricky. She'd never had a problem meeting men, but she certainly had problems getting rid of them. Tommy, on the other hand, seemed safe enough.

"What do you think?" he asked, "Want a couple of roommates?"

"It is an attractive offer, but the wild card is the girl. What if she's got parents? What if some pimp has his hands on her? What if she is a thief, or belongs to a gang? She could be dangerous."

"I know," said Tommy. "Then too, we really don't know each other. You don't belong to a gang, do you?"

"No, no gangs. How about you? Are you using that computer to launder money for a drug cartel?"

"I wish. I bet it pays more than Google."

"How about a trial run?" she said. "Maybe a few days. We'll learn about each other and if it all goes belly up I can move back into my apartment."

"That sounds like a plan," said Tommy. "Let's try it."

And they did.

For a week they shared Tommy's apartment and spent a lot of it trying to guess the little girl's name. No luck. Finally, Kirsten said to her, "We have to have a name we can use, okay? Until we guess your real name?"

The little girl nodded.

"When I was a little girl, I had a favorite cousin named JoAnn but we all called her Jo. Can we use that?"

The little girl paused thoughtfully and then nodded.

"Okay, Jo it is."

Kirsten held out her hand.

"Hello, Jo, I'm Kirsten. Nice to meet you."

The little girl smiled and held out her hand. They shook. Then Kirsten took her over to Tommy, who was deeply engrossed in his computer.

"Tommy," she said, "This is our roommate with a new name. Meet Jo, short for JoAnn. Jo, this is Tommy."

Jo and Tommy solemnly shook hands.

"Nice to meet you, Jo," said Tommy. "We should celebrate. Do you like ice cream?"

Jo nodded happily.

"Chocolate sauce?"

Jo nodded again.

"And whipped cream?"

Jo gave a big thumbs up.

"Okay! Let's do it!"

Later, they watched Tommy's favorite old movie, Nothing to Lose, until Jo nodded off. Then Tommy and Kirsten opened a couple of beers and sat at the kitchen table.

"How did your parents get together?" Tommy asked.

"It was a long shot. My dad was from Norway and my mom was a black woman from Baltimore."

"Ah yes, the old Norway-Baltimore connection. How often have we heard that story?"

Kirsten smiled.

"Okay," said Tommy, "I give up. How did they meet?"

"Dad was a ship captain. Norwegians are famous for going to sea and he studied seamanship in Oslo. Then he got jobs on ships and worked his way up. He rose to captain on Elite Cruises and worked there for twelve years."

"And your mom?"

"She was a singer. She started in church as a little girl with a big voice. She also played the organ."

"Wow, multitalented."

"Damn straight. She moved into blues, rhythm and blues, pop, but never became a big star. She worked nightclubs and casinos, did a few guest shots on TV, and then ended up on cruise ships."

"Was she good?"

"She was killer good. My mom could sing. And she could play jazz piano like Nat King Cole."

"Why wasn't she a star?"

"Back then there was only room for one or two black stars at a time. You people didn't know it, but there was a quota system."

"By 'you people', you mean us white folks?"

"In a word, yes."

"Wow. I didn't know anything about a quota system, but then I'm clueless about the music business.

"You're not into rap? Hip hop? I find that amazing."

"I know. I look like a gangbanger with tons of street cred, but really I'm just a computer guy."

"Damn."

"So your mom got booked on the ship and fell in love with the handsome Norwegian captain, right?"

"Wrong. He fell in love with her first. My mom was a hot number."

"I believe that. Look at you."

"Easy big fella. That was close to a move."

Tommy paused.

"What?"

"Never, in my life, have I been called 'big fella.' I'm going to savor it."

Kirsten laughed.

"So they fell in love on a cruise ship. Storybook romance."

"Yes, but there were problems. Norwegians are pretty good about race but her people were shocked when she brought home that blond-haired white dude with a weird accent. To them he was from outer space."

"But it worked?"

"Oh yes, but they did have some problems on his ship. The passengers were mostly rich Americans and a few were far to the right, as in racist. But my mom had dealt with that all her life and won them over, mostly by being funny, talented, and really strong. She was amazing."

"Where are they now?"

As soon as he said it, Tommy saw he shouldn't have asked.

"You know those ships that were quarantined during the pandemic?"

"Yeah."

"Mom and dad were on one of them. They did their best to help the crew, and then they got sick, and then.... they died."

"Well damn. I'm so sorry."

They sat in silence, drinking their beer. Then Kirsten spoke up,

"Next time, you tell me your story."

"It's like a lot of computer guy stories, filled with lust, power, fortunes won and lost, incredibly beautiful women..."

Kirsten laughed.

"I can't wait to hear it."

"I can't wait to make it up."

CHAPTER 5

K irsten decided to give up her apartment. Tommy was all set to talk to Rick, the manager, but Kirsten stopped him.

"We have to talk."

"Oh oh," said Tommy. "I've heard that before and it's always bad news. Let me guess. You're really a man, a cross-dressing Russian spy sent to torture me and overthrow Google?"

She laughed.

"So close! No, I'm a woman and Google is safe. It's about Rick."

Rick was a big, good-looking dude but Tommy suspected he was a heavy drinker.

"What about him?" he asked.

"It's awkward," said Kirsten, "having him as my landlord."

"Why? I've heard stories of landlords pressuring women, offering them free rent for special favors."

"Special favors? Are you trying to say 'sex'?"

"Well, yes."

"It's not like that."

"What is it like?"

"Rick is my ex-husband."

"Well damn."

"Yeah. Awkward."

"How'd you end up with him as a landlord? More important, is he a martial arts champion who's going to kick the crap out of me because you're in my apartment?"

"No, I think you're safe, and I got him the manager's job. He was desperate."

"And you used to be married to him."

"Yes, and he wasn't a bad guy."

"Wasn't?"

"He's changed. He drinks too much and he's really bitter."

"Hell, half the world is bitter. What happened to him?"

"I did."

"You? I find that hard to believe."

"Really?"

"Really. You seem like a nice person and Jo loves you. You can't be all that bad."

"You might be wrong. You sure you want to hear this?"

"We've got a bottle of wine and a night to kill. It's bound to be better than Jersey Shore."

"Okay. Here's the story. Rick and I worked at the same brokerage house. I was a researcher and he was a rainmaker."

"Like those alpha males in the movies?"

"That's him. He did his homework, he was personable, clients loved him, and he was flying high. I, on the other hand, was great at my job, but I was just analyzing numbers, researching trends."

"Let me guess. He needed research, and you were the go-to person."

"Yes. And we clicked. Soon we were dating, we fell in love, and got married. Both families happy, the jobs going well, a nice home on Bainbridge Island, commuting on the ferry—it should've been idyllic."

"What went wrong?"

"I screwed up."

"I find that hard to believe. What'd you do?"

"He had to go out with a big-money client one night, and I worked late. Then I stopped at the company hangout on the way home and drank too much. I was feeling insignificant, but that's no excuse. Somehow I ended up with a group of Seattle Seahawks."

"Football players? Don't tell me football players turn you on, I'll really be depressed."

"Prepare to be depressed. And it wasn't even one of the stars. Not the quarterback, not the wideout, no, I went to a hotel with the punter."

"Holy Shit. That's like hanging with a rock band and hooking up with the drummer."

"I know, but he was tall, had a degree from Princeton, and was drop-dead gorgeous."

"You had sex with a punter. For some reason that makes me happy."

Kirsten laughed.

"You know the rest of the story. Rick found out, the marriage crumbled, we tried to save it, but failed. Worse, my lawyer was ruthless and I ended up with the house, half the money, and alimony, which wasn't fair. I had a decent job, I didn't need his support."

"Let me guess. He handled it gracefully and still

treats you with love and affection."

"In your dreams. He handled it terribly and drank too much.

Then the crash hit and we both lost our jobs. I sold the house at a huge loss and moved in here."

"How the hell did Rick end up here?"

"I felt sorry for him. I helped him with money, but he kept going downhill. I talked the owners into giving him the manager's job. If he hadn't gotten it and the free apartment, he would've been on the streets."

"All because you slept with a punter. I watch football but I don't even know who the Seattle punter is."

"He's not a Seahawk any more. He got traded."

"Good. Teach that bastard to defile our Seattle women."

"Yeah, I'm sure it was a big life lesson."

"And now you and Rick are both here."

"Yes. And every day I see him at his lowest."

"I bet he's handling that with grace and dignity."

"I think he's handling it with beer and Jim Beam."

"So now we get to tell him you're moving in with me. Are you sure he's not a cage fighter? Should I bring a weapon?"

"No, but maybe I should do the talking."

"Good idea. I don't know if you've noticed, but he is a big dude."

"Ah, but the two of us could take him."

"For sure. You go for the head, I'll go for the midsection."

Kirsten laughed.

"You're not that small."

Tommy treasured those words.

CHAPTER 6

They took the elevator down to talk to Rick, leaving Jo in the apartment playing video games on Tommy's iPhone. Kirsten and Tommy entered and sat on Rick's tattered sofa, with him on a chair across from them. He had the look of an Irish drinker—sandy hair, blue eyes, ruddy complexion.

"I have to give up my apartment," said Kirsten.

"Seriously? I thought you were okay for money."

"I was for awhile, but it's getting tight."

"I know you've been spending time at Tommy's. Are you two a couple?"

From the way he said it, Tommy knew Rick thought the idea ridiculous. In his mind, Tommy morphed into Thor and clubbed him with a giant hammer. Yes, he'd read comic books. Okay, maybe he still did.

"No, we're just friends and I'm helping him take care of the little girl."

"I've seen her around. Is she a relative or something?"

"Yeah," lied Tommy. "She's my daughter. My wife passed away eight months ago."

"How come she just got here?"

"She was living with my wife's parents, but they're

having health issues. She's with me now and she won't be any trouble."

"If she is, you have to send her back. We can't have her bothering the other tenants."

This was bogus, as half of the apartments were unoccupied.

"She'll be good," said Kirsten, "and she's very quiet."

The understatement of the year, thought Tommy.

"So you're moving out of your apartment?" said Rick.

"Yes, I'll be out this afternoon."

"Let me know and I'll come check for damages."

"There aren't any, and it'll be clean."

"I still have to check. It's my job."

"Okay. I guess that's it," said Kirsten, and we all stood.

"You sure you don't want to talk? Come have coffee or something?"

"I'm sure, Rick. There's nothing to say that hasn't been said. I'm sorry."

His face hardened.

"Okay. If that's the way you want it."

Tommy heard the anger in his voice. He opened the door and they stepped out. Rick closed it, a bit too forcefully."

"That went well," said Kirsten, smiling ruefully.

"I don't think he's a happy camper."

"No, and he's getting worse. Thanks for letting me do the talking."

"No problem, but I was dying to ask him how the Seahawks were doing."

She hit him on the shoulder. Hard.

CHAPTER 7

The three of them moved Kirsten's stuff over to his place and locked up her apartment. Tommy went back to fighting off hacker attacks on Google, doing his part to keep the site up and running. Kirsten opened her laptop and spent two hours tracking financial trends around the world. Jo curled up on the couch with Tommy's iPhone. Clearly she'd played with smart phones before.

"You know," said Kirsten, "Lots of parents discourage kids from playing Internet games."

"What do you think?" asked Tommy.

"I think they're idiots. Any kid without computer skills is going to end up flipping burgers."

"I agree. But have you thought about school? Shouldn't she be in one?"

"Sure. I can't wait to talk to the admissions people. Hi, we've got a girl who isn't ours, we don't know her name, she can't talk, and we'd like her to go to your school."

"Yeah, awkward. You know, even if we don't try to get her into school we should get her some paperwork."

"How? We've searched the missing kid files and can't find any information."

"True, but we do have one of the best computer hackers in the country."

"Where?" she said.

"Very funny. Why do you think Google hired me? I applied and they turned me down. So I broke past their firewalls and played hide and seek with their programmers. After a couple weeks they decided I was better than the people they had and hired me."

"You're that good?"

"I'm not one to brag...."

"I think you just did."

"Well, there's that, but here's the thing. I can rig up some paperwork for Jo."

"What if they check it with government files?"

"I guess I'll have to go into them and establish her identity."

"Are we talking theft?"

"No, we're talking creation, as in, 'I am the Lord God of Computers and I say, 'Let there be Jo!'"

"You are really full of yourself."

"And lo," he preached, "Thomas the Omnipotent created JoAnn, and she walketh upon the earth with wondrous identification. Thomas 4:16, Verse 2. Glory Hallelujah!"

"I'm going to bed. I can't take any more of this."

"Wait! You haven't made a donation. The Church of Thomas needs your help."

"You need help alright, but I'm not a mental health professional."

Tommy laughed.

"She'll need a last name, and to avoid trouble I think she should be either your daughter or mine."

"I'd love to have her as my daughter," said Kirsten, "but if Rick gets wind of it he could make trouble. We'd better go with the lie you told him."

"I guess so. She'll have to be my daughter."

"You don't have any ex-wives out there do you? We don't want problems from your side."

"No. I've never been married."

"Are you a virgin?"

"You're still pissed off about the Seahawk remark aren't you."

"Damn straight. That was a low blow. I notice you didn't answer my question."

"No, I'm not a virgin," said Tommy defiantly.

"We're not talking some virtual porn thing are we? We're talking a real, live woman? Naked. In bed?"

"Yes. And I lived with women too!"

"Well good for you! Tommy the stud! Where are they now?"

"In California. One was a punter for the Chargers."

Kirsten leaped up and chased him around the room. Jo clapped and laughed silently.

Tommy spent the evening creating an identity for JoAnn Price, his adopted daughter. It was difficult, because he had to fake the paperwork and then get all the information into the system. Around midnight he was satisfied and stood up to see Kirsten and Jo were long gone, fast asleep in their bedroom. For some reason he felt a deep sense of contentment.

CHAPTER 8

One night after Jo had fallen asleep, Kirsten asked, "Do you have any weapons?"

"I've got a handgun," he said.

"Where is it?"

"On the highest shelf over the stove. I didn't want Jo to get at it."

"Are you good with a gun?"

"Oh hell no. When I bought it I went to a firing range and nailed everything but the targets. If we get attacked by targets, we're doomed.

"I can't say I feel any safer," she said.

"How about you? Do you have a gun?"

"No. I carry a kitchen knife in my purse and I studied martial arts as a kid. Hopefully if we get in trouble some of that will come back to me."

"Our defenses are pretty weak." said Tommy. "I worry about that, especially with Jo here."

"I worry too," she said.

"My solution has been to keep a low profile. I don't go out, I have food delivered, and never tell anyone which apartment I'm in."

"When I was alone I thought about getting a dog,

but I couldn't afford it," she said.

"I thought about getting a dog too but pets are a huge commitment. I decided to start small and work up."

"What'd you get?"

"A goldfish."

"Wow. An attack goldfish. I never thought of that. Did you train it to leap out of the bowl on command?"

"Yeah. It was vicious."

"Did you give it a name?"

"That would be silly, naming a fish."

"Absolutely. Silly. So what did you call it?"

"Well....I called it Woz."

"Woz?"

"Yeah, after Steve Wozniak, the Apple guy"

"I like that. A stealth attack fish named Woz. Where is it now?"

"Gone. I fed it and kept the water clean, but one day I found it floating belly up. I gave it a traditional toilet-flush funeral."

"Impressive. Did you sing? Say a prayer?"

"No, I just said, 'Good bye Woz,' and flushed. I'm not big on ceremony."

"Me neither. I've never really understood weddings and funerals."

"Seriously? I thought I was the only one who felt that way."

"Nope, we're a couple of heartless bastards," she said.

"Yes, and now we've got Jo. I couldn't even handle a goldfish, so how the hell am I going to handle a street kid? Do you feel the same?"

"Yeah. I'm a jock with no parenting skills. Jo could've done better."

"I guess we just do the best we can."

"You know what helps when you feel inadequate?"

"No, what?"

"Beer."

Tommy laughed and went to get a couple Coronas. It had become their beer of choice, a way of poking back at the virus.

They talked into the night. Then Kirsten went in to sleep with Jo and Tommy went back to the computer. He liked working from home.

CHAPTER 9

Tommy had bought the Glock 19 because it was small and fit his hand. He took shooting lessons, but it clearly wasn't his sport. He took it home, unloaded it, and kept it by his bed. Maybe he could scare off an intruder. When Jo moved in he hid it in the kitchen. He'd heard too many stories about kids and guns.

But Jo was full of surprises.

Early one morning he woke early, padded to the kitchen, but stopped in the doorway, shocked.

Jo sat at the table and there, in front of her, was the Glock, fully disassembled. She had all the parts laid out on an old towel and was cleaning them. It was obvious she knew exactly what she was doing. He just gawked and stayed quiet. When she was done, she reassembled the weapon, put in the magazine, ejected it, and using all her strength, racked the slide back and locked it to check the chamber. She looked, looked away, and looked again and then to make doubly sure she put her finger in to check there was no round in the chamber. Then she released the slide and dry fired a few times at the refrigerator. Holy shit!

But that wasn't all. She shoved in the magazine and

checked the clock. Then she magically field-stripped the gun and reassembled it. It seemed to take seconds.

Tommy coughed, not the smartest thing he'd ever done. She spun around and suddenly he was looking down the barrel of his own gun, held professionally in a two-handed grip. His hands shot into the air.

"Jo! Don't shoot!"

She lowered the gun, set it on the table, ran to him and hugged him. Then she backed up and put her hands together and bowed up and down, begging forgiveness. He gathered her up, told her everything was all right and that's how Kirsten found them. She was wearing a huge tee shirt and baggy gym shorts. Tommy wished she wouldn't dress sexy like that. Stop it! He thought. She's your roommate!

It did no good whatsoever.

Kirsten's eyes widened as she saw the gun on the table.

"What the hell is that?"

"It's my pistol," Tommy said. "Jo found it."

"Holy shit," said Kirsten, "She could've killed herself."

"I don't think so."

"What do you mean, you don't think so! Kids do that all the time. Find guns and play with them and then boom! No more kid."

"I want you to see something," Tommy said. "Just sit down at the table. Trust me."

Reluctantly, Kirsten sat.

"Okay, Jo," he said, "show Kirsten what you can do."

Jo picked up the gun and popped the magazine,

racked the slide to lock position, again made doubly sure there was no bullet in the chamber, then dismantled it and reassembled it, very fast. She repeated her earlier moves, ejecting the magazine, checking the chamber to make sure it was empty, and then dry firing at the refrigerator.

That refrigerator didn't stand a chance.

Kirsten was stunned.

"Did you know she could do that?"

"No. I didn't even know she could find my gun."

"Can you do that?"

"Nope, and I'd probably miss the refrigerator."

"You're that bad a shooter?"

"The worst. And I have a really tough time getting the slide back. Jo, can you show me how you rack it?"

Jo nodded. She held the pistol with her right elbow pressed to her body, grabbed the back of the slide in her left fist, and pulled hard. Tommy tried it that way and it worked. Success!

"I think the gun belongs to the wrong person," said Kirsten. "Jo is obviously the Terminator."

Kirsten turned to Jo.

"Can you shoot?"

Jo nodded.

"Are you good?"

Jo nodded again.

"Really good?"

Jo nodded again.

"Well I'll be damned."

"Jo," Tommy said, "go get your drawing pad."

She did and Tommy asked, "Where did you learn to shoot?"

She drew a crude drawing of a firing range and herself as a stick figure with a gun. Next, she drew a larger stick figure of a man.

"Was that your dad?"

She shook her head no.

"Step dad? Foster dad? Someone who took care of you?"

She nodded at the last one.

"And he taught you how to shoot?"

She nodded, and then started drawing the guy's hand with rectangles in it.

"Paper?"

Head shake, no.

Money?"

She nodded.

"He paid for your lessons?"

Jo shook her head, no.

"He was rich?"

No again.

Kirsten tumbled first.

"He made money on you? He made bets?"

Jo nodded yes, smiling.

"I'll be damned," said Kirsten. "Was he a nice man?"

Jo nodded, yes.

"Do you want us to find him?"

Jo thought, then held up her hands in a fifty-fifty move.

"You're not sure?"

Jo nodded.

"What should we do about the gun?" Tommy asked.

"We should hide it again," said Kirsten. "And if ever there's a home invasion, I put my money on Jo."

Jo smiled.

Tommy reluctantly agreed. All his Wyatt Earp dreams flew out the window.

"Jo," he said, "I know you can shoot, but this is a really big question. Have you ever shot anybody?"

She smiled a strange little smile. Then she held up her thumb and forefinger, a little bit apart.

"You shot someone a little bit?" asked Kirsten.

Jo nodded and pointed to her foot.

"You shot someone in the foot?"

Jo nodded.

"By accident?"

A shake of the head, no.

"On purpose? You shot someone in the foot on purpose?"

Jo nodded.

"Was he a bad man?"

Jo nodded.

"Was he going to attack you?"

Another nod.

"And that stopped him?"

A nod.

"But it wasn't the man at the range, was it? The one who was nice to you? Did you shoot him?"

Jo shook her head, emphatic no.

"And then you left?"

Yes. She pantomimed running.

"I don't think we're going to get the full story until she can read and write."

"I guess."

"Okay," Tommy said to Jo, "here's the deal. Kirsten and I should be the ones protecting you. And we all are going to be really, really careful with that gun. Innocent people could get hurt."

"Especially if Tommy's the one doing the shooting," added Kirsten.

"Well, there is that. Jo, do you understand?"

She nodded, slowly, but Tommy could see she had a question. He tried to guess what it would be.

"Are you wondering what you should do if Kirsten or I were in trouble? Like if bad people were going to hurt us?"

She nodded yes.

"First, we have to be smart. With guns, too many things can go wrong. Bystanders get shot. Bullets bounce off surfaces or go through walls and who knows what they'll hit. So a gun is our last option."

She nodded yes.

"You know how I handled trouble when I was a kid? I ran. People say you should fight back but I was always the littlest kid in class. There was no way I could fight big kids. You're little too and I bet you've run away from stuff. There's nothing wrong with that. We have to be smart and do whatever works. Okay? Shooting is our last resort."

She nodded again.

He didn't tell her that deep in his heart he dreamed of being Jackie Chan or Jason Statham. Or Thor. Life was confusing enough.

CHAPTER 10

Kirsten and Tommy drank morning coffee. They heard the bedroom door open and Jo stepped out rubbing her eyes.

"Did we wake you sweetie," asked Kirsten.

She shook her head, no.

"Did you have bad dreams?"

She nodded, and walked over to sit between them.

"I have a really serious, important question," Tommy said.

They looked at him.

"Do we like waffles or pancakes?"

Kirsten giggled. Jo held up two fingers.

"Both?"

She nodded.

"You're kidding! There is no way you could eat both waffles and pancakes!"

Jo rubbed her stomach and nodded emphatically yes.

Tommy complied.

"We have groceries coming today," said Tommy over breakfast. "I ordered everything we put on the list."

Jo looked up quizzically.

"Yes," said Tommy, "I ordered ice cream. I got dirt ice cream, asparagus ice cream, refried bean ice cream..."

Jo looked at him like he was an idiot.

"No?" he said, "You didn't order those?"

Jo gave him a big thumbs down.

"How about strawberry?"

Jo grinned.

"And chocolate?"

Bigger grin.

"Chocolate sauce?"

She clapped.

"Okay," he said, "That's what I ordered. But I'm really going to miss asparagus ice cream. It's my favorite."

Jo scrunched up her face in disgust.

"Did you order shampoo?" asked Kirsten, "and conditioner?"

"Yes. I noticed we were running low. I got a good deal on asparagus shampoo."

"It's my favorite," said Kirsten, straight faced.

"Actually, I ordered the products you wanted. I've never heard of any of them."

"I hate to break this to you, but our hair is different."

"I know that. Because I'm really observant and clued in to black culture."

"Dream on."

"Anyway, I got your products."

"Jo," she said, "My hair just accepted Tommy as its personal savior."

Later, the buzzer buzzed. Tommy pushed the button and asked, "Groceries?"

"Yes, delivery for Price," said a male voice.

"Be right down," said Tommy.

"How should we do this," asked Kirsten. "There will be a lot to carry."

"Why don't I go down, get the boxes inside and lock up, then you two can come down and help me get them in the elevator."

"Okay," said Kirsten. "Make sure it's the right guy."

"I will."

Tommy rode the elevator down, checked the guy's credentials, then opened up and helped him bring the boxes into the lobby.

"Want me to help you get them upstairs?" asked the kid, who towered over Tommy.

"No thanks."

"It would just take a minute."

"No, I'll be fine. Just give me the bill."

"You're sure? It's a lot of stuff."

"I'm sure. I'll handle it."

Reluctantly the kid handed him the bill and Tommy paid. He tipped the boy, and carefully locked the locks on the front door. Then he shoved the boxes over to the elevator. He glanced outside and the boy was still standing there, watching. Tommy stared at him until he turned and walked back to his truck. Tommy watched until he drove away.

He called Kirsten and she and Jo came down to help load the boxes into the elevator."

"That kid worries me," said Tommy.

"The grocery guy?"

"Yeah. He's a bit too helpful."

"I bet it's the same guy," said Kirsten. "We'll have to be extra careful."

Tommy checked the bill to make sure everything was there.

"Damn," he said, "no asparagus ice cream!"

Jo rolled her eyes.

CHAPTER 11

They sat out on the balcony that evening, the apartment pool below them, empty of water. No boats at the dock, no music, no tenants in lounge chairs sipping cocktails.

"Remember the parties they used to have down there?" asked Kirsten.

"I remember watching them. I wasn't much of a party animal."

"I find that hard to believe. I picture you as a tequila-shooter kind of guy doing cannonballs off the diving board and chasing ladies."

"That's me. Very perceptive."

"I wasn't much of a party person either." she said.

"Really? I would think you'd like pool parties. You could dazzle people in your bikini, have your choice of guys...."

"I hate that. I don't like people looking at my body and I don't like being hit upon by strange men. Thanks again, by the way, for not hitting on me."

"No problem. If there's one thing I'm really good at, it's not hitting on women."

"For what it's worth, I think you're really nice."

"Oh God, don't say that!"

"What?"

"Nice. For a guy, that's the kiss of death. With women, axe murderers have a better chance than nice guys."

"No way."

"Think of all the nice guys you've known. How many were studs?"

"Okay, maybe you've got a point."

"I bet Rick wasn't nice."

"I thought he was."

"Really?"

"Well, I suspected he had a dark side."

"And that made him interesting, didn't it?"

"Yes," she said reluctantly. "I guess so."

"I rest my case. Now promise never to call me nice again. Deep down I'm a man of mystery, a dangerous renegade with a sinister past."

"If you say so. What do you think, Jo, is Tommy nice?"

Jo nodded.

"Damn. I will never date again."

Jo looked down and grabbed Kirsten's sleeve. She pointed.

It was getting dark, but they could make out two figures by the pool. One was Rick, but it was hard to make out the other. He looked young, carrying a six pack.

"Hey," whispered Kirsten, "is that the grocery guy?"

"It could be. What would he be doing with Rick?"

They watched as the two sat in deck chairs three floors below and popped open beers, but they couldn't pick up the conversation.

"I don't trust that guy," whispered Kirsten.

"I don't either. He was trying to find which apartments we were in."

"He can just ask Rick now. Are we sure it's the same one?"

"Not really," said Tommy, "but he might be."

They sat in the stillness with the murmuring of voices from below and the pop tops of beer cans opening.

The two figures got up. It was almost completely dark and they still couldn't make out Rick's buddy.

Kirsten and Jo went to bed but Tommy, wide awake, worked on the computer. He was deeply into it when he heard a key in the lock. He tip toed over and sure enough the door handle was turning. It was silly because he had three other locks on the door. He also had a metal bar he could put across it. He picked it up and gently slid it in. He was startled when the door handle shook in frustration and then someone pounded on the door.

"Kirsten!" Rick yelled drunkenly, "I know you're in there! We have to talk!"

"Hold it down!" said Tommy in a soft voice. "Kirsten's asleep. You can talk tomorrow."

"No!" he yelled, "I want to talk to her now!"

"Not going to happen," said Tommy. "It's late at night. Go home. We can talk tomorrow."

"I don't want to talk to you, you little shit. I want to talk to my wife!"

"Ex-wife, and she's asleep. Go away!"

Tommy looked behind him and saw Kirsten and Jo in the door to their bedroom, wide eyed. He put a finger to his lips. Rick pounded some more.

"Open this fucking door! I know she's in there! We're going to have this out once and for all."

"No way," said Tommy. "You've got to calm down. You're going to lose your job."

"Fuck the job. I hate this job and I hate you. Now let me in. I want to talk to Kirsten."

"I can't do that. Go home."

"I'm staying here until you open this door!"

More pounding.

"Okay," said Tommy, "knock yourself out. I'm going to get coffee. You like The Foo Fighters?"

"Open this fucking door you little shit!"

Tommy pulled both of his speakers over to the door. They were Bose, the kind people bought back when the economy was strong. He put on "Best of You" and cranked up the sound. Rick's pounding and yelling were drowned out.

Kirsten and Jo just stared and Tommy motioned them into the kitchen.

"The neighbors aren't going to like that," said Kirsten.

"What neighbors? Half the apartments are empty. I know there's no one on either side and I think downstairs is vacant too."

"You're right," she said, "I forgot."

"Rick won't last."

In time, Rick gave up. Tommy didn't open the door to see if he was gone. It could've been a trick. They were wide awake now, so Kirsten figured a midnight snack was in order. They sat around the table, nibbling Oreos.

"I'm really sorry," Kirsten said.

"For what?" Said Tommy. "You didn't do anything. The guy's an asshole."

"He might do this again. Or he might pick a fight

with you. I'm worried that he's out of control."

"Jo," said Tommy, "What do we do in times of crisis?"

Jo stared at him.

"We run, don't we?"

Jo nodded.

"Run?" asked Kirsten.

"It's a thought," said Tommy. "The city is messed up, and it might be time to find a better place, even for just a few weeks. As long as Rick is living here he's going to be a pain in the butt, so why not hit the road?"

"It's a thought. We should make plans."

They talked some more and then Kirsten and Jo went to bed. Tommy, wide awake from the excitement, went back to work.

CHAPTER 12

Kirsten slept with Jo cuddled up next to her. The next thing she knew she got hit in the face by a small fist and Jo was thrashing around. Kirsten woke her up.

"It's only a dream, baby. You're safe now, I'm here and I'll hold you."

The girl snuggled in and Kirsten felt the wetness of tears on her shoulder, but still there were no sounds from Jo. Eventually she drifted off to sleep.

Kirsten told Tommy about it in the morning.

"She has terrible dreams and there's nothing I can do. I just hold her and talk and eventually she goes back to sleep. Do I have a bruise on my cheek? She caught me a good one as she was thrashing around."

"I don't see anything. I wish we could take turns, let you get a full night's sleep," he said, "but it wouldn't be right for her to sleep with me."

"Your bed is a king, isn't it" she asked.

"Yeah. I need it when three or four women come over for wild sex."

"Does that happen often?"

"Constantly. I have them sneak in after you've gone to sleep."

"See? I knew you were a nice guy. Always thinking of your roommates."

Tommy laughed.

"Fantasies aside, you do have a king-sized bed and we could all sleep in it. We put Jo in the middle and she'll feel protected, but you'll have to wear clothes to sleep. We don't want her to think you're a pervert."

"I can wear jeans and sweatshirts, like Jo. It'll be doubly good because you won't see my body and get excited."

"I'll try to contain myself."

"Okay," Tommy said. "We can try it, but if she hits me during one of her nightmares it's your fault."

So that's how they did it. Tommy in jeans and sweatshirt, Kirsten in workout shorts and sweatshirt, and Jo between them cuddling first one, then the other. Safe. Tommy had dreams of Kirsten, but never told her. She probably had dreams of him too, he thought, and was afraid he'd reject her.

CHAPTER 13

"I have cabin fever," said Kirsten one night.

"Me too, but we're stuck in this apartment until something changes."

Jo listened attentively. She set the iPhone down and pointed at them and then herself. Then she pointed to the door with a questioning look on her face. Kirsten picked up on it first.

"Jo, we'd like to go outside, but it's too dangerous."

Jo smiled. Then she pointed at herself, walked to the door and motioned them to follow her.

"You'll take us out?" asked Kirsten. "Now, at night?"

Jo nodded.

Then she led Tommy over to his closet and pointed to a dark pair of jeans, dark sweatshirt, and black sneakers. He nodded, and she led Kirsten to the other bedroom while Tommy dressed. He walked to the living room and waited until they came out, also dressed in black clothes. Okay, ninja family on the prowl.

Jo led them to the elevator and down to the basement garage. How did she know about the basement? It was a parking garage filled with dust-covered cars. Tommy yearned to drive his Honda Civic, but there was no sense chancing a joy ride only to get carjacked.

Jo led them through to the back wall, climbed onto the bumper of an SUV, and pushed aside a piece of metal grate that Tommy had never noticed before. How the hell did she know this? And then he realized that when he found her it wasn't the first time she'd been in the building.

Once through, she motioned for them to follow.

Tommy climbed onto the bumper and pulled himself through, getting his sweatshirt covered in dirt. Oh well, he thought, camouflage. Kirsten pulled herself effortlessly through the opening. Showoff.

They were outside! Breathing the night air! It was glorious.

Jo led them down a hidden path through the shrubbery to the water's edge. The dock was off to their left, and Tommy and Kirsten remembered when there were boats tied up and people partying. It was empty now. Forlorn.

They caught faint odors along the water's edge— seaweed, wet sand, fishy smells. Nice. Jo led them south along the water, past large houses that faced the lake with unkempt lawns running down to the water. Some had lights, some were dark— either empty or the people asleep. They heard sounds of crickets and frogs and the distant barking of dogs. Other animals had drifted back into town and people had actually seen cougars roaming the streets. Weird.

They sneaked under the huge beams that held up the approaches to the floating bridge and I-90. It was dark back in there, and a hundred yards back they saw the flicker of flames. Homeless people with a fire in a barrel. The three of them stayed down by the water and sneaked under the overpass of I-90.

"Where are we going?" whispered Kirsten.

"Hell if I know," said Tommy softly, "but I'm enjoying this."

"Same here. I hope Jo knows what she's doing."

Ahead was a huge house with a large, overgrown lawn that led down to the lake. At the water's edge they saw a boathouse and inside there was a dim light, and voices.

Jo walked up and knocked softly.

The door opened a crack and then flew wide.

"Penny!" a whispered exclamation. "You're back!"

Jo (or "Penny" to these people) motioned Tommy and Kirsten in and they entered a room lit by a Coleman lantern turned low. In the gloom they could see five women sitting around a table off to the side, glasses of wine in front of them. In the water was a fine old speedboat, maybe a Chris Craft, probably mahogany.

"Holy cow," said Tommy. "That's a beautiful boat."

"Thank you," said one of the ladies. "My husband and I had some great times on it. It's a shame we can't take it out any more."

The five women crowded around hugging Jo, or Penny. She still didn't say a word.

Then they turned to Tommy and Kirsten and the lady with the boat introduced them.

"This is Connie, Karen, Marsha and Pat. I'm Wendy and this is my boathouse. There are two men with us, but they're outside keeping watch up by the street. Sometimes we get vandals."

"I'm Kirsten and this is Tommy," said Kirsten. "And I guess you know our young friend here."

"How did you find Penny?" Wendy asked. She seemed to be the leader, a stocky woman with short gray hair and a commanding presence.

MIKE NEUN

"I found her in the doorway of our apartment building," Tommy said. "I assumed she was homeless and cold, so I brought her in. She's been living with us for awhile."

"Are you his wife?" asked the woman named Pat.

Kirsten smiled and said, "No, we were neighbors but when Tommy asked for help with Jo we joined forces. We couldn't guess her name so we called her JoAnn."

"Well," said the woman, "We call her Penny but we don't know her real name either. She came to my house one night and knocked on the door, begging for food. I had to take her in didn't I? I think she has a hideout around here somewhere and I never knew when she would show up. Then one day she was gone and we haven't seen her in weeks."

"That fits. She's been with us. So this is your boathouse and that's your house up by the road?"

"It is, and we have this secret book club. It's fun to sneak down here, drink wine and talk about our latest reads."

"You all live around here?" Tommy asked.

"We used to," said the one named Pat, "but there's safety in numbers so now we live in Wendy's house."

"And you have two men?" asked Kirsten.

"Yes. They like to patrol the area and play soldier. Actually, Charlie was a real soldier, in the army for years. He's married to Pat. The rest of us are divorced or widowed."

"And you all got to know Jo, er, Penny?"

"Why yes. Isn't she just a darling little girl? Such a shame she can't talk. We figured it was trauma."

"We did too," said Kirsten.

"Where do you two live?" asked Wendy.

"We're in Sherwood Apartments on the other side of the bridge," Tommy said.

"Oh that used to be so nice," said Karen. "I went to parties there when I was in college. Out on the dock, drinking, sailing. What a great place to live."

"It's a lot quieter now," said Tommy.

"I'll bet. Such a shame."

Jo sat at the table, being fussed over by the ladies and it made Tommy nervous. He didn't want to lose her. For one thing, he'd grown attached to the quiet girl. For another, she'd brought Kirsten into his life and that was awesome. Deep down, he knew he was in love, but he'd also been in love with Beyonce and the chances of anything happening were about the same. Beyonce never called, never wrote.

They heard a soft knock at the door, and it opened. Two guys came in, both well over sixty.

"Ah," said one, "We have visitors! And Penny's back!"

"Charlie and Walter," said Wendy, "This is Tommy and Kirsten. Penny brought them."

"Hi," said the one with white hair. He was slim, just under six feet in height, and stood straight. Definitely a military man. The other had a roundness about him, not fat, but a bit overweight with a pleasant face and a bald head. "I'm Charlie," said the first, "and this is Walter. Nice to meet you both. Any friend of Penny's is a friend of ours."

They shook hands, and the two old guys opened bottles of beer. Kirsten and Tommy already had glasses of wine and the ladies had found a Coke for Jo.

"Remember those beautiful days when we could

ride our bikes around the lake?" mused Wendy.

"I sure do," said Kirsten, "and I'd give anything to go running again."

"It'll happen. We just have to be patient. We've also talked about going somewhere safer."

"You have any ideas?" asked Kirsten.

"Not really. Have you?"

"I've been surfing the Internet," said Tommy, "and some of the small towns seem interesting. I used to go skiing with my family in Idaho and Ketchum seems pretty calm."

"Oh yes, near Sun Valley? We used to go there too! It's a great area."

"We worry that if we leave the house it might not be here when we get back." said Wendy. "Either that or it could be taken over by squatters."

"That would be bad," said Kirsten.

Tommy looked at Jo. She was sitting between Connie and Pat, cuddling up and listening intently.

"We talk about it a lot," said Wendy. "Maybe we'll ride it out until things improve."

"Or," said Tommy, "We could go to my default position—run like hell and start over."

"That would be a great title for a book," said Walter. "Run Like Hell and Start Over. Tony Robbins would be so jealous."

"I just wish we could go back in time." said Pat wistfully, "I'd love to be in another one of those parties on your dock. We could take Wendy's boat over and swim and drink margaritas and dance..."

"It's so dangerous now," said Connie. "Tell them about the break in."

"You had a break in?"

"It was no big deal," Wendy said, "just some kids. Charlie chased them off."

"Charlie?" Tommy asked.

"People don't mess with Charlie," said Connie. "He spent time in Afghanistan and Iraq, but he won't talk about it. When he started shouting at those kids, I got scared."

Charlie raised his beer and smiled.

"Hell, I was scared too," he said. "Those kids could've beat the crap out of me. Luckily it was dark and they didn't realize I was a geezer."

"Did they take anything?" asked Kirsten.

"We don't think so, but they were pretty unruly."

"It's not as bad as it was," said Kirsten. "Things have calmed down. I think in a couple of weeks I can go running again."

"Maybe," said Wendy, "but I wouldn't rush it. It's going to take awhile to get back to normal."

"I don't think we'll ever get back to normal," said Walter. "That third wave was a disaster."

"It sure was," said Kirsten. "Hard to believe a mutant strain could develop so fast."

"Thank God it didn't take as long to find the second vaccine, but it sure destroyed the recovery."

"It'll be a long haul now," said Kirsten.

The conversation wandered to other things and Tommy and Kirsten could see Jo cheered them all up. She made the rounds, sitting with everyone and Tommy had the thought it might not be fair to take her away from these friends.

They left around eleven and Jo came with them as

if it was the natural thing to do, setting Tommy's mind at ease. As they sneaked under the eastbound spans of the floating bridge they could hear an argument break out in the darkness further in. Some sort of homeless confrontation, and they hurried along the water's edge, eager to keep their presence secret.

CHAPTER 14

A huge crash blasted them out of sleep. Tommy and Kirsten leaped out of bed and rushed to the living room, but it was too late, the front door had been sledge-hammered open. Rick and the grocery guy stood there, triumphant, drunk, grinning stupidly.

"Honey, I'm home!" Rick shouted, laughing.

"Rick," said Kirsten coldly, "You're drunk."

"Absolutely. I'm drunk and I don't give a shit. We're going to have this out once and for all but first I need more liquor. You got any booze in this place?"

Rick's hair was wild, his eyes half shut, his tee shirt damp from spilled beer and he weaved around as he stood there waving an empty Rainier beer bottle.

"Shake and I are really thirsty."

"Rick," said Kirsten, "You can't do this. You're drunk and you're breaking and entering. That's a crime."

"Oh hell," he said, "I run the place! And the police are way too busy to bother with shit like this. How are you doing, wife of mine? Happy to see me?"

"No," she said. "I want you to leave. Now."

Shake, the grocery guy, laughed. He too was stumbling drunk but much more menacing. His sleeveless tee shirt showed lots of tattoos—tigers, dragons, knives, gang symbols, a swastika—no wonder he wore long sleeves at work. He seemed bigger now, with ropey muscles and a nasty grin.

"Yo, Rick, she doesn't seem happy to see us. Come on, lady, this is your true love, come to rescue you from this little fuck. We're going to take you home!"

"This is my home. Now get the hell out."

Shake walked over and tried to slap her, but she threw up a forearm and blocked it.

"Whoa!" said Shake, "good move!"

Then he feinted with his left and caught her with a punch to the stomach. She went down, gasping for air.

"Hey!" Tommy yelled. "You son of a bitch!"

"Shut the fuck up, little man. This is our party and I'll do what the fuck I want."

Tommy rushed him and Shake swatted him aside like a bug. He slammed against the wall.

"Okay," said Shake, "We got that settled. Now my friend Rick has told me how you—he pointed at Kirsten—screwed him four ways from Sunday and it's time for a little retribution, a little payback."

"Rick," said Kirsten, on her knees clutching her stomach, "What's happened to you? How'd you get this way?"

"I got fucked!" yelled Rick, waving his beer bottle. "I got fucked by my wife, I got fucked by my job, I got fucked by lawyers, and I got fucked by this fucking apartment house and I'm tired of getting fucked. Tonight is my night! It's your turn to get fucked and I'm just the guy!"

"Absolutely!" said Shake. "Think of this as a connubial visit. Rick is going to have a couple hours with

CHASING EXES

63

his wife, just like old times. And while he does that, I'm going to go through this apartment and see if there's any money, watches, laptops—portable stuff. But first, we need more liquor! What the fuck kind of hosts are you people? Booze, get some fucking booze!"

Tommy and Kirsten struggled to their feet, dazed and scared.

"Come on little man, go get me some booze! And no tricks or I take it out on the lady here. God damn she's a nice piece of ass. Maybe Rick is into sharing. Go, damn it, get a bottle!"

Tommy, hating himself, limped to the kitchen and turned on the light. He grabbed a bottle of Jack Daniels and turned to see Jo standing by the door, the Glock in her hand, with a finger to her lips. She pointed to him and made talking motions. Tommy understood. He'd talk, she'd handle the weapon. Tommy hoped she was as good as she thought she was.

He came out of the kitchen holding the bottle, and Shake and Rick turned to look.

"I'd better tell you something," said Tommy.

"What," snarled Rick, "That we should be nice? That we should leave? Well fat fucking chance little man. We're going to party! Now hand over that bottle."

"You're not going to believe this, but you're in grave danger."

"From what? You?"

"No, her."

Then Jo stepped out, Glock in hand. With her left hand she grabbed the slide and with all her strength, racked it. Then she stood, pistol in a two-handed grip, feet spread.

"You're joking. She's just a kid! I'm going to come over there and take that pop gun away."

Jo pulled the trigger, a loud bang rocked them, and Shake looked down to see a hole in his baggy jeans, about five inches below his private parts. He froze.

"Rick," Tommy said, "Stand real still. Maybe you should put your feet apart. We don't want an accident. Jo, can you do the same to him?"

She pulled the trigger again, another explosion, and a hole appeared in Rick's pants, similarly placed. Rick had suddenly sobered up.

"What the fuck?"

"Okay," said Tommy. "Now I think Shake here is the real badass and we should convince him that we mean business. Can you put a hole in his pants about an inch higher? Shake, you should stand real still for this."

"Fuck you!" said Shake, and before it was out of his mouth Jo shot a hole an inch higher than the first one.

"Fuck!" he yelled, and froze.

"Want to try one more? Just a bit higher?"

"No," he yelled. "Make her stop."

"We can keep doing this," said Tommy, "or you can lie down on the floor, face down, hands behind your heads. Your choice."

"No way!" said Shake. "No fucking way!"

Jo, without being told, put another hole in his pants, very close to all he held dear.

"Stop!" he yelled. "Stop shooting!"

"On the ground, now!" said Tommy. "Face down, hands behind your heads."

They really didn't want to do it, but the gunshots had rocked their befuddled world. The possibility of losing their family jewels had a definite sobering effect.

"Jo," said Tommy, "We should help them decide. One more for each of them, just a tiny bit higher."

"No!" yelled Rick. "I'll lie down."

He knelt down on the floor and laid out flat, hands behind his head.

The grocery guy, Shake, really wanted to press his luck, but then his shoulders slumped and he did the same.

"Don't move," said Tommy. "Jo, if they even twitch, you can do some more target practice. Kirsten, there's duct tape in the kitchen drawer. Can you go get it?"

Kirsten was stunned, but she managed to go to the kitchen and come back with the tape. They used it to bind the wrists and ankles of the two invaders. Then Kirsten motioned Jo and Tommy into the kitchen.

"We have every right to kill them," whispered Kirsten, "but I think we've painted ourselves into a corner."

"What do you mean?"

"If we'd shot them when they broke in, we'd be legally within our rights. But if we shoot them now, when they're tied up, we could get sent up for manslaughter or murder."

"Damn," said Tommy, "you're right. But I'm glad Jo didn't shoot to kill. You did good, Jo. They do deserve to die though."

"I'm not sure I could pull the trigger," said Kirsten. "I could've earlier, when they broke in. Now? In cold blood? Maybe not."

"Same here. I don't think I can shoot them in the back, all taped up. Where's Rambo when you need him? What the hell do we do?"

"We should document this," said Kirsten, "in case we

ever get to press charges. Police and courts are beginning to regroup."

"Great idea. Let's take lots of photos, especially the beer bottles and sledge hammer. If it ever gets to trial they can test them for fingerprints."

They took pictures of everything, including Rick and Shake, the caved-in door, the mess in the living room, and the bruise on Kirsten's cheek.

Then they used more duct tape, going for the mummy look because they were pissed off, and went through their pockets. They found wallets, some money, keys and a wicked-looking knife in grocery boy's front pocket.

"You guys were going to hurt us bad, weren't you," said Tommy.

No answer.

"Jo, take another shot at Shake. His legs are together, so there'll probably be a blood. Can't be helped. Stay still, son, we don't want to hit an artery."

"No! Wait! Yes, we were going to hurt you. Rick wanted revenge and he wanted to mess you guys up. He paid me! He paid me to do this!"

"Shut up you fucker," said Rick.

"My god, Rick," said Kirsten. "You've lost your mind. You're a fucking psychopath!"

"You did it!" he snarled. "This is all your fault and I'll get you. I swear I'll get you."

"Well shit," said Tommy, "that really presents a problem. What are we going to do with these guys?"

"I wish we could get the police," said Kirsten.

"Fuck you," said Shake, "the police don't care. Unless there's murders, they're not coming."

"That's true," said Kirsten. "So what do we do?"

"We could maim them," said Tommy, winking at Kirsten and Jo. "Shoot them in the knees. It's hard to chase people in a wheelchair."

Rick got very quiet.

Kirsten picked up on it.

"Okay, and I get to do grocery boy here. By the way, what the hell kind of a name is 'Shake'?"

"None of your fucking business."

"Is it short for 'Shake 'n Bake'? Do you get twitchy? You like milk shakes? Help me out here, I'm running out of ideas."

"It's my DJ name, bitch. I work the clubs."

"And Rick paid you to do this?"

"Just shut up, Shake," snarled Rick.

"Yeah, he paid me. Said it'd be a piece of cake. Stupid bastard."

"Fuck you," said Rick.

"Fuck you too," said Shake. No honor among thieves.

"Tommy," said Kirsten, "we have to talk in private."

"Okay. Let me tape their mouths."

He did, and they walked into the bedroom with Jo.

"This is complicated," said Kirsten. "The obvious solution is to shoot them. They're a danger to us and to everyone else and the police aren't an option."

"I see two problems with that," said Tommy. "Maybe more."

"Same here. If we shoot them, it would open up a bag of worms. Once we have two dead guys, we will have police. How do we explain Jo?"

"And we didn't shoot them breaking and entering, we shot them taped up on the floor. Hard to claim self-defense."

"True. If we kill them, we lose Jo and we could go to prison. Either that or we shoot them and run like hell with police chasing us forever. I vote against both of those."

"Me too. Now what?"

"Disable them? Shoot them in the leg?"

"And then what? Let them bleed out? Or try to patch them up? And again, if the police ever do get involved we're fucked. No self-defense and we lose Jo."

"We can't just let them go free, not after what they did," said Kirsten. "Have you got a baseball bat? Can we break their legs?"

"And then what? Call a doctor? If they're not treated, they could die from that."

"Fuck," she said. "What the hell do we do?"

"I think we should leave them here and disappear. Get out of Dodge."

"That could work. Rick's got no money so he can't chase us."

"How about Shake?"

"He ratted out Rick, so they're sure not a team any more. I think he'll split."

"Can we scare the shit out of them before we leave?"

"It would only be fair. They sure scared the shit out of me."

"Jo, can you unload the gun? Make doubly sure."

Jo did that, and they walked back into the living room. Tommy ripped the tape off the two intruder's faces.

"Okay," he said. "We can only think of one solution. You guys have got to be stopped, right now. Any last words?"

"You can't shoot us," said Shake. "You haven't got the guts."

Tommy knelt down beside him and cocked the gun. Then he held it to Shake's temple.

"Fuck you!" Shake yelled.

Tommy pulled the trigger. There was a click of metal on metal, and Shake peed himself.

"Damn. Must've been a misfire. Let's try Rick."

He knelt beside Rick and put the gun to his head.

"Don't," he pleaded. "Please, Kirsten, stop him. I'm so sorry. You loved me, you can't let him do this. Please...."

Tommy pulled the trigger. Click. Rick whimpered.

"Jo," said Tommy, "what's wrong with the gun? Can you fix it?"

"Please," begged Rick. "Don't do this."

Kirsten spoke up.

"Rick, look at me."

He met her eyes.

"We're leaving town and I'm buying a gun. If I ever see you again, anywhere, anytime, I'm going to shoot you. Dead. Do you believe me?"

Rick stared. He'd never seen her like this.

"Say it."

"I believe you."

"Shake," she said. "What about you?"

"I'm out of this. He didn't pay me enough for this shit."

"Okay. Tommy, how do we to this?"

"I say we leave them here and call the cops in a day or so. With luck, they'll come get them."

"Don't do that!" cried Shake. "The cops won't come. We could die!"

"Works for me," said Tommy.

"No," moaned Rick.

　　　　　　　　　　　　　　MIKE NEUN

"I'd put your odds at fifty-fifty," said Tommy, "and I guess we're leaving town. Is that okay with you, Jo?"

Jo nodded.

"I just hope nothing happens to us before we make that call. It would really be bad luck for these guys."

"Karma," said Kirsten, "is a bitch."

"I found a car key in Shake's pocket," said Tommy. "It's got an "H" on it. What are you driving, Shake, a Honda? A Hyundai?"

No answer.

Tommy, surprising himself, kicked Shake hard in the ribs.

"Ow! Fuck! It's a Hummer!" he yelled. "It's a Hummer. H2."

Tommy had no idea what "H2" meant but he knew Hummers were huge.

"A Hummer!" exclaimed Tommy. "What the hell are you doing with a Hummer?"

"It was my dad's. The virus got him and I got the Hummer. It's an H2 and it's a stupid fucking SUV but you can't take it."

"Why not?"

"As soon as we get free I'll report it stolen."

"Was that a threat? Seriously? You just added five hours onto the time before we call the cops. Want to try for more?"

"No, don't. I won't report the car."

"Go ahead. That police thing works both ways. They're understaffed and overwhelmed so I don't think they'll bother with a stolen SUV. Where's it parked?"

"In the basement. Rick let me in."

"Let's go take a look. It might be better for a road

trip than my car."

Kirsten put tape over their mouths, and they took the elevator down to the garage. The Hummer was huge and black, with heavily tinted windows.

"We have a choice," said Tommy. "My Honda Civic is over there, or we can take this."

"I'd feel safer in this," said Kirsten, "and we could carry more stuff. What do you think?"

"I agree. Let's do it."

They took the elevator back upstairs. Shake and Rick, taped up like parcels, hadn't moved. Tommy pulled the tape off Shake's mouth.

"We're taking your Hummer."

"You can't do that!"

"We can do any damn thing we please. You're just fucking lucky we can't have you thrown in prison. Home invasion, attempted rape and murder? You guys would've been doing hard time."

"You can't just leave us here. What if nobody comes?"

"Boy, that would be terrible," Tommy said. "A long, slow death. If the cops don't come, maybe we'll call someone else to come get you, or maybe we'll still be pissed off and forget. You better pray for the first one, but right now I'd vote for door number two.

"Water! You can't leave us without water."

"We could, and it would serve you right. What do you think, Kirsten? Jo? Water for these guys?"

"Please," begged Rick.

Kirsten and Jo nodded. Water was okay.

"We'll do water, but we have to tape your mouths so you can't yell. I'll cut a hole in the tape and tape a straw in it. You can sip water through that."

They finished with the taping up and arranged two bowls of water and straws.

"Wait a minute," Kirsten said. "What if someone gets curious? We should leave a note."

They took awhile composing it.

To Whom It May Concern,

These two men broke into our apartment using that sledge hammer (their fingerprints should be on it) and assaulted me and my friend, Tommy Price. They also threatened me, Kirsten Haugen, with rape.

We managed to overcome them, but we no longer feel safe so we're leaving town.

Rick is the apartment manager and my ex-husband. Shake, the other guy, delivers groceries to this building. They were armed, drunk and dangerous. Please call the police.

We have photos of everything and will be happy to testify if law enforcement returns to normal.

If you live in this building, we advise you to get out unless both of these men are taken into custody.

Sincerely,

Kirsten Haugen

They propped the note up on the little table by the door where it couldn't be missed, in an envelope that read, "Read this before releasing the guys on the floor."

They tried to think of everything they'd need for their trip. They packed it up and took trips down to load it into the Hummer. After an hour they couldn't think of anything else, so they pulled the apartment door shut as best they could and Kirsten hung a makeshift "Under construction" sign on the knob. The hummer was huge, and Tommy loved the dark-tinted windows. People couldn't see inside and maybe carjackers would think twice before attacking.

He looked over the dust-covered cars and picked out a Nissan. He took a screwdriver and switched license plates. Now even if grocery boy called it in they'd be harder to find.

The beast-on-wheels barely fit under the overhang as Tommy pulled out of Sherwood Apartments. As he drove around and up onto the floating bridge, Kirsten called Wendy, put her on speaker, and explained why they had to leave town.

"We had a home invasion." said Kirsten.

"Oh my god," said Wendy, "are you okay?"

"We're fine, but it was a close call and now they're all taped up in Tommy's apartment. Can you do us a favor? Can you call the cops in a couple of days? If they won't come, can you to get someone to go over and cut them loose? We want them to suffer and fear for their lives, but we don't want to get charged with murder."

It sounded really bizarre to Wendy, but she promised to do as they asked.

Tommy, Kirsten and Jo left Seattle in the Hummer, with Tommy's feet barely reaching the pedals. He felt like an elf driving a cruise ship.

CHAPTER 15

"I'm so happy we're leaving," said Kirsten. "I had a terminal case of cabin fever. Two more weeks and I would've taken a high dive off the balcony."

"I think the world is getting cabin fever." said Tommy. "It's crazy out there and I feel like I'm chained to that damn computer. If I lose my job I don't know how long I can support the three of us."

"We can go cheap. I don't mind sleeping in this thing, and I'm sure Jo will think it's an adventure."

Jo nodded happily.

"That'll save motel money and none of us are big eaters. We should be okay."

"I guess we don't have much choice."

"I'm still shaking," said Kirsten. "I've never been through anything like that."

"Me neither. Jo, are you okay?"

Surprisingly, Jo seemed the calmest of all. Maybe life as a street urchin prepared her for home invasions and shootouts.

Tommy drove toward Snoqualmie Pass and after a few miles they calmed down. Tommy tried to get Kirsten talking to take her mind off their narrow escape.

"How did you spend your time before we got together?"

"I kept researching the markets. If I ever get hired again I want to be up to date. I also exercised, watched a lot of movies, played games, read books and putted on my carpet."

"You're a golfer?"

"Nope, but I had my dad's old clubs in the closet so I practiced putting. I counted the attempts. I was up to eleven thousand when Jo came along and saved me from trying to commit hari-kari with a golf club."

"That's two suicide mentions in the last fifteen minutes. You're not trying to tell me something are you?"

"No. My life is much better with you and Jo. And no putting."

"Eleven thousand attempts. How many did you make?"

"I'm not goal oriented. I just tried to putt over a dime, but I didn't keep track. That's much too anal for me."

Tommy giggled.

"What?"

"You said 'anal'"

"What are you? A third grader?"

"No. But I heard that word in a movie when I was a kid and I always laugh. It was comedic highlight of my grade school years."

"You are some piece of work."

"I'm sorry. Computer geeks set the humor bar really low."

"Infantile."

Tommy looked over and realized Jo was zonked out.

The night's excitement had worn her out.

"Rick is a real head case, isn't he? I knew the guy was screwed up but I didn't realize how bad it was. I bet he was pissed off when we told him you were giving up your apartment."

"He sure was. And I don't think you're his favorite person."

"Especially not now. A couple shots to the crotch and duct taping a guy to the floor is probably not a good start to a friendship."

"Thank you for saving me, by the way."

"You can credit that to Jo. I was useless."

"I don't think so. You sure took charge after she tuned them up."

"I think it was a flashback to all those years I was bullied. What a joy it was to turn the tables on those bastards. I just wish I'd had Jo with me in high school. I'd have kicked ass."

"I think schools frown on little girls with Glocks."

"They are so picky," said Tommy.

"We also have her to thank for bringing our little family together."

"Isn't that the truth? Even after you brought the wine over that night I still had to work up courage to talk to you."

"Why did you need courage to talk to me?"

"Be serious. I need courage to talk to anyone, much less a woman like you."

"That's really weird."

"I've also been called weird before."

"I didn't call you weird. I said it was weird you had a problem talking to me. We were neighbors."

"That made it even harder. If I said something stupid I'd have to see you every day and be reminded of it."

"You haven't said anything stupid yet. Oh wait, I forgot the Seahawk remark after our talk with Rick. You will live to regret that one."

"I already do. I still have a bruise on my shoulder."

"Other than that, I can't think of any stupid thing you've said."

"Give me time. I'm a black belt in blurting out the wrong thing."

An hour later they neared the top of Snoqualmie Pass. Jo woke up and the green forests and crisp air were a wonderful change after weeks cooped up in the apartment. There was no snow at the ski areas, and the chairlifts hung over cleared grassy runs. Tommy had skied at Snoqualmie and Alpental when he was younger and the drive brought memories of times up there with family and friends.

They stopped in Ellensburg for fuel. The Hummer drank gas until Tommy thought the pump was going to tap out. He paid and realized that at some point he and Kirsten were going to have to come up with more ways to make money. Oh well, if an economist and a computer hacker couldn't find a way to top up their cash, what hope was there?

They drove thirty-seven miles to Yakima, ate Pizza Hut takeout and realized they were exhausted. No sleep, the confrontation with Rick and Shake, the packing and driving, all combined to make them call it quits.

"You okay with sleeping in the Hummer?" asked Kirsten.

"It works for me," said Tommy, "but where should we park?"

"How about near the police station? That would be safe."

"You might want to re-think that. We're driving the most conspicuous stolen car in America with plates off an old Nissan. If the cops run them we're dead."

"Damn. Maybe not a good plan."

"Let's see what we find."

Near the freeway they found a truck stop, filled with semis, delivery trucks and other working vehicles. The Hummer fit in and they parked near the back of the lot.

They folded down the back seats and laid out sleeping bags, but then found they were still too buzzed to sleep. With the heavily tinted windows, Tommy figured it was safe to do a little work on his laptop, putting patches on patches, helping to keep Google up and running. Jo played on Tommy's iPhone while Kirsten checked the markets around the world on her laptop. Between them, they had the world's knowledge at their fingertips, but not a bed. Life was weird.

After a few minutes, Kirsten and Jo climbed into their sleeping bags and soon they'd drifted off to sleep. Tommy was about to join them when he had another thought. The Hummer. If he could whip up a fake I.D. for Jo and get it in the system, why not do the same with the beast-on-wheels? The idea brought back the joys of hacking and he spent two hours creating registration, insurance, matching the plates, and entering it all into the system. If they could find a Kinkos the next day he could print up registration and insurance forms that would get them through a police stop.

They slept late and ate at the truck stop cafe, which actually had a decent breakfast. They shared eggs, waffles, toast, crisp bacon, orange juice and coffee, enjoying a stress-free beginning to the day.

But then two policemen came in and walked over to the booth.

"You folks just passing through?" The bigger one asked. He looked like a linebacker who hadn't seen a gym in awhile. There was a weariness about him.

"That's right, officer," Tommy said. "We're on our way to Idaho."

"That your Hummer outside?"

"Yes."

"That's a valuable vehicle these days. Gangs love Hummers. I'd be real careful if I were you."

"Damn," said Kirsten. "Do you have any suggestions? How can we get to Idaho without being attacked?"

"A police escort would help," he said, smiling.

Tommy saw where this was heading. Like everyone else, the cops had taken huge hits in salary and layoffs. They were open to side jobs—security, body-guarding, payoffs.

"That sounds really good, but we both lost our jobs. We couldn't afford to pay you," lied Tommy. He didn't want to get ripped off.

"That's unfortunate," he said. "If you're broke, we might have to run you in for vagrancy."

"We've got enough money to get to Idaho, and that's about it. Why are you doing this to us?"

"It's nothing personal, we're strapped for cash. I've got three kids and they're close to being hungry. Roy, here, he's got kids too and his wife is sick. We're both living on the edge and we're desperate."

"I'm sorry to hear that," said Kirsten.

The cop looked at Jo.

"I'm sure you understand, having a child yourself. What's your name little girl?"

Jo stared at him and Kirsten jumped in.

"She can't talk," she said. "She never could. But she's smart and hears everything."

"Well isn't that a shame," said the cop, and turned back to Jo, "Are you enjoying the trip?"

Jo nodded. Then she pointed to her breakfast and gave a thumbs up.

"I see she can make do without talking."

"Especially if there's food involved," Tommy said.

"Is there any reason you're headed to Idaho? Are there jobs there? Is it safer?"

"To tell you the truth," Tommy said, "we got attacked in Seattle and we're trying to get away. Idaho is about as far as we can afford to go. My family used to go skiing there and we figured we could hide in a small town in the mountains."

"I'll tell you what," said the cop. "If you buy us some burgers for our families, we'll escort you out of town and about 50 miles down the road. We'd go further but the city only pays for so much gas."

Tommy looked at Kirsten. It seemed like a good deal and it could never hurt to help out cops.

"We can do that," he said. "You go order what you want and we'll finish up here."

The two policemen went up to the counter and ordered. When they got their food, Tommy paid and they walked out. The big cop gave him his card—his name was Chuck Fisher—and Tommy gave him his.

"This is my partner, Roy Pryor."

Roy was a smaller, less macho version of Chuck and needed a haircut. Tommy guessed Chuck was about forty, Roy about ten years younger. They shook hands and Tommy gave them his card.

"Google? You worked for Google?"

"Yep. It was a great job, but they laid off hundreds of us."

"Isn't that a pisser? It's happening all over. We're just barely hanging on."

"If you ever get to Idaho," Tommy said, "Look us up. I'm thinking we'll be in a tiny cabin somewhere but you'll always be welcome."

"That's good of you," he said, "and if you're ever back this way look us up. Hopefully things will improve. I feel terrible begging for food, but my family needs it."

Tommy made a mental note to send some money if they could spare it.

"You mind if we stop at my house and drop off the food? It's on the way and Roy's family can come over and get their share."

"No problem. Oh wait, we need to stop at a Kinkos. It'll just take a couple of minutes. Is there one near here?"

"Not too far. We'll go there first and then to my house."

"We'll follow you."

The two cops climbed into their patrol car and Tommy, Kirsten and Jo climbed into the Hummer. They followed the police to Kinkos and Tommy took in a thumb drive. Odd, he thought, getting a police escort to print up stuff to fake out the police. Smiling, he printed up registration and insurance forms for the Hummer.

When he finished, the cops led them to a small

house on the way out of Yakima and Chuck carried in the food. Then they followed the police car out of town and ' down the highway.

"I feel like royalty," said Kirsten.

"Me too," said Tommy. "I've never had a police escort before."

"You can't blame them for trying to feed their families."

"I guess not, but it's sure sad."

An hour later the two cops pulled over and waved the Hummer on.

CHAPTER 16

"Hard to believe we lived next door for months and never talked," said Tommy as they drove.

"I know. I guess it's kind of a big city thing. And we still know next to nothing about Jo."

"Yeah."

"Jo? You sure you can't talk? You're not playing a big joke on us are you?"

Jo smiled and shook her head.

"Okay, but if you wake up some day and start reciting Shakespeare I'm really going to be upset."

Jo had no clue who Shakespeare was so she smiled again.

"Well, we can't save the world but we can give Jo a good home. That's got to count for something."

"I'm not sure running away in a Hummer counts as a good home."

"Hey, it's the best we can do."

"Jo, I know you've lived on the streets and seen a lot of bad stuff," said Tommy. "You're not playing us, are you? You're not going to knock us out and steal our Hummer are you?"

"You've seen too many Chuckie movies," said Kirsten. "Jo, your dad is talking trash, but we give it right back, don't we?"

They gave each other a fist bump.

"I do feel clueless sometimes."

"Maybe you do. I'm right on top of this," Kirsten laughed. "We may never know Jo's past, but I still don't know much about yours either. What's your story?"

"Pretty mundane. I grew up in Eugene, was always the smallest kid in class, only child, loved computers.... sort of Bill Gates without the money."

"And you went to Stanford?"

"Yeah. I got a scholarship. After graduation I joined a startup. When that failed I joined two other startups that failed." "Wow. You must be a hell of a businessman."

"I love computers and hate business. It's not a good combination. Finally, with no money coming in, I applied at Google. I told you that story. When I got hired they treated me well, the money was good, and all I really wanted to do was quit and try another startup."

"Why don't you?"

"I don't know if you've noticed, but unemployment is at thirty percent, people are scared, and hunger is a real problem. The thought of actual wages is a powerful incentive."

"So you're working for Google and able to feed yourself. These days you're the one percent."

"Why don't I feel like that? I still feel like the college nerd who never figured out people. I can run through video games in no time but I still have no clue what my parents were all about. I loved them, but as far as I was concerned they were on another planet."

"Seriously?"

"Sure, and they didn't know what to make of me. My dad played sports, ran a restaurant, and took two years to figure out a smart phone."

"So you really bonded."

"I can't remember us ever having a conversation longer than ten minutes."

"That's kind of sad."

"Not really. We knew we loved each other. We just had no common ground."

"How about your mom?"

"We loved each other but she thought I was a bit odd. She helped my dad at the restaurant, kept the books."

"What kind of restaurant."

"Italian. My dad loved to cook and started out with a tiny hole-in-the wall pizza place. When that became successful he kept making it a little bigger and a little better. It was always crowded, and they made a good living."

"Are they still alive?"

"No. Cancer got my mom, and my dad died of a heart attack a year later. That was about five years ago. His old manager owns the restaurant now. Dad left it to her because he knew I had no interest in the business."

"Were you okay with that?"

"Sure. His manager is a great lady and she's doing really well. I would've run it into the ground."

"How do you know?"

"Just saying. I had no interest in it and I was doing fine with Google when they passed away. It worked out for the best."

"Did the restaurant survive the pandemic?"

"It's still hanging on. Luckily dad made part of it a sidewalk cafe, so she was able to serve customers outdoors."

"What's it like, being small?"

"Boy, you get right to the hard part, don't you?"

"I know for you it's a big deal so we might as well get it out in the open."

"Okay. First of all, it eliminates about 80% of the women on Tinder. I looked into it. Then I did extensive research on Google and YouTube and it's biological."

"Wow, Google and YouTube. You really are a scholar. I bet you know all about Sasquatch and UFOs too."

"Well, I did drift off into moon-landing conspiracies. I like to be well-rounded."

"So what did you find in all this research?"

"Women don't want a guy who's shorter than they are. It's a primitive urge to have a big guy who can protect them."

"But aren't we breaking down those barriers?"

"Look around. How many tall women do you see with short guys?"

Kirsten paused.

"I'll give you a clue. I've been looking for years and I can count my sightings on one hand. So my dating opportunities are severely limited. Now, where do computer nerds rank on the scale of desirable men?"

"I don't know."

"Right up there with sanitation workers and loan sharks."

"You're kidding."

"Not much."

"But now you're a computer geek with a job. That

puts you in the one percent, so I'm thinking you're a high roller. A stud."

"I wish. Apparently women still put a lot of stock in things like empathy and awareness. How stupid is that? We nerds, on the other hand, are notoriously self-centered."

"Are you that way?"

"Of course. Who are you and what are you doing in my car?"

Kirsten smiled. They kept driving.

Once they got out of Pendleton, it was Tommy's turn.

"Okay," he said, "how about you? What's it like to be tall?"

"Ah!" she said. "If your theory about women wanting taller men holds true, it eliminates eighty-five percent of the men from my dating scene. You know what's really weird? Fifty-eight percent of male CEOs are six feet or taller."

"Shit. There go my CEO dreams. I missed by seven inches."

"Well I'm five-eleven, so my choices are really limited if I go with the flow. That could be why I'm single."

"I doubt it. You're a hot chick, so you must've had lots of opportunities."

"Hot chick? Are you from another century?"

"In the dating scene I'm from another galaxy. If we walk into a club, the chances of you picking up a date are about ten thousand times better than mine."

"Ah, but we haven't talked about the race thing. I don't know if you've noticed, but I'm half black."

"You're kidding!"

MIKE NEUN

"I know it's a terrible shock. You just thought I had a great tan."

"No, you told me about your mom, so I'm right on top of this racial stuff."

"Seriously?"

"Of course not. I'm the oblivious white guy. I'm amazed I haven't blurted out something insensitive already."

"Why, are you a racist?"

"You would know by now."

"Okay, you're not a racist. Why are you scared to talk about me being black?"

"Half black."

"You know what that makes me in this country? Black."

"I know. How stupid is that?"

"That's a point for you. Good going."

"So how does that apply to relationships?"

"Well first I have to weed out the racists and the guys who think it's a status thing to date a black chick."

"You're right. Complications. But at least you have guys coming up to you. I never have women coming up to me."

"Okay, but that's not always a good thing. My good-guy radar sucks. I seem to have a knack for picking out the worst guy in any situation."

"So you've had a lot of bad relationships?"

"Oh have I! It's depressing."

"So which is worse, bad relationships or none at all."

"None? You've never had a relationship?"

"This is supposed to be about you, remember? Later on I'll tell you about my dating history. It's awesome."

"Okay. The answer is yes, I've had bad relation-ships."

"How bad?"

"Well, not abusive. I was an athlete and my mom put me in martial arts when I was five."

"Really?"

"Yeah. My dad was her second husband. Her first was a nasty drunk and she swore if I ever got in that situation I'd be able to take the guy down."

"How did she handle the drunken husband?"

"With a frying pan. Mom didn't fuck around."

"So your dad was her second husband?"

"Yes, and in between she dated some losers too. Mom's good-guy radar was as bad as mine. She finally got lucky with my dad."

"Where did you live?"

"In Ballard, Seattle's little Norway."

"Did you have brothers and sisters?

"No. I was an only child."

"What sports did you play?"

"All of them, especially in high school. Then I got a basketball scholarship at the UW and in the spring I competed in track. I was a pole vaulter."

"You'll find this hard to believe," said Tommy, "but I was never recruited for either one of those. I think the coaches were a bunch of heightists."

She smiled.

"You know what's weird?" said Tommy, "I love sports. I watch them all the time on TV. Maybe it's a guy thing."

"Did you play any of them?"

"A little, but the only ones I was good at were

skateboarding, snowboarding and skiing. Size doesn't matter in those and I loved them. How good were you?

"Pretty good but I wasn't world class. Also, I liked school. Economics fascinated me."

"Holy shit. You were an actual student-athlete!"

"Damn straight. And lots of times I was the only girl in my classes. Not a lot of women major in Econ."

"When you got out, did you like the work? Were you a Wall Street geek?"

"Not really. There's a lot of ruthlessness and sleazy dealing in the financial world and that bothered me."

"Wait a minute. You're saying high finance isn't honest and above board? This is a huge shock."

"I know. I hate to shatter your illusions. And now we're in a third-world economy and you know what upsets me?"

"What?"

"I'm the woman I never dreamed I'd be. I'm damn near broke and depending on a man to get me through. I feel like I've regressed seventy-five years."

"Well, maybe if we just look at ourselves as people, not man-woman, we can deal with it. If you had a friend who was in trouble, would you help them?"

"Yeah, I would."

"Okay. So that's what this is. Take the gender thing out of it. It's one person helping another. Besides I get a lot out of it too."

"What?"

"Friendship. I'm not good at that and it's really important to me. Also a chance to help Jo. I couldn't do that alone."

"That's nice."

"And I get the glory of walking around with a hot black chick."

"You had to wreck it, didn't you?"

"Hey, I'm a guy. That's my job."

CHAPTER 17

"Jo, I'm worried about your diet," said Kirsten. "Tommy keeps feeding you pizza and ice cream."

"What's wrong with pizza and ice cream? I've spent my life on Red Bull and Doritos, the diet of computer geeks everywhere. Pizza and ice cream are a step up."

"Jo, your father is dangerous. We strong women need healthy food, and Tommy does too."

"Well, I'll try to eat better," said Tommy, "but it goes against all my lifestyle choices."

Whatever the food, Jo was looking better. Tommy was happy to notice she still favored his jeans and shirts, even when they were a bit big. Maybe she felt safer in them, but it was nice.

He had given her his old iPhone and she loved downloading apps and games. Tommy brought up maps and tried to get her to point out where she came from, but she either couldn't or wouldn't do it. They realized she never wanted to go back.

Jo had to go to the bathroom so they stopped at a rest stop outside La Grande, Oregon. Tommy didn't want to because rest stops were deserted and could be dangerous, but they had no choice. Jo grabbed her backpack and they stood guard outside the toilet while she ran in. Sure enough, a large pickup truck stopped next to their Hummer and a tall guy got out—work boots, cowboy hat, tee shirt, tattoos—everything setting off alarms in Tommy's head. He looked to be in his early thirties, maybe a construction worker.

"Hi folks, nice day isn't it?"

They agreed.

"Where you headed?" he asked.

"East," Kirsten said. No sense giving away their destination.

"Good idea," he said, "Don't tell people where you're going. There are some bad guys out there."

Tommy decided to bite the bullet.

"Are you one of them?"

He laughed.

"Boy, you don't beat around the bush, do you? Nope, I'm just a guy headed home to see my family. Looking for a job like everyone else. You don't need a carpenter do you?"

"I wish we did," Kirsten said. "We're looking for work too."

"That's okay, I have to ask."

"I'll tell you what," Tommy said. "Give us your phone number and if we hear of anything we'll give you a call."

"That's decent of you," he said. "I'm Ted, and this is my number."

He gave it to them and headed into the men's room. Just then a biker rode up on a Harley. Fuck.

"Well hello!" he said, dismounting. He was huge, fat in a hard way, dressed in dirty jeans, boots, muscle shirt and one of those tiny helmets that satisfy the law and offer no protection at all. A sandy-colored full beard covered much of his face and his long hair hung in a straggly pony tail down his back. He took off the helmet, hung it on the handle bars, then strode over to them.

"Why aren't you the cute couple! How you doing little man?"

Tommy hated being called little man.

"We're just leaving," he said.

"Well that's not neighborly. Why don't we take a few minutes and have a chat?"

"We don't want to talk," said Kirsten. "We want to move on. Would you please step out of the way?"

"I don't think so. Did you know this highway is a toll road?"

"Well shit," Tommy said, "and I suppose you're the collector."

"I am! Let's see, I make it fifty for you and two hundred for the woman, because she is a fine-looking piece of action. So, two-hundred fifty dollars, plus tip. Let's call it an even three hundred."

"Nope," said Kirsten, "We're not paying you a dime. Now get out of our way."

Just then Ted walked out of the toilet. Thank god, Tommy thought, we've got some support. He was wrong.

"Hi Ted," said the biker. "I was just explaining our toll procedures."

"Hi Jupe," said Ted. "Sorry folks, I was making up all that shit I told you, just trying to keep you here for my friend. How much is he charging?"

"Three hundred bucks," said Kirsten, "but we're not paying."

"Oh that's too bad," said Ted. "Now it just went up to three fifty, plus a little fun with the lady. Jupe and I haven't been around a woman like you in a long time and you want to hear the good news? We're not prejudiced! We will jump the bones of any beautiful woman, no matter what race, creed or color."

"Nope," Tommy said. "That's not going to happen. She's with me."

"Well fuck me. Aren't you the salty little prick! What are you going to do, take us on?"

"I will stop you somehow. Trust me."

"Nope, not going to happen," said Ted. "Okay darling, we'll just go back behind the restrooms."

"No," Tommy said, "you won't."

Jupe thought that was really funny.

"Stop messing around little man. Unless you're packing an Uzi we're going to do whatever the fuck we feel like doing."

Ted started to approach Kirsten and two things happened.

A shot rang out and Ted's hat flew off. Everyone froze, then Jupe turned to look and Kirsten side-kicked him hard in the nuts. Jupe doubled over.

"What the fuck?" yelled Ted.

"Aaaaugh," groaned Jupe.

A second bullet caught Ted in the butt. He cried out, stumbled and fell to the sidewalk.

Jupe was in pain and befuddled by all the noise, but he slowly straightened up and this time Kirsten kicked high and caught him in the face. Blood spurted and Tommy realized she'd just broken his nose. Apparently she hadn't been kidding about the martial arts training and she wasn't making the same mistake she'd made with Shake. Kick first, talk later. Jupe went down.

Another shot rang out and a bullet caught the sidewalk sending chips into Ted's face.

"Stop!" he yelled. "Stop shooting! We give up!"

"Fuck that!" said Jupe and he started to turn, only to have a bullet take off part of his ear. Now he was bleeding from his nose and ear. He rethought his options.

"God damn it!" he yelled. Stop shooting!"

Jo walked out with the Glock aimed at them.

"What the fuck!" exclaimed Ted, "It's a fucking little girl!"

He struggled to stand up and Jo sent a bullet whizzing past his head. He froze.

"I should warn you," said Tommy. "She's a champion with that pistol. Next time you move she's going to start shooting off body parts. Do you want a demonstration?

"No," said Ted sullenly, "we believe you."

"You sure? She could take off a couple toes or fingers if you want. I don't want you to think she tricked you."

"No," snarled Ted, truly pissed off, "we believe you."

"Okay," said Kirsten. "You guys lie on your stomachs with your hands behind your heads. We have to decide what to do."

"I'm shot!" exclaimed Ted. "I'm bleeding."

"I think we can safely call that a flesh wound," said Kirsten. You won't die. Now stay down on the ground and shut up."

Tommy took Kirsten and Jo aside.

"We should call the police and turn them in."

"How do we explain the stolen Hummer? And Jo? Police would take her away for sure."

"Damn. This is déjà vu. We can't just leave them here, they're too dangerous."

Ted overheard that.

"Fucking right," he said, "you guys are dead meat."

Tommy looked at Kirsten and Jo and winked. They'd played this scene before.

"There's nothing we can do. We have to kill them."

"I agree," said Kirsten.

"Now wait," said Jupe, as reality hit, "you can't do that."

"Why not," said Tommy. "You were going to do it to us, and worse. I don't have any problem with it."

"We were just having fun," said Ted, "We weren't really going to hurt you. We need the money."

"Bullshit," said Tommy, amazed at how brave he could be with Jo holding a gun on the bad guys.

"I don't see any other way," said Kirsten. "Do you?"

"Come on," said Jupe. "You don't want to do that. You just go away and we'll leave you alone. Seriously."

"You're joking." said Tommy. "Sorry, but we can't do that."

"We've waited too long," said Kirsten, winking at Jo. "Give Tommy the gun. Let's get this over with."

"No!" said Ted. "Take our money, our truck, our motorcycle, whatever you want."

Tommy got thoughtful.

"You know," he said to Kirsten, "That Hummer has been too conspicuous. I think we should shoot them and take Ted's truck."

"No," snarled Ted, "Just take the truck and leave us. We'll stay here. We won't bother you again."

"Ted, you should run for office. That kind of bullshit could take you to the White House."

MIKE NEUN

"Is that truck yours?" asked Kirsten.

"Yeah."

"You got the title and registration?"

"In the glove compartment."

"I'll go get it," she said, "While I do that, Ted, you empty out your pockets. Very, very slowly. Jo, if he makes one quick move shoot the bastard."

She went to get the papers while Ted emptied his pockets of a wallet, keys, pocket change, a big pocket knife, some cigarettes and a Bic lighter.

"Okay," Tommy said. "Now you, Jupe. Very slowly. By the way, what the hell kind of name is that?"

"It's a nickname, short for Jupiter, 'cause I'm big like the planet."

Jupe put his stuff in front of him. Same stuff, almost the same knife.

"You got guns?"

"No."

"Jo, shoot him in the leg."

"No! Wait! Ted has a gun in the truck."

Kirsten came back with the papers and a handgun from the pickup.

"Guess what else I found?" she said.

"What?"

"Rope." She held it up. "I've heard it comes in handy in situations like this."

"Here's what's going to happen," said Tommy. "We're going to trade you the Hummer for the pickup."

"I don't believe you," said Ted. "That Hummer's worth more."

"There's a tiny catch," Tommy said. "The Hummer is stolen."

"Stolen? Who the hell are you people?"

"You don't want to know. The bad news is the guys we stole it from are dangerous, and they're seriously pissed off. So you should either hide the Hummer or get it as far as you can from Seattle. The good news is we papered it and the documents should get you through a police check."

"You papered it? How the fuck did you do that?"

"As Liam Nielson would say, 'We have skills you never dreamed of.'"

"Fuck me. Seriously, who are you?"

"Ah," said Tommy, "just a family out for a drive."

He turned to Kirsten.

"You got the papers?"

"Just sign here and here," said Kirsten to Ted, "and we'll be good to go."

He signed.

"Keep them covered, Jo," said Tommy, and he tied their wrists tightly behind their backs, using Ted's knife to cut the rope. Then he tied their ankles.

"One other thing," Tommy said. "I'm going to do some damage to the Hummer and the Harley. When you guys get loose you can patch up your wounds and hoof it to the next truck stop. Maybe call someone to come get the vehicles.

"Oh, and here's something to think about. We're not the only family like this. Think of us as a terrorist organization. There are lots of us. So remember this before you ever fuck with any family ever again. We're tired of this gangster shit. Spread the word."

"If we ever see you again, anywhere, anytime," said Kirsten, "we will shoot to kill. No questions."

"Also," said Tommy, "I'm taking your wallets. I'm going to loot your bank accounts and fuck up your identities. You should never piss off a hacker."

They gathered up their stuff and Jo and Kirsten kept them covered while Tommy got a tire iron and randomly bashed the engines in the Hummer and the Harley. Then Jo covered the two hijackers while Tommy and Kirsten moved their stuff into the pickup. It was big, with four doors, so they could put their valuables inside. The rest they threw in the cargo bed. Then they walked back, got Jo, and backed away from the two men on the ground.

"You're sure we shouldn't kill them?" asked Tommy. "It'll just take a second."

"That makes it too complicated," said Kirsten, "but if they try again we'll have to."

They jumped in the truck, a Dodge Ram 1500, and drove out of the rest stop.

CHAPTER 18

"Damn," said Kirsten. "I'm not sure I like this. People attacking us from all sides."

"I agree," said Tommy. "We've definitely got to go underground."

"Jo," said Kirsten, "come here, sweetie and give me a hug. That's twice you've saved us, and no little girl should ever have to do that. We are going to figure out a way for us to protect you from now on."

Jo nodded and buried herself in Kirsten's arms.

"That's right, Jo," said Tommy. "We want you to be with us always and we want to protect you."

Kirsten turned to Tommy.

"Terrorist families?"

"Well, it could happen," he said. "And by the way, nice kicks! You really laid that guy out."

"He was distracted. There's no way I could take him in a fair fight."

"It was still impressive. How'd you like the way I beat up those engines?"

"They didn't stand a chance."

The tension was wearing off, replaced by giddiness over their escape.

"Thanks for sticking up for me," said Kirsten.

"But I couldn't do anything to help you."

"You tried. That means a lot."

"I think from now on I'm going to strap dynamite to my body. Next time bad guys come I'll show them how a real terrorist family operates."

"And you can go to heaven with seventy-two virgins."

"If only I were a believer...."

"Seventy three counting you."

"Ha! Not even close. I am a legendary lover."

"Virgin."

"Legend."

Jo smiled, put a fresh clip in the Glock, and put it back in her backpack.

Kirsten looked down at Ted's gun.

"What the hell do I do with this?"

Jo took it, unloaded it, broke it down, and put the pieces in her backpack.

They stopped in Boise. It was only two hours to Ketchum, but they were exhausted and wanted food and a place to sleep. They thought about sleeping in the truck but the lure of a soft bed, a shower, and high-speed Wi-Fi was too appealing. They decided on a motel, something big and cheap away from the highway. They found a Best Western, got a room in back with a king-sized bed, and moved in.

"You'll never guess what I saw on the way in," said Kirsten.

"What's that?"

"A Thai restaurant."

"They have those in Idaho?"

"Apparently they do," she said. "Do you like Thai food?"

"I love Thai food. Jo, have you ever had Thai food?"

She seemed kind of bewildered and shook her head no.

"Well," said Kirsten, "You are in for a treat. You know where Thailand is?"

Again, a head shake.

Kirsten brought up Google maps and showed her Thailand.

"When I was a little girl," she said, "My parents took me on a big ship and we went to Thailand. We loved it and the food was the best! Someday, when the world gets back to normal, Tommy and I will take you there. Okay?"

Jo nodded happily. Tommy did too. The three of them? Traveling the world? It was the stuff of dreams.

"Anyway, Thai food is really, really good and I haven't had any in months."

"Let's do it," said Tommy, and they drove to Chaipon's Siam Restaurant. In true Thai style they ordered four different dishes and shared everything, with Kirsten teaching Jo how to eat with a fork and spoon like the Thais did. Jo loved everything except Tom Yung Goong, the spicy Thai soup that made her nose run and her eyes water. They enjoyed the quiet meal, and the Thai lady who served them took a liking to Jo. Soon they were fluent in hand signals and facial expressions as Jo pointed out her favorite foods.

They paid the bill, tipped, and the lady gave Jo a little carved wooden elephant when they left. Jo was delighted and Tommy and Kirsten marveled at her ability to make friends wherever they went. Well, with the possible exceptions of Ted, Jupe, Rick and Shake. Some people just didn't get the concept.

"You know what we need to do?" said Kirsten the next morning.

"What?"

"Check to see if Wendy called the cops to get Rick and Shake. With all the stuff going on I forgot about the situation in Seattle."

"Damn, me too. We don't want a murder rap hanging over our heads. I wonder if the police will do anything."

Kirsten called Wendy and put it on speaker.

"Hi Kirsten," she said, "How's your trip?"

"Very eventful," said Kirsten. "Yesterday we got attacked by hijackers."

"You're joking."

"No, it's the truth, but we're safe now. We'll tell you all about it later. The reason we're calling is to find out about Rick and the other guy we left taped up. Did you call the police?"

"We tried the police, but they're understaffed and breaking and entering is low on their list. Walter and Charlie had to go over and ring buzzers until someone answered."

"What happened?"

"They spread the word on the speaker and a bunch of tenants went up. They found your note and Rick and Shake in bad shape. They released them, but they didn't like what they saw. Some tenants moved out."

"Good. I'd like to see Rick explain that to the owners."

"We'll try to find out what happens. He should be out of a job unless he does some really fast talking."

"He used to be good at that. Okay, let us know what you hear."

"We'll do that. And we can't wait to hear the hijacker story. Give our love to Jo."

"She's right here, and she misses you all."

"We'll meet again, Jo. You can count on it."
"Thanks for helping us, and we'll keep in touch."
"We will too. Stay safe."
"Bye."
"Bye.".

CHAPTER 19

The drive to Ketchum took under two hours and when they pulled into town it was more upscale than Tommy remembered. Sadly, a lot of the stores were boarded up. He saw names from the past—The Pioneer Saloon, Louie's Pizza, the Casino bar, Whiskey Jaques. Long ago he'd had dinners with his parents at all but The Casino Bar, which wasn't a casino but an old bar frequented by local drinkers and pool shooters.

Tommy saw Mount Baldy off to the left, with the familiar ski runs carved into the trees. They had a couple weeks until ski season and Tommy wondered if the mountain would even be open.

He had Kirsten turn left, toward the Big Wood River. His family had stayed in a cabin down there but he couldn't find it. They drove back to main-street and then out to the Sun Valley Resort, but it too looked almost deserted. It was low season, between summer and winter tourists, but he wondered if any skiers would come this year. He hoped so because ever since they'd left Seattle he'd dreamed of getting up on the mountain.

They parked and walked aimlessly up Main Street. Kirsten saw a sign for Valley Real Estate and they checked out the listings in the front window. Lots of condos, cabins and houses for sale or rent so they walked inside. There were four desks but only one was occupied. A lady, about thirty-five, tanned and healthy, stood up to greet them. She had long black hair, dark eyes, a beautiful smile, and was wearing jeans, boots and a Pendleton shirt—pretty much the uniform of Idaho.

"Hello," she said, "I'm Joyce Flowers. Can I get you some coffee? We've got a machine here and the espresso's not bad."

"Sounds good to me," Tommy said. "Kirsten?"

"Sure thing."

"How about your girl? Would she like a 7-Up?"

Jo nodded.

"Two coffees and a 7-Up," Tommy said. "Thank you. And my name's Tommy. This is Kirsten and this is Jo, short for Jo Ann."

"Nice to meet you," said Joyce. "Are you new to Idaho?"

"They are," Tommy said. "I skied here years ago with my family, but everything's changed."

"It sure has. We don't even know if we'll have a ski season this year. The crash killed everything."

"It's the same everywhere," said Kirsten. "We came from Seattle and people are really hurting. I lost my job and we're just lucky Tommy is hanging on to his."

"I know that feeling," said Joyce. "Two years ago my business was booming. I had three people working for me and a couple months ago I had to lay them off. If they can dig up any business I pay them commissions but pickings are really slim."

"We're not going to help much," Tommy said. "We're

MIKE NEUN

just looking to rent something bare bones. Maybe a cheap cabin out in the woods."

"I don't know if I'd live in the woods," said Joyce. "We've got problems with rough guys roaming around. They've been breaking into cabins, stealing stuff and vandalizing cars. We even had a murder six months ago. Also, we've got a dog problem. People all thought it was a mountain thing to have big dogs—huskies mostly—and when they left town a lot of them left the dogs behind. They run in packs out in the woods. Sometimes they take down deer.

"Damn," Kirsten said. "We just wanted something safe and cheap. We figured it'd cost too much to live in town."

"Not these days. We've got tons of empty condos, apartments, houses, cabins you name it. And owners would be happy to get anything they can. I'd be glad to show you some places."

"That sounds good," said Kirsten. "Is there somewhere we can stay tonight?"

"You could get a room at the lodge, but I've got a better idea. You can stay in my house, really cheap, and I'll make dinner and breakfast. It'll help you and God knows I could use the money."

"That sounds just fine," said Kirsten. Tommy agreed.

They spent the afternoon touring empty condos, cabins, houses and apartments and eventually Jo made the choice. It was an old log cabin down by the foot of River Run, one of the two main ski lifts up the mountain. In normal times, rent would cost a bundle but now it was within their range and Jo loved it. She ran around looking in the rooms and then outside, where the yard ran down to the Big Wood River. Tommy had to admit it was perfect and Kirsten agreed.

Before they signed, Tommy asked Jo if she could swim. They would be close to the river and he didn't want to worry. She nodded yes, she could swim.

"Your daughter is a quiet little thing, isn't she?" said Joyce.

"She doesn't talk at all," said Kirsten. "She never has. But she's really smart and after awhile you don't even notice. I think she likes you."

"Well I like her too. And don't worry, darling, I can talk enough for both of us, especially if I've had a beer or two."

Jo smiled.

They finalized the deal and Joyce took them to her house for the night. She had an A-frame cabin out toward Warm Springs and they cleaned up while she put together a dinner of spaghetti, salad and garlic bread. Tommy brought some wine in from the pickup and they ate and talked.

"The pandemic hit us hard," said Joyce. "It was kind of a shock because we thought it was mostly a big city thing. We lost a bunch of old people, including my father."

"Oh that's a shame," said Kirsten.

"It wasn't too surprising," said Joyce, "He was in his seventies and had diabetes, firmly in the high-risk group. I'm just sorry he was in quarantine and I wasn't able to be with him at the end."

"Do you have other family up here?"

"No. I came here fifteen years ago to be a ski bum and snowboarder and just stayed. Dad came to live with me when mom died, so at least we had a couple years together. When I first came I did the usual—waited tables, tended bar, worked at the lodge—and then I got into real estate."

"Ever been married?"

"Yeah, but it didn't last. Had a few boyfriends first, but they were ski bums too. I was happy on the mountain and had no desire to be tied down. Later on I married a nice guy but it didn't work out."

"We're sorry to hear that."

"Hey, it's life. You have to move on. How about you two? What's your story?"

"Oh we were neighbors," said Kirsten. "Then we joined forces when Jo came to live with Tommy. She's a wonderful kid and I'm trying to help out."

"These days whatever works is okay."

"That's for sure."

They talked some more and then Joyce showed them to the loft bedroom and the three of them went to bed, Jo in the middle. Safe.

CHAPTER 20

Rick Bryson, Kirsten's ex, was pissed off. Three years ago he was a big-time broker with a hot wife, a fine house and a BMW. Then the roof caved in. His wife cheated on him, the market crashed, he lost big in the divorce, he lost his job and now he was a fucking gofer in an apartment house. Oh sure, his title was manager but he spent his days listening to complaints and trying to fix stuff he knew nothing about. Plumbing, for Christ's sake! How did he go from big-money stock transactions to fixing toilets?

And if that weren't enough, his ex-wife moved in with that fucking computer jockey. Then he and Shake pounded down a few beers and went up to have a little fun and that fucking little girl shot the shit out of them! He couldn't forget those holes in his pants, way too close to his private parts, and the two days on the floor with Shake, all taped up, pissing his pants, terrified no one was going to find them. Fuck. That was the worst! Then that bunch of tenants came in, saw the two of them taped up and stinking, and read that fucking note. The tenants called the cops but no one showed up so the tenants cut them loose. Shake disappeared, and Rick tried desperately to come up with an explanation. It didn't work.

Now Kirsten, the computer jockey and the little girl from hell were long gone. Tenants had bailed out—not many people want to live in a building where the manager gets ripped and breaks into apartments—and the only saving grace was that the owners were camping somewhere in Colorado and couldn't be reached. He had a feeling the owners were in deep shit too and hiding from tax collectors. But when they found out they were sure to fire his ass. He was damn near catatonic, and his life was crap. The only friends he had were the guys on the websites who'd gone through the same divorce hell he had.

Thank God they hadn't had kids or Kirsten's lawyer would've taken them too. Fucking lawyers. He spent his spare time on the computer, trading vengeance-filled posts about the havoc they would cause. Revenge of the ex-husbands!

Oh sure, there was one tiny problem. He was broke. He was fucking poor! And he hated it. That's when he thought of the Honda Accord in the basement parking lot. Sure, why not?

The old couple who owned it had died from the virus months ago and all their stuff was in a locker downstairs. He'd been waiting for some relative to come claim everything, but nobody had. It was a shame to let that thing just sit there.

He got the master keys and opened the locker. It took him awhile to find the paperwork and car keys, and a lot longer to forge the signatures. If anyone asked, he'd just tell them he'd bought the car fair and square. Perfect.

He sold the two-year-old Accord for half of what it

was worth—almost twelve thousand bucks—and bought a used Toyota. He had a car. He had cash. He was an angry ex-husband on a mission.

Then he thought about the Volvo SUV in the corner of the garage. Same story! The owner, a single guy, had died and no one had come to claim the belongings. It had been months, surely that meant no one was coming. Why not?

Three days later, Rick had over twenty thousand dollars in the bank. He was back in business.

That's when he logged onto the websites and found the story about the attempted hijacking in La Grange. A short guy, a tall black woman, and a little girl with a gun. He'd found the bitch! And there were those two guys talking about it on the Get-The-Bitches website. They were pissed off, Rick was pissed off, why not join forces? He had money. He hired Ted and Jupe.

CHAPTER 21

The Ketchum rental cabin was old, built back in the days when the ski resort was owned by the Union Pacific Railroad. Sun Valley had been famous back then, with movie stars taking the train up from Hollywood to go skiing.

Their log cabin must've been built by locals and over the years it had been refined with a modern kitchen and bathroom. It had two bedrooms, one with a king-sized bed, perfect for the three of them. The other was a loft with a double bed. The fireplace was large and there were cords of wood stacked neatly outside. All in all, a great cabin at a really cheap price.

Tommy got on the computer that night, and using Ted and Jupe's driver's licenses dug deep into their identities. He destroyed their credit ratings. Then, using Ted's checkbook they'd found in the truck, he donated all the money to Planned Parenthood and the ACLU. If that didn't piss Ted off, nothing would. He couldn't get into Jupe's bank account, but he did max out his credit cards. He also did a background check and found Ted had been kicked out of high school for severely assaulting a classmate and had been booked as an adult for DUIs and resisting arrest. He'd spent six months in jail.

He couldn't find anything on Jupiter until the last few months, where apparently he'd gone off the deep end— barroom fights, a drunk and disorderly conviction, and a motorcycle crash. He couldn't find what had brought all that on. Finally he got sleepy so he logged off and went to bed.

Tommy couldn't wait to get up on the mountain. Some of his the happiest times had been spent skiing and he wanted to share that with Jo and Kirsten. The next morning he logged on to Ebay to check out used gear. He found a family selling three pairs of two-year-old K-2 skis and Scott poles for next to nothing. They were leaving town and needed cash. He knew nothing about the recent advances in equipment but checked online and these looked excellent. Also, years ago he'd skied on K-2s and liked them so he called the family and bought the skis. He was surprised to find Sturtevant's ski shop still in business. They drove into town and walked in. A bored college-age kid stood behind the counter and Tommy asked him about the plans for the mountain.

"From what I hear," said the kid, "They're only going to open the River Run side and just two or three chair lifts. The lift tickets are going to be cheap, so maybe it'll be okay for the locals. I hope I can keep this job long enough to get a season pass and make it through the winter."

Tommy brought in their used skis and asked him what he thought.

"Those are top-of-the-line skis and bindings," he said, "and you got a great deal."

"We need boots, goggles, parkas, jumpsuits, gloves and everything else," said Tommy. You know someone who wants to sell used stuff?"

"I can do better than that," said the kid. "We got new rental gear last year and there's no way we're going to need it now. I can sell you everything cheap if you don't mind last year's models. You sure you can pay for all this?"

"I think so. Let's add it up and see."

The prices were amazingly low, and Kirsten and Jo had great fun picking out their new ski outfits. Tommy took them aside and told them to get muted colors, again in an attempt to maintain a low profile. No pinks or yellows. They pretended to pout, but neither of them were girly girls so it wasn't a big deal. The boy added it up and Tommy realized it was going to put a decent dent in his paycheck. He paid the kid, who told him it was the biggest sale he'd had in months.

Their plan was to lie low. It wouldn't be easy, because Kirsten would stand out in Ketchum. Not a lot of tall, black women in Idaho, especially ones hanging out with a short guy and a little girl who couldn't talk. They might as well carry posters. "Over here! People who don't fit in!"

Maybe lying low just wasn't an option. In the past few weeks they'd tried to stay under the radar and even so they'd been attacked by Rick, Shake, Ted and Jupe. Rick, they could understand, but Ted and Jupe had come out of nowhere. Would they give up? Who knew?

Tommy wanted the pickup ready for a getaway, so he asked Joyce if there was a good mechanic in town.

"Jerry over at the Shell station is the best. You can trust him."

Tommy drove to the gas station and asked for Jerry. A guy about thirty-five walked out in coveralls but he looked more like a California surfer than a mechanic. With longish blond hair and an outdoors tan, only his grease-stained hands and coveralls gave him away. Tommy told him Joyce sent him.

"Good for her," he said. "I can always use the business. What do you need?"

"Can you do a tune-up, lube and oil, check everything out and fix anything that needs to be fixed?"

"You really trust her judgment, don't you." he said.

"I guess so. Let me know if there's anything expensive, and we may have to think about it. If it's a belt, or brake fluid, stuff like that, go ahead and do it."

"You got it. It runs okay now?"

"Yeah. Should I get snow tires? Or chains?"

Jerry checked the tires.

"These should be fine. They're pretty good about plowing the roads around here and if you get a set of chains you'll be okay if we get a snow storm. We can also drop a couple of sand bags in the cargo bed, put a little weight on the back tires."

"Sounds good to me. I just want to depend on it. By the way, do you know any way we can get a camper shell for that cargo bed?"

They'd talked about this and it would have advantages. One, it would change the look of the truck. Two, if they did have to make a run for it they could sleep in back. And three, they could lock up their skis and gear.

"Let me check around," said Jerry. "I might be able to find something."

"If you do, let me know what it costs and you can go ahead and put it on."

"I'll do that. Give me a day or two, and I'll call when it's done."

Two days later the truck was outfitted for winter and tuned

up. Jerry replaced a couple of belts and put in a new battery. Best of all, he'd found a used black camper shell and installed it. It was faded but serviceable, and extremely cheap. The price for everything was more than fair.

"Thank you," said Tommy. "Joyce was right about you."

"She's a good person," said Jerry. "I ought to know, I was married to her."

"Ah! So you're the one. She said she'd been married to a guy in town but she didn't tell me it was you."

"Yep, I'm the guy."

"She said you're a good person."

"Nice of her. It was sad that it didn't work out, but we're over it."

"I'm impressed," said Tommy. "I've seen a lot of bitter divorces."

"Life's too short, and we were both ski bums. If nothing else, we know how to move on from our mistakes. I hope she's doing okay."

"She's struggling, but we'll try to help if she gets desperate."

"I will too. I hope she knows that."

"Thanks for getting the truck in shape. I feel a lot safer now."

They shook hands and Tommy drove back to the cabin.

CHAPTER 22

"I don't like guns," said Kirsten one night as they sat in front of the fireplace, Tommy and Kirsten with laptops, Jo with her iPhone and ear buds.

"I don't either," said Tommy. "What brought that up?"

"I just realized that Jo and the Glock saved us twice from scary situations. Do you think we should revise our thinking?"

"Maybe, but you know there are all those statistics that say you're more apt to kill yourself than an intruder."

"Is that what they say?"

"Something like that. Accidents, kids playing with them, guys shooting themselves while cleaning them, suicides, domestic disputes—there are all kinds of ways to kill yourself with a gun."

"And yet we may have two hijackers chasing us and you know they'll be armed next time."

"I know. My first choice is to outwit them. My second is to run like hell, my third is to steal all their money so they can't buy gas to chase us, and my fourth is to buy weapons."

"Can we do all four?" asked Kirsten.

"I've already taken their money and we have the pistol from Ted's truck. I don't even know what kind it is. Should we ask Jo?"

"It just seems so weird, having our little girl as our authority."

"Hey, the whole world is weird. We fit right in. Jo took that gun apart and put it in her backpack, didn't she?

"I think so."

"Hey Jo," he said loudly, and she took out her ear buds. "Can you get your backpack? We want to look at that other handgun."

Jo ran to the bedroom and brought the back pack. She pulled out the pieces of Ted's pistol and assembled it, leaving the magazine out.

Tommy could see the brand, Smith & Wesson.

"Jo, is this a good gun?"

She stripped it down again. She looked through the barrel, checked the mechanism, and reassembled it, leaving out the magazine and checking the chamber to make sure it was empty. Then she racked it, took aim at the refrigerator and dry fired it. It was good she didn't play with loaded guns or they'd be leaving a trail of dead refrigerators.

"Is it okay?"

She nodded.

"Look, Jo," said Kirsten, "Tommy and I don't like guns. You know that, don't you?"

She nodded.

"But these are dangerous times and we have to be prepared for the worst. Should we each have a handgun?"

Jo thought about it, and nodded.

"Okay. From now on, the Glock is yours. You

certainly know how to use it. Tommy can have this Smith and Wesson and I guess I should get one too. What kind should I get?"

Jo pointed at the Glock 19. It made sense. Might as well get the same weapon for both of them.

"Okay," Tommy said. "We'll go find a gun store tomorrow. Jo, can you teach us to shoot?"

Jo nodded.

The next day they drove ten miles south to Western Sports in Hailey. The guy behind the counter wore boots, jeans, a cowboy shirt, and was probably about fifty. He looked like a mountain man, grizzled, with bushy eyebrows and a heavy black beard. To his credit he didn't seem startled to see a tall black woman, a short white guy and a mixed-race girl walk in his store.

"Hi folks, can I help you find something?"

"I need to buy a pistol," said Kirsten.

"We've got a lot of those. What were you thinking?"

"Do you have a Glock 19?"

"We sure do. Got a couple of them."

He brought them out and laid them on the counter.

"I don't know anything about guns," said Kirsten. "What's the difference?"

"This one's new, and this one we got on a trade-in. It's cheaper but it's used. The good news is it should be easier to cock. The slide can be a little stiffer on the new ones."

Kirsten wanted Jo to look at the used one but it wouldn't do to have this guy see a little girl strip down a weapon.

"Can you take it apart for me? I don't know how to do that."

The guy field-stripped the handgun, and laid the pieces on a felt pad on the counter.

"Honey," said Kirsten, "have you ever seen a gun all taken apart?"

Jo shook her head. We'd briefed her coming in.

"Here, come take a look. It's like a puzzle."

Jo came over, stood on tip toes at the showcase and looked at the disassembled weapon. She picked up the various pieces, entranced, and the salesman watched.

"We shouldn't let kids play with the weapons," he said.

"As long as it's apart she can't do any harm. If we buy one we'll keep in way out of reach and unloaded. We're both scared of guns."

"That's a good way to be. Do you know how to shoot?"

"No, but we have a friend who's an instructor. Don't worry, we are going to do this the right way."

Kirsten turned down to Jo.

"Pretty complicated isn't it, sweetie?"

Jo nodded.

"Should we buy it?"

Jo nodded again.

Kirsten laughed.

"Well, we've got one vote for this gun. I don't have a clue. Tommy, what do you think?"

"The price is good for the used one," he said, "and we're strapped for cash. Let's go with that.

"Okay," said Kirsten, "I guess this one will do. Do you think it's okay?"

"It's a good gun. Probably as good as the new one, but don't tell the boss I said that."

"Our lips are sealed," said Kirsten. "We'll take it. We should get ear protectors and glasses too,"

The next couple of weeks while they waited for snow, Tommy drove them out into the country and Jo taught them how to shoot their new pistols. They wore the ear protectors and yellow eyewear. Odd, none of those gunslingers at the OK Corral wore ear protectors and wrap-around glasses. Amateurs.

Kirsten had wonderful hand-eye coordination and soon was knocking beer cans off logs with great abandon. Tommy, on the other hand, would have to go to shooting school in the little bus. He was a slow learner but eventually he could at least hit the log. They shot up a lot of ammunition and Jo taught them how to strip down and clean the guns after every session.

"As long as I think of this as a sport," said Kirsten, "I can do it. But I'm not sure I could ever shoot a person, even if he was coming at me."

"What if he was coming at Jo?" Tommy asked.

Kirsten smiled.

"That sucker is dead."

"Maybe that's the way we have to look at it. We protect each other."

"So you'll be protecting me?"

"Absolutely."

"I'm a dead woman."

"Hey, I'm getting better."

"That's not saying much, but I know your heart's in the right place."

Tommy laughed, but deep down he knew he was going to try harder.

CHAPTER 23

Winter arrived in December. It was just light flurries when they went to sleep, but the next morning they awoke to find six inches of snow on the ground. In no time Jo and Kirsten had thrown on their jumpsuits and parkas and were outside winging snowballs. Tommy wondered if it was the first time Jo had ever seen snow. Clearly she loved it.

Ski season was upon them. Sun Valley always has a short season and as soon as the River Run lifts opened up, Tommy began teaching Kirsten and Jo. He loved skiing, a sport where small people could excel, especially in slalom and mogul skiing. Quick turns? He could do those. He taught them the way the young instructors had taught him—by playing follow the leader on the easy runs. He kept snow plowing to a minimum, taught them the value of edges, and how to keep weight on the downhill ski. Soon they were carving turns on the gentle slopes and Kirsten and Jo were finally impressed with something he could do. It was hard to dazzle people with programming skills.

They bought cheap family lift tickets and skied every day. It was a quick trip from their cabin to the mountain and that was good in case they had to leave town in a hurry. They timed it, and they could get down the mountain, drive to the cabin, load up and be headed out of town in less than forty-five minutes. They had all the essential stuff pre-loaded into the truck.

One night they were sitting in the cabin with Tommy working on the computer, Kirsten checking the markets, and Jo watching K-pop music videos. How she found them they never knew, but she was definitely hooked. Then Kirsten's phone rang.

"It's Wendy!" she exclaimed, and put it on speaker.

"Hi Wendy, how are you doing?"

"We're just fine. We called to see how you are. Did you make it to Ketchum?"

"We did. We had that adventure along the way but we're safe now."

"Happy to hear that. Tell us about it."

"We ran into hijackers outside of La Grande and it was a close call. Jo saved us."

"Thank heaven for that. Is Jo okay?"

"She's here beside me and she's really happy you called."

"And Tommy?"

"He's here too, doing nerdy stuff on the computer."

"Don't knock it. It's those nerds who are keeping us afloat these days."

"You can say that again," said Tommy. "In fact I wish you would. I can't convince them how important I am."

Wendy laughed.

"The reason we called," said Wendy, "is that we're all feeling cooped up and it's too much work protecting the house. We're thinking of getting out of town."

MIKE NEUN

"I tell you, Wendy," said Kirsten, "It sure felt great when we did it."

"How's Ketchum?"

"We love it here. Tommy taught us to ski!"

"Wait a minute! You found a nerd who can ski?"

"Yeah, and he's good at it too."

"Well I think you hit the mother-load. Hang on to that boy."

"We plan to. Jo and I would be lost without him."

Tommy felt his heart surge. He should've recorded the call.

"We are thinking of leaving Seattle and we thought Ketchum might be a good place for us too."

Kirsten paused.

"We'd love to have you, but there might be a problem."

"What's that?"

"We're not sure about those hijackers. They threatened to come after us and we're set to bail out at a moment's notice."

"It sounds serious."

"They were serious guys. Scary. Do you think you could hold off for a week or two until we think it's safe?"

"Let me ask the others. Hang on for a second."

There was a pause.

"It's unanimous. We'll wait, but let us know when it's safe. We all miss Jo."

Jo beamed.

"Tell her she's got seven grandparents waiting to come visit and we don't want to be put off too long."

"We'll do everything we can to figure out what's going on," said Kirsten.

They talked awhile longer and then hung up.

"You know," said Tommy, "The only way we're going to know if those guys are still after us is if they come after us."

"I know," said Kirsten. "I hope they don't but the suspense is killing me. In some ways I wish they would come so at least we could deal with it."

"Same here. All we can do is stay prepared and surf the Internet, see what they're up to. Can you think of any way they'd be connected with Rick?"

"I don't know how. I don't think he's ever been to La Grande in his life."

Jo loved the cabin. The furniture was rustic, covered in Indian blankets, and the walls had pictures of Ketchum in the old days. One had a herd of sheep filling up Main Street. Others showed old movie stars and Austrian ski instructors in baggy ski pants and leather boots.

Outside, Jo explored the woods around the cabin and down by the river, which was icy cold. Tommy warned her not to get too close and slip in. Jo seemed perfectly happy but Tommy worried about Kirsten.

"What do you think?" He said. "Do you like Ketchum or is it too small?"

"I'm not sure. I love the cabin and the skiing, but I don't like everyone knowing us. Privacy isn't a big deal around here, is it?"

"No. In the city you could be anonymous, hide out in the crowds. Here, if anyone wants to find you they just ask the first person they meet."

"Well, we're not forced to stay. We can leave any time."

CHAPTER 24

Joyce invited them into town for coffee at Jitters, a little coffeehouse on the road to Sun Valley. They sat, drinking cappuccinos with a hot chocolate for Jo.

"How are you doing?" Kirsten asked.

"To tell you the truth," said Joyce, "I'm really struggling. Nobody's buying or renting and I'm behind on my office rent. My house is paid for, but I'm not sure I'm going to have money for food or heat and winter's coming."

"Anything we can do to help?"

"Sure. Buy a house. Buy a really big one with a giant commission that'll get me through the winter."

"I wish we could," said Kirsten. "You know, you can always come eat with us. We have enough food and we're certainly willing to share. And if you lose your heat, you can come sleep in our cabin. It's not much but it's warm."

Joyce's eyes welled up.

"You don't know how much that means," she said. "I was really worried about winter and I've got no place to go."

"No relatives? No family?"

"Not really. I grew up in Minnesota and came out here after high school. There's a big Minnesota-Sun Valley connection that started years ago and no one knows why. Anyway, I was a ski bum and I did all the jobs—dishwasher, barmaid, house cleaner—anything to get money for lift tickets."

"It sounds kind of hard," said Kirsten.

"Actually, it was the best time of my life. We crashed at friends' houses, had lots of parties, the skiing was sensational, and we were all young and beautiful."

"That does sound exciting. Lots of romance?"

"Oh hell yes. The guys were long-haired and tanned, funny, willing to try anything. It was a young girl's dream."

"What happened?"

"We got older. It's hard to sustain that lifestyle and of course younger kids came in. Before I knew it, I was a 29-year-old ski bum, my friends had all gotten married and the guys were after the younger girls. Then prices went up and minimum wage jobs wouldn't even get me lift tickets."

"What'd you do?"

"I tried to settle down. Jerry and I lived together awhile and then we got married."

"Not a good move?"

"It wasn't horrible. Jerry's a great guy, but our interests were miles apart. He's the one who worked on your truck, so Tommy knows him. We just drifted apart and got divorced. No big drama."

"So then you got into real estate?"

"I tried other stuff first. I managed this coffee shop and a little boutique, but they didn't pay much. Luckily, an older lady hired me in the real estate business and when she retired I took over. It was good for about five years, but then the pandemic hit and the crash followed that."

"Okay," said Kirsten. "Our offer stands. You're welcome at the cabin anytime and as of today you and Tommy are our official ski instructors. Can we pay you with food and a warm bed?"

"Absolutely," said Joyce.

As Tommy, Jo and Kirsten walked back to the pickup, Tommy said, "That was pretty quick. Are you sure about bringing her into our life? We don't know anything about her."

"Actually I do," she said. "While you were working yesterday I researched her on social media and Google. I did a pretty extensive background check."

"Why?"

"Because I want us to be safe. If we're going to deal with the people in this town I want to know as much as I can about them."

"What'd you find out?"

"Everything she told us was true. Also I like her thinking on important things and her friends seem to hold her in high regard. I think she's a good person."

"What about her ex-husband, Jerry? He did good work on the truck and I liked him. He seems like a nice guy and he said good things about her."

"She still likes him too. They keep in touch on Twitter and their conversations are respectful."

"That's a weird concept. Should we tell them how a real divorce is supposed to work? Lots of anger, hate, home invasions, gunfire?"

"For sure. My divorce was much more exciting. Where's the adventure in two people acting rationally?"

"Boring."

"She does seem to be one of the good people in town and I'm happy to help her out."

"Works for me," Tommy said. "What do you think, Jo? Do you like Joyce?"

Jo nodded yes, happily, and it was settled.

MIKE NEUN

CHAPTER 25

Ketchum life was idyllic, but they never forgot that Ted and Jupiter might be coming after them. And who knew what Rick was up to? Tommy and Kirsten filled Joyce in on their problems. She spread the word among her friends to watch for strangers, especially any guys in a black Hummer. Hopefully chances of them finding the little cabin in Ketchum were slim, but it would've been foolish not to be prepared.

On the positive side, Jo loved skiing. Kirsten, the athlete, caught on fast but Jo was a driving force from the start. She wanted to be first in the lift line every morning and last down the mountain at night, which was fine with Tommy. He didn't want to push them, but they both learned so quickly it wasn't a problem. Soon they were on intermediate runs, racing each other down the mountain.

They'd ski all day and then Tommy would try to drink enough coffee to get his computer work done in the evenings. It was wearing him out but luckily Joyce volunteered to ski with Kirsten and Jo so Tommy could take days off and catch up. Joyce was a better skier than Tommy—it's tough to beat years on the mountain—and Tommy bought her a cheap lift pass. Their ski family had grown to four.

Tommy had prided himself on his skiing, but Joyce was an expert and soon he and the girls were learning new skills—using the tops of moguls to unweight the skis, slipping down into the troughs, using the backsides of the bumps to brake, knees working like pistons, and Tommy rejoiced in his new techniques. Also, by getting up early they were able to get some powder days in and soon were good enough to get off the packed runs and into the trees.

They loved to watch Joyce and realized she was indeed a ski bum. Her moves were effortless.

Joyce often stayed overnight in the cabin and that was fine too. She was a quiet woman, easy to get along with, and she fell in love with Jo just like Kirsten and Tommy had. Life was good. They tried to keep a low profile but good luck with that. Soon they had friends all over town and everyone knew about the tall black woman, the short guy and the little girl who didn't talk.

So far there'd been no sightings of the Hummer. Regular SUVs and pickups made up most of the vehicles in Ketchum, so a Hummer would definitely stick out. Sure enough, one evening Joyce's phone rang and she had a quick conversation.

"Trouble," she said. "A black Hummer just drove into town. Jerry said it pulled in for gas, looked like it came up from Boise. Two guys in it, one of them really big with a bandage on his nose and one on his ear."

"Okay," said Tommy. "Emergency drill!"

They threw their gear into the pickup, along with pre-packed backpacks. Sleeping bags, ski gear and other survival stuff were already in the cargo bed, locked under the camper shell. They were ready to go in ten minutes. Joyce came with them. It would've been silly to leave her there unprotected.

MIKE NEUN

Kirsten drove, Joyce navigated and they cruised quietly out of town using back roads. But they had a big problem. There were only two ways out of town. North led you up to Stanley and into the back country. South took you to Twin Falls and civilization.

They chose north, and it was hard leaving Ketchum. Their time on the mountain had changed them, especially Jo. She had a skier's tan, with the raccoon paleness where goggles covered her upper face, and she moved with new athletic grace and confidence. Tommy too felt better than he had in years and he realized he couldn't spend his life glued to a computer. Kirsten felt alive again, and her failed marriage and loss of job seemed like something from a past life.

"We shall return," said Kirsten softly as they drove away.

They headed to Stanley, knowing they had choices once they got there and each one would make it harder for any followers to find them. The truck had a full tank, it was dirty and nondescript and wouldn't be noticed.

This whole thing was baffling. Surely Rick didn't have enough money to afford hired guns and Tommy had looted all the money from Ted and Jupe. Who the hell was financing these guys? Was there anyone else who had that kind of a grudge against Tommy? Or Kirsten? Or Jo? It didn't make any sense.

"I'm putting my money on Rick," Tommy said. "He's definitely dangerous and he hates you. I have no idea how he hooked up with Ted and Jupe, but he's the obvious choice."

"I don't know," said Kirsten. "I bet you broke some girl's heart and she's gone insane with lust."

"That could be," said Tommy. "Down in California I was known as Mighty Stallion."

Kirsten looked at Jo and rolled her eyes.

"Your dad just left the planet," said Kirsten.

"I worry for the child," said Joyce. "Jo, your father is really weird."

Jo nodded happily.

"From what you've told me," said Joyce, "It has to be Rick."

"I agree," said Tommy. "I think he's overreacting to the fact that we shot at him and left him tied up for two days. Some guys have no sense of humor."

"He's really screwed up." said Kirsten. "How could he turn from a nice guy into a psycho bent on revenge?"

"I think it's all your fault," said Tommy. "I bet he was a righteous man until you twisted him into a drunken, sex-crazed lunatic."

"Got me," laughed Kirsten. "But how would he know people like Ted and Jupiter."

"Jupiter?" asked Joyce. "What kind of a name is that?"

"It's a nickname. He's a huge guy so it fits."

"I have to admit it's inventive," she said.

"Anyway, how would he hook up with guys like that?"

"The Internet?" said Joyce. "Some divorced guys group? Dumped guys with a grudge?"

"It could be. There are certainly groups like that out there. But it's pretty far-fetched."

"Can we dig deeper into Rick? See what he's doing?"

"Maybe Tommy can do that when we stop tonight. His hacker skills are better than mine."

MIKE NEUN

"Did you hear that, Jo?" said Tommy. "Kirsten thinks my skills are better than hers."

Jo rolled her eyes. She was becoming a professional eye roller. Tommy was so proud.

"He's better at one tiny thing, Jo. Remember, girl power!"

Jo and Kirsten did a fist bump, Joyce joined in. Kirsten continued,

"I still think it's some wacko out of Tommy's past. Maybe Microsoft agents out to bring down Google. Russians who hate his Twitter posts. But I'm still going with old girlfriends whose lives he ruined."

"Hey," Tommy said, "Don't be flippant. I can be a heartbreaker too. I had girlfriends."

"How many?" asked Joyce.

"Let me count. This may take awhile."

"We're waiting."

"Two."

"You sex-crazed womanizer!" exclaimed Joyce. "No wonder people are after us! You've left a trail of broken hearts."

"Not really. They both left me. And my ex-girlfriends weren't physical threats. They were both just over five feet tall and as far as I know, neither of them were gangbangers."

"Did you hook up with them in Seattle?"

"No, California. One in Santa Monica, the other in Palo Alto. I knew them when I first started with Google and lived down there."

"Why did they leave you?"

"I don't know. I tried to be a good guy. Maybe they were driven off by excessive masculinity. Testosterone poisoning."

"Ease up, tough guy. You're forgetting we saw you tear up at the end of Titanic."

"Never. I was crying because there weren't any Kung Fu fights or explosions. What kind of movie is that?"

"So you were a perfect boyfriend?"

"Okay, maybe I spent too much time on the computer."

"Were you in love?"

"With the computer? Maybe."

"With the women, idiot. Were you in love?"

"I thought so, but I'm not all that sure what love is. I was so thrilled to have a woman in my bed that I didn't think much about it."

"Were they good women?"

"Who knows? I thought they liked me but then they left me for other guys. What kind of woman would do that?"

"The kind that figured out you weren't a mighty stallion?"

"Maybe. To tell you the truth, I wasn't that confident in bed."

"Were they geeks?"

"No. One was a hair dresser and one was a DJ."

"Whoo boy, I bet you had a lot to talk about!"

"You have a point. They did come from different worlds. I don't think we connected very well."

"How did you meet a DJ? Were you out raving? Tearing up the dance floor and she begged you to take her home?"

"No, I met her at Starbucks and she had a massive hangover. All the tables were full and I offered her a seat. She said okay, but only if I promised not to talk. She didn't want her head to explode."

138   MIKE NEUN

"What'd you do?"

"I didn't talk. I wrote code on my laptop. Quietly. When she was finished with her coffee I got her another one. She asked me how I knew she needed more and I just smiled and gave it to her. Then she wrote something on her napkin, gave it to me and left."

"Her phone number?"

"Her email address. I wrote to her and thanked her for a quiet hour at Starbucks. Two months later she was living with me."

"Wow, sexual magnetism."

"I like to think so, but she was broke and my apartment was probably a big part of my appeal."

"So she took advantage of you?"

"I didn't care. There was a naked lady in my bed. She could've been a North Korean spy and I would've been a happy camper."

"Ahah! She was Asian!"

"No way! The North Koreans wouldn't be that stupid."

"How long was she with you?"

"About a year. Maybe the best year of my life. Then she met that other guy and moved on."

"Damn."

"Yeah. I was crushed."

"How about the hairdresser?"

"I met her when I lived in Palo Alto. It was random. I was walking home from work and saw a salon across the street. Best haircut of my life and we talked. She was petite, blonde and amazingly beautiful so I figured she was out of my league. Then she asked if I wanted to have lunch the next day. I was stunned."

"So you dazzled her at lunch?"

"Not really. I figured my best bet was to shut up and

let her do the talking. I guess it worked."

"How long were you with her?"

"A little over a year. Same story. She found another guy and walked out on me."

"So neither of them are out to get you? No crazy women running around hiring hit men?"

"No, unless I missed that entirely. Actually, it's possible. I don't read people very well."

"How about work? And disgruntled fellow workers? Any sexual harassment problems?"

"No, I was the quiet guy who did his job, didn't bother people. Still am. Sometimes I wish I were more assertive but it seems like a lot of work."

They drove some more.

"We better talk about the other possibility," Tommy said.

"Jo?"

"Yeah. We know nothing about her except for the guy at the gun range. We don't know if she hung out with gangs, pimps, Russian sex traffickers, white supremacists, whatever. Anyone could be after her and we wouldn't have a clue."

"True," said Kirsten, "and I admit I'm not sure I want to know. It might break my heart."

"Same here. I can understand a lot of criminal impulses, but the thought of hurting kids makes me sick."

"How will we handle it if we ever do find out?"

"I don't know," said Tommy. "That's the one thing that could turn me into a sniper vigilante."

"Oh god no. The damage you could do with a rifle chills me to my soul."

"Hey, it could be a hidden talent. I might be lousy

with pistols and a deadly marksman with a rifle."

"Oh heck yes, and I could be a genius at quantum physics. The odds are about the same."

"Jo," said Tommy, "Can you think of anyone who would be after you? Any bad guys in your past?"

Jo turned thoughtful, then shook her head no.

"I guess the best we can hope for is that she's just another runaway and we caught her before really terrible things could happen."

"But Jo can't talk."

"There is that. And the obvious cause would be trauma."

"Jo, did something bad happen? Is that why you can't talk?"

Jo thought seriously and shook her head.

"Could you ever talk?"

She lifted her hands in an "I don't know" gesture.

"Well, so much for our psychiatric skills," said Kirsten. "Jo, we love you just the way you are, so don't ever worry about it. Talking's not that big a deal."

"Let's keep researching," said Tommy. "Check out all our lives, see if there's a wacko in our past."

"It's the best we can do."

"In the end it doesn't matter who sent them. We just have to deal with the problem."

CHAPTER 26

They pulled off in Stanley and stopped for dinner at the High Mountain Resort, the only restaurant with lights on. It had a motel next door, and obviously both had seen better days. Some of the letters in the sign were out and the restaurant was deserted. When they sat down they found half the items on the menu blacked out.

"You sure know how to show a girl a good time," said Kirsten.

"Nothing but the best for my ladies," said Tommy. "I recommend the meat loaf."

"They have a great selection of wines here too. Red or white."

"Tough decision but I think I'll go with beer."

The meatloaf was actually quite tasty—a pleasant surprise—and they ate and talked.

"You told me about your problems," Joyce said as they were eating, "but now they sound worse than I thought. Have I stepped into a Die Hard movie?"

"We didn't think it would affect you," said Kirsten, "but now those guys might know you were staying at our cabin. We're so sorry we got you involved."

"I think once we're gone for three or four days," said Tommy, "we can get you back to Ketchum. They're after us, not you."

"I like Ketchum," said Joyce, "but the truth is I was going under in a big way. I've got nothing to go back to, unless you count starving. Would you mind if I tag along for awhile? If you give me food, I'll do my best to help out, and maybe the country will start to recover."

"Oh heck yes," said Kirsten. "We need all the help we can get."

"I hate to ask this," Tommy said, "but are you any good with weapons?"

"I lived fifteen years in Idaho," said Joyce, "alone in a town full of randy cowboys and drunken skiers. Or maybe it was drunken cowboys and randy skiers. I can never get that straight. Anyway, I've got a gun. I never needed it, but I'm a pretty good shot."

"That's good to know. Kirsten and I have been practicing but Jo is our resident gun expert."

"Seriously?"

"Yes. She saved us twice already."

"That is the weirdest thing I ever heard," she said. She looked at Jo.

"You can shoot?"

Jo smiled and nodded.

"I'm sorry to hear that. You're too young to handle guns."

Jo nodded again, and smiled ruefully.

"And you two are just learning?" asked Joyce.

"Yes," said Kirsten. "We both have handguns, but I'm not sure I could shoot anyone and Tommy is a danger to us all."

"Hey," said Tommy, "I'm getting better."

"Just make sure you stand behind him. He's kind of a free range marksman."

"I'll keep that in mind," said Joyce.

They finished their meal.

"We need two things," Kirsten said. "A place to stay and high-speed Wi-Fi. I thought we could camp out, but Tommy should spend time researching."

"We can check in next door," said Tommy. "The motel is open and I have a cunning plan."

"My God," said Joyce, "Don't tell me you're a Black Adder fan!"

"Hell yes! We could be the only two in all of Idaho."

"Black Adder?" asked Kirsten.

"One of the greatest TV shows ever," said Joyce. "We've got to find it for you."

Tommy checked into the motel as Joyce and Jo crouched low in the back seat. They only needed one room, made sure it had Wi-Fi, and drove the truck to the far side of the parking lot and backed in, ready for a quick getaway. The motel was a two-story wood frame building and they'd booked a room on the second floor.

They showered and changed into warm clothes, then took their stuff back out to the truck and laid out sleeping bags in the front and back seat of the cab. The room would be a trap so they didn't want to be in it, but the showers were great and they could use the motel Wi-Fi. Joyce and Jo bedded down in the back seat of the pickup, Tommy sat shotgun so he could work on his laptop, and Kirsten took the driver's seat. They had quilts, sleeping bags and pillows and would get through the night the best they could.

MIKE NEUN

Tommy got on his laptop and began searching.

"What's Rick's last name?" He asked.

"Bryson, and he's from southern Oregon. Medford I think. Went to college at the University of Oregon and worked for Harrison, Noble and Fitch in Seattle. Just to be sure, what are your ex-girlfriends' names?"

"Holly Carlson was the hairdresser in Palo Alto. Jody Robinson was the DJ. She came from Detroit and lived in Santa Monica. I met her when I was down there for a convention."

"Okay, you do research on Rick. I'll get a start on your girlfriends. I'm going to be pretty pissed if I find one of them is a Muslim jihadist. Did either of them wear a burka?"

"I might've noticed that."

"Really?"

"Okay, maybe not."

She smiled.

Joyce, in the back seat with Jo, reached into her backpack and took out a pistol.

Kirsten glanced over her shoulder and saw it.

"I just want to see if what you're telling me is true," said Joyce.

She handed the gun to Jo, who popped out the magazine, racked the slide and checked the chamber. Then in about fifteen seconds she field-stripped the weapon and laid the pieces on the sleeping bag.

"Okay," said Joyce, "I'm impressed."

Jo reassembled the gun, again checked to make sure the chamber was empty and the magazine out, then dry fired it out the side window using her two-handed grip. She aimed at a tree, as apparently all the refrigerators had gone into hiding. She nodded her approval and gave it back to Joyce.

"What kind of guns do you have?" Joyce asked Kirsten.

"Jo and I have Glocks and Tommy has a Smith & Wesson we took from Ted. What's yours?"

"A Sig Sauer. Apparently Jo knows all kinds of weapons."

"You can say that again. We don't have to bother with toys, we can just go to any gun shop."

Jo gave them a questioning look.

"That's okay, sweetie," said Joyce, "Kirsten's making jokes. We're amazed at your skills, and I have to admit, a little worried. Guns and kids are usually a horrible combination."

Jo nodded, and smiled again.

"Where's your gun?" asked Joyce.

Jo reached into her backpack and pulled out the Glock. She showed it to Joyce, carefully keeping it aimed away with her finger off the trigger.

"That's a nice pistol," she said. "Well, at least were going first class when it comes to weapons."

"It feels like we're the James Gang," said Kirsten. "I'll be so happy when we can get back to a normal life."

Joyce and Jo put their weapons back in their backpacks while Tommy's fingers flew over the keyboard.

"You were right, Joyce," said Tommy. "Rick belongs to a bunch of online men's groups, full of pissed-off divorced guys. There's a lot of stuff in here about guys who lost everything—houses, kids, savings—and they sound pretty violent.

"Has Rick posted anything?" asked Kirsten.

"Yeah," he said, "but you might not want to hear it."

"Go ahead, I've heard it all before."

"He posted how you cheated on him, took all his money, made him lose his job."

"Damn. Some of it's true, but I didn't make him lose his job. We both lost our jobs."

"How about the cheating part?" asked Joyce.

"It's true. One drunken night and I wrecked our marriage."

"With a punter," Tommy added. Kirsten glared daggers at him.

"A punter?" asked Joyce. "Like in football?"

"Put a sock in it," Kirsten said to Tommy. "Joyce, I feel bad enough. Let's move on."

"Okay," Joyce said. "So he's in these radical men's groups. How about Ted and Jupiter? Ted's a common name but does Jupiter show up anywhere? Or Jupe?"

"I searched, and there's one in Eastern Oregon. Got to be the same guy."

"Any pictures?"

"No, but this guy loves Harleys and he's supposed to be huge. That can't be a coincidence."

"I think we found our pursuers," said Kirsten. "I haven't found much about your old girlfriends. There are a ton of Holly Carlsons in California. I cross referenced the name with hairdressers and came up with a possible."

"Really."

"Yeah. She married a tall, good-looking guy who hates computers. She says it's the best thing that ever happened to her, especially after spending a year with a dweeb at Google."

"You're making that up."

"No way. Oh look, here she says the Google guy was clueless in bed and had a terrible sense of humor."

"Now I know you're making that up. I'm a tiger in bed and my sense of humor is world class."

"One more punter remark and I'm going to tell everyone her pet name for you."

"She didn't have a pet name for me."

"Does 'Needledick' ring a bell?"

Tommy grabbed her laptop. The screen was blank.

"Gotcha!" she crowed.

"You did," he admitted. "I guess I deserved it."

"Payback is a bitch."

"Okay. I did find more stuff about Rick."

"Really? What?"

"The Seahawks just signed him to do their kicking."

Kirsten punched him. Hard. Then she jumped on him and started punching some more. Tommy begged for mercy. Joyce and Jo joined in, laughing and pummeling him. Finally, Kirsten started laughing too.

"I'll get you for that," said Kirsten.

"I think you already have. I'm going to have bruises. If this town has a sheriff I'm going to report roommate abuse."

Kirsten hit him in the arm again.

"Report that you bastard."

Tommy threw up his hands in surrender. They calmed down and Kirsten reported on his DJ, Jody Robinson.

"It looks like her DJ career never hit the big time so she tried acting. I found some head shots and she was quite a looker. Tommy, you stud! I'm impressed. But the acting didn't work out and she married a guy who owns a Les Schwab franchise. They've got a couple of kids. I don't think she has any revenge fantasies about you. I don't think she even remembers you.

"Holly Carlson is different," she continued. "After she left you she married a guy in Reno. Later she filed police complaints of domestic abuse. Then, get this, her husband disappeared. It was a big deal in Reno, made all the papers. The police found blood traces and strongly suspected murder, but they couldn't find the body or pin anything on her. It all sounds kind of scary. Did she scare you when you knew her?"

"No. She seemed nice enough. I don't have a lot of dating rules, but I try to steer clear of murderers."

"Nice to know you have boundaries. I'll keep searching. Maybe there's more about her."

"Okay, but I'm getting sleepy. How about all of you?"

Jo was already asleep, wrapped in her sleeping bag.

They decided to call it a night and arranged themselves as best they could in the cramped conditions, snuggled into sleeping bags, quilts and pillows. It had been a long day.

CHAPTER 27

Jo heard the engine first, about 4 a.m.

She roused the others quietly and they saw their old friend, the Hummer. They stayed low as it pulled up to the office and Ted got out and limped in. Apparently a flesh wound in the butt takes time to heal. It took him awhile to wake the clerk, but then he walked back out and he and Jupe drove over and parked about thirty feet away from the stairs. They got out and looked at the truck. Everyone was scrunched down and it appeared empty. They walked quietly over to the steps and began sneaking up. Watching Jupiter, a three-hundred-pound biker with a heavily bandaged nose and ear, try to sneak up old wooden steps was a treat. Jo had her window cracked open and they could hear the wood creaking from across the parking lot.

"We should've charged admission," whispered Kirsten. "You getting all this?"

Tommy was taking video with his iPhone.

"Yeah."

Into his phone he whispered, "And now, on this installment of Criminal Fails, we are watching two masterminds pull off a motel break-in."

Ted and Jupe made it up the steps and eased down the wide outside passageway to the motel room. In the truck, Jo moved as planned. She reached into her backpack, took out the Glock and under a pillow, quietly cocked it.

Tommy continued his video commentary.

"You've seen them sneak up on quiet cat feet, now comes the action."

Joyce had taped the latch open, and the only thing holding the door closed was a tiny amount of friction.

Jupe stood outside the motel door, back to the railing. He pushed off with one foot and charged. His shoulder hit the door at full speed and met no resistance whatsoever. The door flew open and he plunged across the room off balance and crashed into a full-length mirror on the opposite side. They heard the crash and tinkle of glass and then a large thump as he toppled back onto the floor. Ted, sensing a trap, rushed in to do battle and found the room empty except for his partner, bleeding from tiny cuts, thrashing and cursing on the floor.

Under all that noise, Kirsten started the truck and pulled out quietly. She cruised past the back of the Hummer as Jo lowered her window and blasted off six shots at the back tires. Ted came flying out of the room and Kirsten floored the pickup. Ted watched helplessly as she careened out of the parking lot, turned right, and sped toward the highway.

"Do you hit the tires?" Tommy asked.

Jo nodded, and held up one finger. That was okay. One flat tire would stop them from chasing. They wouldn't be able to follow them to the highway and see which way the pickup turned. Kirsten turned right, back toward Ketchum, hoping to confuse the hijackers.

"I can't wait to post this," said Tommy.

"Hell," said Kirsten, "That's YouTube stuff. I think we're talking Darwin Awards."

"We'll teach those fuckers not to piss off computer people."

After a few miles, Kirsten spoke up.

"There's something wrong. There's no way they could've followed us here, yet they found us. Are they using some kind of tracking device? Are they locating our phones? We've got to figure this out or they'll just follow us back to Ketchum."

"You're right," Tommy said. "We can't stop to look for a tracking device but we should take the batteries out of our phones."

"How?" asked Kirsten. "We've all got Apple stuff and you can't get into the cases. You're a hacker, can you do it?"

"I can, but not in a moving truck and we don't want to stop. The best we can do is turn them off."

"I've got an idea," said Joyce. "There's a big metal tool box in back. Can we put everything in it? It should cut off the signals."

"Great thinking!"

Kirsten pulled onto the shoulder and stopped. They grabbed their phones and laptops and rushed back to put them in. They locked it, jumped back into the truck and Kirsten spun gravel accelerating back onto the highway.

"That solves that," said Kirsten. "How about a tracking device? Some kind of theft protection? LoJack?"

"Hard to believe on a 4-year-old pickup," said Tommy, "but maybe. Wait. If Rick hired them he's got our numbers in his records. If Ted's got a hacker friend he could trace our phones. That has to be the way they're doing it, and the best way to stop it is to get new gear and SIM cards. I vote for that."

Kirsten drove hard for Ketchum. They figured they had at least a thirty-minute head start, more if Jo had managed to hit two tires. More if the police answered quickly to shots fired and Ted and Jupiter were wrestling with the tires when the cops got there.

CHAPTER 28

Ted and Jupe knew the cops would be coming to investigate the shots, so they didn't bother to change the one tire Jo had hit. They jumped in the Hummer and drove out across town on the flat tire. They pulled behind a deserted gas station and leaped out to change it there, guessing the police response in Stanley, Idaho, might be a bit slow. Jupe was a mechanic and still bleeding from tiny cuts, he and Ted worked fast. They jacked up the Hummer, threw on the spare and plunged back onto the highway in fifteen minutes. Jupe drove as Ted checked his laptop and located the pickup truck headed back to Ketchum.

"Got 'em," he said. "Turn right at the highway."

The Hummer wasn't fast, but Jupiter floored it and soon it was rumbling along at seventy on the straights. They had to catch these people or they'd be screwed. The Seattle guy didn't like fuckups and they needed the money.

"Are we close?" asked Jupiter, wiping traces of blood off his face.

"They got a pretty good head start. Oh oh."

"What?"

"We just lost the signal. They must've dumped their phones. God damn it."

"They've got to be headed for Ketchum, maybe we can catch them before they get there."

Ted heard a rustling sound behind him. He started to turn.

"Don't even think of moving," said a soft voice behind him.

"What the fuck!!!" blurted Ted as he started to turn his head. A pistol slammed into him from behind.

"Ow! Fuck me!"

"I said don't move," it was a woman's voice, but it was steely strong. "Next time I'll shoot. You got it?"

"We got it," said Ted. "Who the fuck are you? What are you doing here?"

"We should get this straight. I'm behind you, I've got a gun, and I'll be asking the questions. Does that work for you?"

She poked him in the neck with her pistol.

"Yes ma'am," said Ted. "Whatever you say."

"Okay. Now who are you guys?"

"The guy driving is Jupiter," said Ted.

"Jupiter? Really?"

"It's a nickname," said Jupiter, "because I'm big."

"Okay. So who are you? Mercury? Because you're fast?"

"No, I'm Ted."

"Ted? That's it? No fancy nickname?"

"No. Just Ted."

"You better call the nickname police. You got robbed."

"Who are you?"

She nudged him again in the neck with her pistol.

"Are we forgetting who's asking the questions here?"

"Sorry."

"You can call me Holly. Why are you after the people in the pickup?"

"We're after them because a guy is paying us a lot of money to catch that black woman."

"What guy?"

"Just a guy on the Internet. His name is Rick and he sent us money and said we'd get twice as much if we bring him that woman in the pickup.

"How'd you know where the woman was?"

"It's a long story."

"I bet you could make it shorter."

"It's kind of embarrassing."

"More embarrassing than getting shot?"

"No."

"Okay, go for it."

"We tried to hijack them at a rest stop outside La Grande and had the man and woman cornered when someone started shooting at us from behind. There was nothing we could do. The embarrassing part was the shooter walked out and it was a goddam little girl. She could really shoot."

"I'm liking this more and more. You got taken out by a little girl with a pistol?"

"She was a fucking wizard with that gun. She could shoot the caps off beer bottles."

"How awesome is that? I've got to meet that girl."

"She's all yours. Anyway, that pickup truck up there is mine. They stole it and left us with this fucking Hummer."

"And you didn't chase them?"

"Er, no. They trashed the engines on the Hummer and Jupe's Harley. They took our phones, I.D., money, everything. We couldn't even call for help. So we had to hike back to town. It wasn't easy.

"What happened to Jupiter's nose?"

"The woman kicked him and broke it. The little girl shot his ear too."

"No shit? They shot you? Broke his nose? You guys sure know how to pick your victims. Who are you going after next? The Russian mafia?"

"They caught us by surprise. We had them until that fucking little girl came out with the gun."

"This is priceless. Obviously she didn't shoot to kill, where'd she get you?"

Long pause.

"In the butt."

"A little girl shot you in the butt? My God, this just keeps getting better and better. Don't stop now."

"Some guys picked us up and thought it was pretty funny."

"Embarrassing."

"Yeah, it was. Then the bastard went on the Internet, stole our money and wrecked our credit ratings."

"Whoo boy, I bet your credit ratings were way up there too. Must've been a huge financial blow."

"Fuck you, we're doing the best we can."

"And you're after that woman?"

"The guy too. He fucked us over."

"So let's see if I've got this straight. We're in their Hummer chasing your pickup, right?"

"Right."

"And there's a little girl up there who is armed and dangerous."

"Yes."

"I love it. I can tell this story to my grandkids. Oh sure, they'll never believe it..."

"What do you want with Ted and me?" asked Jupe. "You going to take our Hummer?"

"Was that a question? Are you asking the questions now?"

She poked the back of the driver's seat hard with the pistol.

"No ma'am. I forgot."

"Okay. I'm going to have you guys help me. Who all is in the pickup?"

"A guy named Tommy, a woman named Kirsten, and that goddam little girl with the pistol. Now there's another woman too. We don't know who the hell she is."

"Four people."

"Yes. And that damn kid shoots like Wild Bill Hickok."

"You," she said to Ted, "what's on the computer?"

"We had their position. One of the guys on the Internet traced the guy's phone and we were using that to find them."

"He must be good. Who is he?"

"I don't know. He's in our group on the Internet."

"What group is that?"

"Just a group. A bunch of guys."

"What's the name of the group?"

"It doesn't matter, it's just a group."

"Here's a thought. You could tell me the name of the group or I could put a bullet through the back of your seat. I bet it hits a vital organ."

"Okay, okay. But the name doesn't matter, really."

"Three...., two...."

"Wait! The name of the group is 'Take Down the Bitches.'"

"Really. So it's kind of an anti-woman group?"

"I guess so. We're all divorced, we all lost a lot of money, and some guys lost their kids."

"So it's a bunch of pissed off ex-husbands."

"Yeah, I guess so."

"You know what's funny?" she said.

"What?"

"I'm divorced too."

"Shit."

"Yeah, only it went the other way. I lost my business, my house, everything, just because of a few moments in my life that didn't sound too good. You want to hear about those moments?"

"I don't think so."

"Sure you do. How are you going to take down the bitch if you don't know what she did?"

"I don't want to take you down."

"Sure you do. I'm a bitch, I fit the profile."

"Look, we're just doing a job here."

"Ask me about the moments."

"Okay, what did you do?"

"It started with my first husband. I had this hair salon and I was living with a guy who was okay but not too exciting. Then I met this other guy, fell in love, and dumped the first one.

Big mistake."

"Why? Wait, sorry, that was a question."

"That's okay, that one keeps the story moving. Why? Because the new guy was not a nice man. We got married, we moved into his big house in Reno, what could go wrong?"

"I'm guessing it didn't end well."

"Nope, it was a disaster. Turned out he was a mean drunk with violent tendencies."

"Wow, bad combination. What happened?"

"Well, he kept punching me out and I kept getting hurt. Bad. I came back from the hospital after one of these episodes and that night he disappeared. Poof! Just like that! One day I was stuck with this abusive bastard and the next, all my problems were solved! How cool is that!"

"Yeah. Cool."

"Wouldn't you know it, the police found blood spots and thought I killed him! How silly is that? Me, a tiny little woman, kill a big man like that? I told the cops he'd run off with another woman. Oddly, they couldn't locate him or this other woman, so they searched the house, dug up the yard, and canvassed the neighborhood but couldn't find anything. Then it got in the papers and you'd have thought I was Jack the Ripper. The police kept on it for awhile, but couldn't find anything. Lucky, eh?"

"Yeah. Lucky."

"He just disappeared," she said. "Oh sure, I had to leave town, but hey, problem solved."

"Did you do it?"

"Do you really want to know? Do you want to have information that could put me on death row?"

"No!" said Jupe, quickly. "We don't want to know."

"Then I met other guys, but I was more choosey. I lived with a musician for awhile, kind of nice, but we

MIKE NEUN

broke up. Then I met the man of my dreams and we got married. Perfect, don't you think?"

"I guess so."

"He lived in Los Gatos. Nice house, living the dream. But I caught him chasing around. Fuck me, I can pick 'em, can't I? There I was, turning over a new leaf and the guy was cheating on me! I figured turnabout, you know? So I screwed a bunch of his friends, did some shoplifting, threatened his girlfriend with a machete, you know, little relationship moves that bother people. He divorced me, his evil bastard of a lawyer dug all that up, plus the police reports on my first husband, and I lost everything. My new beauty salon, house, money, all of it gone. Also, the judge, the bitch, put a restraining order on me."

"I've never heard of that before. Usually they put the restraining order on the guy."

"I like to break new legal ground."

"So he disappeared too?"

"No, but he's kind of traumatized. Nervous. Jumps at shadows. Someone must've thrown a real scare into him. I've got visitation rights that the lady judge doesn't even know about.

"Visitation rights?"

"Yeah, sometimes I visit him and he never seems happy to see me. Then he pays me to go away."

"He pays you? What do you give him?"

"His life. You'd be amazed how nice he is to me."

"Fuck. You are one scary Bi..... woman."

"Oh, that was close. Did you almost call me a bitch?"

"No."

"You sure?"

"Yes."

She laughed.

"You men are all alike. One little woman in the back seat with a gun and you get all soft and cuddly."

"So why are you after the people in the pickup and how the hell did you find us?"

"Easy. When I left that second rat bastard of a husband I realized that my life choices weren't the greatest and that first guy, the one I'd been living with before I ran off with the abusive fucker, was the best guy I'd ever been with. He's Tommy, the guy in that truck, and he's the love of my life and I didn't even know it. Isn't that a hoot?"

"You're chasing this guy because you love him?"

"Yeah. Some people would call it stalking, but I think that's kind of harsh, don't you?"

"Yeah, harsh. How did you find him? And us?"

"Oh I tracked him to Seattle. That was easy. I just went to Palo Alto and cozied up to the secretaries at Google. I mentioned I'd lived with him and did they know him? One did, and she got me his address in Seattle."

"What then?"

"I flew up to Seattle, got to his apartment building and couldn't get in, but I sweet-talked one of the tenants, said I was trying to find Tommy. He told me the story about the break-in and how Tommy had left with the tall woman and the little girl."

"The break-in?"

"Oh my, that sounded like a question."

"Sorry. We didn't know about any break-in."

"Apparently that woman's ex-husband is a nut case and he broke into their apartment. Didn't work out too well. Hey, he's the guy who hired you, isn't he?"

"I guess."

"Well, he's fucking Looney Tunes. I hope you got your money up front."

"Half. We got half up front."

"Well, this guy, Rick, her ex-husband, was the manager of the place. He got fired. Hard to believe. He bailed out of Seattle so I checked him out Twitter and Facebook. I friended him and he posted all this shit about you guys and how he hired you to find his wife. I figured if you were chasing her I'd just tag along and find Tommy. Smart move by the way, getting someone to track their phones. Stupid move, posting your adventures online. That's how I found you two were going to Ketchum in a Hummer. You do know this is not a stealth vehicle. It's like trying to sneak around in a parade float."

"Hey," said Ted, "It's all we've got," said Ted. "Those fuckers stole my pickup."

"So," said Holly, "I caught a flight to Hailey, rented a car, drove up to Ketchum and asked around for the Hummer. I followed you guys to Stanley and when you stopped for gas I ditched the rental and jumped in the back seat when you went in to buy snacks. Next thing I know you're driving to that motel and playing SWAT team on their motel room, but then all hell breaks loose. Someone's shooting the hell out of the Hummer with me in the back seat. Lucky I didn't get killed!"

"Yeah, lucky."

"Call me crazy, but that didn't sound sincere," she said, prodding him with the handgun.

"Sorry."

"So," said Jupe, "You're after the guy and we're after the woman."

"Correct. So I thought what the hell, we'll join forces."

"You could've just asked."

"Oh hell yes. Walk up to two hired thugs and say, 'Hi, can I join your gang?' How do you see that working out?"

"Okay, maybe not. What about the woman?" asked Jupe. "The ex-wife? You got any problem with her?"

"The tall one? I hate tall women. They get all the tall guys and we little girls are left with the shrimps. She really pisses me off, and if she gets in my way I'll hand her over to you. But the little girl? She's a chip off the old block. She's a keeper."

Ted realized he was dealing with the ultimate psycho bitch from hell and she was in the back seat with a pistol trained on him. He knew Jupiter felt the same. Fuck.

"Are we getting closer?" asked Holly.

"I don't know. We lost the signal, but they have to be in front of us. This piece-of-crap Hummer is slow as hell."

"Put the pedal to the metal boys, true love doesn't like to be kept waiting."

CHAPTER 29

Carlos Gonzales opened the door of his Nissan Almera and climbed in, happy to be leaving town. For the last twenty-three years he'd owned a gun store and firing range in Elko, Nevada, and he was happy to watch it disappear in his rear view mirror.

It was a long story, how he'd gone from being a fledgling novelist in Berkeley to peddling guns in Elko, and he didn't like to dwell on it. Life was a crap shoot. The pandemic had wiped out the economy and the economy had wiped him out, especially after the little girl ran away. For awhile he'd actually enjoyed his life and she'd been the reason. Then two fucked-up dudes had wrecked it.

He drove the Nissan because it was a boring car and no policeman in his right mind would ever stop it. It was a grandpa car, brown and slow, and Carlos fit the driver profile. Fifty-six years old with unkempt gray hair and dark features. Skinny. Glasses. Tall for a Mexican. He looked like a grandpa, and he could play the part. But you had to be careful of old guys. Carlos had learned a lot over the years. He'd dealt with all kinds of people. He'd won and lost fairly large amounts at the poker tables. He had lived an eventful life.

He kept in touch with some of his buddies—other quiet ones, former customers—and put out feelers about the girl. He asked if anyone had heard stories about a kid who could shoot the filters off cigarettes. He'd won a bet on that one, standing Marlboros on nails ten feet downrange. The guy deserved to be hustled, because he'd hustled Carlos at the poker table.

The bastard's name was Hardwick and he looked like a doofus, with a bow tie and horn-rimmed glasses. Who would've thought he was a card shark? So the hell with him. Carlos invited him to the gun shop after the disastrous all-night poker session and showed him around. Then he took Hardwick out to the range and they shot some guns while the little girl moped around, sweeping up casings.

"You've obviously been around guns. Nice shooting."

"I'm not great," said Hardwick, "but I'm okay."

"You ever seen the cigarette guy?"

"No."

"He's a hustler, goes around shooting the filters off cigarettes. Kind of a legend at firing ranges."

"You ever seen him?"

"Nope, but I've tried it and I can't do it."

"You're hustling me aren't you?"

"Nope. We can try it. No money. Just to see what it's like. We've all tried it and now and then someone gets a lucky shot, but that's it."

Carlos got a fresh pack of Marlboros from behind the counter and walked back out. He set up a board with nails driven through it and stuck five cigarettes on the nails.

"Go ahead, give it a try," he said.

"No money."

"No money."

Hardwick managed to blast a cigarette, but no way could he shoot off a filter.

That's when the little girl tapped him and motioned that she wanted to try.

"Go away," said Carlos.

"That your daughter?" asked Hardwick.

"Yeah, but there's something wrong with her. She can't talk."

"You let her shoot?"

"Sometimes. What the hell, she likes it and there's not much else for her here."

"Hell," said Hardwick, "Come on, little girl, if you hit one of those cigarettes I'll give you a dollar."

"The girl smiled. A couple other guys who'd been shooting came over and offered dollars too."

"How many shots?" asked Carlos.

"Five. How about five?" said one of the guys.

"Done," said Hardwick.

Carlos gave her ear protectors, glasses, pulled up a chair for her to stand on, and racked the slide on a small .32 automatic for her. She picked it up, smiled a happy, stupid smile, and fired off some random shots. Not even close.

"Good shooting, little girl," said Carlos. She smiled gaily and gave him back the gun.

"She's easily pleased," said Carlos.

"Let's keep shooting," said one of the guys, winking at Carlos. "Twenty bucks to the first guy who hits a filter."

"You're on," Carlos said, and they took turns. No one could do it.

Again, the little girl tapped Hardwick on the shoulder.

"She wants to shoot some more," he said.

"Okay by me," said Carlos.

"I'll bet you ten to one she can't shoot a filter," said one of the guys.

"No way," said Carlos.

"Hey, come on. You got a bunch of my money last week in poker, give me a chance to win it back."

"Okay," said Carlos, laughing, "I'll put up ten bucks to your hundred."

"I want some of that," said the other. "Come on, Carlos, you been living off our money for months. A hundred to your ten."

"This is stupid," said Carlos. "But I can afford twenty bucks."

"I'll go two hundred," said Hardwick, "but I want better odds. Five to one, my two hundred to your forty."

"Maybe, if you give her a hundred shots to hit a filter."

Hardwick laughed.

"Not a chance."

"Five shots," said one of the guys.

"I can't afford it," said Carlos. "This guy took all my money last night and it's a stupid bet. I want twenty to one."

"Ten to one. That's as good as you get."

"Okay," said Carlos reluctantly. "Five shots, two hundred to me if she shoots one of the filters, I pay twenty if she doesn't hit any."

"But she has to leave at least half of the cigarette standing, or it doesn't count."

"Jesus Christ, you guys are relentless!"

"What if she shoots more than one?" asked one of the shills.

"Okay, same bet for each filter. You all good with that?"

Everyone agreed, but Hardwick was starting to tumble. Too late.

The little girl put ear protectors and glasses back on. Carlos picked up her favorite Glock 43, racked it and gave it to her. She took a police stance with the gun in a two-handed grip, and shot five filters off the Marlboros.

The two guys paid up. Hardwick had no choice. He looked at the girl, then at Carlos and nodded.

"Well done," he said dryly. "Nice hustle. It took me seven hours to win that poker money and you got back most of it in five minutes."

"Hey, what goes around comes around."

"You know what? It was worth it just to see her shoot. Little girl, you are a genius."

When he was gone. Carlos gave the money back to the other two, plus a hundred for their help, and pocketed his eight hundred. The little girl went back to sweeping up the spent shell casings.

Carlos missed the little girl. He still didn't know where she came from, as he'd found her on the front step of his shop one morning. He could see she was hungry, and he fed her. Then she washed all the dishes and spent the day sweeping and cleaning. In return he fed her lunch and dinner. She wanted to sleep on the couch, but he knew that was too dangerous. Single Mexican guy with a little girl in his apartment? Not a chance. He'd be looking at years in prison. On the other hand, his store was spotless for the first time in months. Hell, he was getting free maid service.

He thought about it, and then took a bunch of blankets and a cushion out to the range and rigged up a makeshift bed under the counter down at the end. If anyone asked, he could say he didn't know she was there. Just a runaway, hiding out. The little girl nodded and burrowed in among the blankets. In minutes she was asleep.

CHAPTER 30

This arrangement lasted and daily she put in hours cleaning the shop, the range, and his apartment. She became a fixture at the place and when people asked, he told them he was watching her for his sick sister. The little girl fit the picture, obviously mixed race of some sort, so what the hell.

Carlos was a decent man, just kind of lazy and he didn't like guns that much. He been trapped in his business for years and he knew the girl was a stroke of luck. Free maid service, no complaining, and a tireless worker.

One day he was cleaning a pistol, and she stood by the table, mesmerized. He put the gun back together, and then slowly took it apart. She watched every move. Then he slowly reassembled it and showed her how to make sure the magazine was out and there was no bullet in the chamber. She repeated his moves. Then he showed her, a step at a time how to dismantle and reassemble the gun. To her it was a toy and she played with it for hours, until she knew every tiny piece of it. She'd seen people fire guns on the range, and she would make doubly sure it was empty, and then dry fire it at the clock or the deer head mounted on the wall across from the counter.

Carlos made her promise never to point it at a person. Never, ever. And she nodded.

For a week she played with the pistol every chance she got. Then Carlos showed her he could disassemble and reassemble the gun blindfolded. She thought that was a great game and soon she could do that too. They moved on to other handguns, learning each of them intimately, and then into rifles and shotguns.

The clothes she was wearing were awful so he logged on to Amazon, girl's clothes, and let her pick things out. She ignored dresses and went straight to jeans, tee shirts and jackets. Then she pointed at shoes and he nodded. She picked out a pair of Converse All Stars and he put in the order. She danced around in excitement. When the clothes came, she was ecstatic, and hugged him. He patted her shoulder and went back to work.

One day, Carlos was busy with a customer and another guy wanted to see a .45 automatic. The girl was sweeping behind the counter, so she reached into the showcase and got it, ejected the magazine, checked the chamber, and gave it to him. The guy was impressed.

"Hey Carlos, your little girl here knows weapons."

"She does," said Carlos. "Better than you."

"I doubt it. I grew up with guns. My dad was military."

"Bet you ten bucks she can field strip that .45 faster than you."

"No way. Put your money on the counter."

Carlos did, and that was the first money he made off the little girl. After the guy was gone, he showed her how to fumble a bit and make the contest close. That way he could get the guy double or nothing. Then he rewarded her with a Three Musketeers, her favorite.

He liked to fool around with his cell phone and realized she was fascinated by it. He showed her how it worked and soon she was playing with that too. He showed her how to download apps and kids' games. She loved that and then he realized she was downloading games that were more complicated. That night he took her to Best Buy and got her a low-priced Samsung. You would've thought he'd bought her the moon. She hugged him and for the next few weeks she was on it all the time.

One day, Carlos was trying to teach a boy how to shoot. The boy was about twelve and his dad wanted him to man up, but it was obvious the kid was not enthused. He looked like a bookish little boy, and the noises scared him, even with the ear protectors.

"Come on, son," shouted the dad. "Be a man! You've seen guns on TV. Just shoot the damn thing."

The boy started crying, and Carlos steered the father away. He didn't want to lose a customer, so he took him into the shop for coffee, calming him down.

The girl was sweeping up loose shells and saw it all. She went over to the boy and led him to a table. She got her favorite Glock 43, emptied it, checked it twice to make sure, and then took it apart while the little boy watched. She showed him all the pieces, how they fit together, how it was like a puzzle, taking it apart and putting it back together. Soon she'd taught the boy, slowly and painstakingly, how to field strip the pistol. It was no longer scary. She brought a couple of chairs over to the shooting position and they climbed up. She showed him how to always take out the bullets. He wasn't strong enough to rack the slide, but she could do it if she used all her strength and good technique. She showed him the stance, and the grip, and how to dry fire the gun. She had him dry firing at targets. The clicks were not scary. There was no recoil.

Finally, she showed him how to put on the ear protectors, glasses, and load one bullet into the gun, always pointing it downrange. She pantomimed a huge explosion, and the boy laughed. She pantomimed how the gun would jump up, and he laughed again. Then she showed him the two-handed stance and she put the gun in his hands. She pantomimed how scared she was, how big the explosion would be, and he aimed at the target and squeezed the trigger. Bam!

Carlos and the father came tearing out, only to see the girl lock the slide, clear the gun, check the chamber, and lay it on the bench pointed downrange. The boy, still wearing ear protectors and goggles, was laughing and pointing. Not a bulls-eye, but he'd hit the target. The father was stunned. Carlos speechless. The boy puffed up like Mike Tyson after a knockout.

Carlos taught her how to shoot, and she was a natural. All those weeks field-stripping weapons had made them familiar to her. She knew the feel and weight of each gun and the idiosyncrasies of all of them, so the actual firing was almost anticlimactic. At times he thought about how much the ammo was costing, but then he realized she made up for it as a house cleaner, semi-salesperson and good luck charm. Carlos didn't like the business and sometimes it showed. She diverted people's attention and sales improved, so he let her shoot whenever she wanted. His regulars noticed this, and soon there were competitions. She'd lose on purpose now and then, just to keep them interested, and Carlos made money. She was a little gold mine.

MIKE NEUN

CHAPTER 31

Rough guys came into the shop. Ex-military, military wannabes, militia members, and guys with distant looks in their eyes and voices in their heads, survivors of faraway wars and unknown conflicts. It was not a good place for a little girl, but mostly she charmed the customers and became a mascot. The regulars protected her, and Carlos did too, but he knew that might not always be enough. Only some close friends knew his story, and they weren't talking. Others in Elko thought he was a tough, gun-loving Mexican, but they were way off the mark. He certainly wasn't a warrior. Far from it. He knew the look of the bad ones who frequented his store and tried to keep the girl out of the way when he saw them coming.

One day, though, he'd gone to the toilet and when he came back he knew he had a problem. The two guys who came in, one black, one white, were bad dudes. He knew it immediately.

"Little girl," he said, "Go upstairs and make some coffee okay?"

She started out, but the white guy grabbed her arm. He was a nasty piece of work, skinny but muscled, with lots of tattoos. His front teeth were chipped and he had a scar across one cheek. His voice was raspy and harsh.

"Sorry old man, but this is a stickup and she stays here."

He pulled back his shirt and Carlos saw the butt of the handgun stuck in his Levis.

"We need money and my friend here needs a gun, so everyone's just going to act natural and calm."

The little girl tried to pull away.

"Don't run away girl, we're just here to get money. Stay here and talk to us."

"You can have whatever you want. Just let her go make coffee. She doesn't need to see this."

"She can do that later. We're just going to talk, aren't we little girl. You remind me of good times. Remember that, Bro? When we had little girls to play with?"

The black guy smiled thinly. He looked like a body builder, maybe six feet tall, wearing a dark green muscle shirt and camo cargo pants. He had a shaved head and a gold tooth. His voice was deep and melodic.

"Yeah, I remember. But that shit don't fly over here. Keep your eye on the prize, man. Money and a gun. In and out."

"Tell you what, old man, why don't you close up for an hour or so and we'll have a party here. Just us. You got any liquor? By the look of you, I'm guessing a bottle of tequila is around here somewhere."

Carlos knew this was big trouble. All he could do was play for time and hope someone else came. Fat chance. It was Monday afternoon, a slow day. Damn.

"Come on, guys. You're scaring my daughter. You don't want to do that. She can't talk. She's got a problem."

MIKE NEUN

"No shit?" said the scar-faced guy, "She can't talk? I never had a silent one before. Now I am excited. But we need booze. You got some?"

"I've got whiskey behind the counter."

"Bart, you go with him, make sure it's just whiskey he's going for. I'll stay here with little Miss Silent, get to know her."

"Don't be fuckin' with that girl, Ess, and we don't need no whiskey. Old man, we just need money and a weapon, okay? No muss, no fuss, and we'll be long gone."

"Anything you say," said Carlos.

"Tell you what," said the nasty white guy, "we'll compromise. One drink, a quickie for the road, and we'll hit the bricks. How about that?"

"Okay," said Bart. "Just one, then we're out of here."

Carlos, with Bart close beside him, walked over behind the counter and opened a high cabinet. Sometimes buddies came over after hours for a drink and he had a bottle of Jack Daniels up there. He pulled it out, with two glasses, and brought them back.

"Please," he said, "you can have my money, anything in the shop, but let the girl alone."

"You know why they call me Ess?" asked the white dude.

"No."

"Stupid name, don't you think? Ess. It's short for Esso because I greased a lot of guys."

Bart nodded and poured himself a shot. Ess poured half a glass.

"We call him Bart, because he loves the Simpsons. Over there he had CDs and he'd watch them over and over."

"Best show ever."

"Bart, this is like old times. Whiskey, guns and a little girl. What more could a guy want?"

Bart nodded.

"What's your name, boss?"

"Carlos."

"Okay Carlos, we want to see your best handgun. None of that cheap shit, we want the absolute best."

"Okay, I'll get it."

"Oh hell yes! We're here holding up your store and you think you're going to get your hands on a weapon? What's your best handgun?"

"I got a Sig Sauer P320 and a Browning High Power. Most guys think they're the best."

"Little girl, do you know what a Browning High Power is?"

The girl looked confused. She looked at Carlos. He caught on.

"You know the one," he said slowly, "the big black one in the middle."

She thought hard, then nodded stupidly.

"She's not the brightest bulb in the chandelier is she?" said Bart.

Carlos knew she was playing them, and had to admire her guts. God damn she was a piece of work.

"You sure you know which gun I want?"

The girl nodded.

"You go get it out of the showcase," said Ess, "along with a box of ammo, and bring it to us, okay?"

The little girl looked at Carlos.

"It's okay. You go get the gun. And you know where the ammo is. Get them and be very careful."

She went to get the pistol, and Carlos turned to the two men, thinking how to distract them.

"I never let her handle the merchandise. Kids and guns don't mix."

"Good thinking old man. Can never be too careful."

"You see that deer head over there?"

They looked.

"See that hole in the forehead? A kid did that. Dumb fuck of a father let his kid hold a Glock, thought it was unloaded. Scared the shit out of us."

He grabbed the bottle and poured more whiskey, anything to keep them distracted. As he set the bottle down he knocked over a glass, spilling it on Esso, who jumped up and took a swing at Carlos, knocking him down. Carlos swore loudly.

"Fucking stupid old man," said Esso, and Bart laughed. His laugh was cut short by a gunshot, and the whiskey bottle exploded. Ess, Bart and Carlos looked up to see the girl behind the counter, a Glock in two hands, deadly serious.

"What the fuck?" said Bart.

"Little girl," said Ess, "You just put that down. Someone could get hurt."

He took a step toward her, and she shot him in the foot.

"Fuck!" he yelled, as he crumpled to the floor, grabbing his boot. "Bart, get that crazy little bitch!"

Bart leaped toward her, but her next bullet caught him in the thigh. She was not shooting to kill, but she was definitely going to put him out of commission. Bart grabbed his thigh and moaned, blood leaking through his fingers.

"Gentlemen," said Carlos, "she is not fucking around. But you guys are just dumb enough to try again so I want you to think about it. Little girl, clip the white guy's ear. Ess, I suggest you don't move a muscle."

Esso froze, five feet away, and the little girl shot off part of his ear lobe.

"Fuck!" he screamed.

"Bart," said Carlos, "Your turn. Stand very, very still. Little girl, show him that ear shot wasn't a fluke."

"I believe!" yelled Bart.

"Too late," said Carlos. "Stand real still. We don't want an ugly accident do we?"

The girl gave a little grin and shot off the top of his ear.

"God damn it," yelled Bart, grabbing his ear. "That's enough."

"I bet those little girls in some foreign land were saying the same thing and I bet you fuckers didn't stop, did you? If I had my way, I'd let her shoot off parts of your bodies just to teach you a lesson. Now, Ess, get up and put your hands against the wall and step back, way back.

"I can't. She shot me in the foot."

"Want her to shoot you in the other foot?"

Ess struggled up, using the table, and limped over to the wall.

Bart, you do the same. Little girl, if they move, shoot 'em again."

Carlos reached around and pulled Esso's gun out of his jeans.

Then he took out his phone and called the cops. The Elko cops were stretched thin but all of them knew Carlos. They used his range for target practice and all of them had come for a drink and conversation at one time or another.

The police car slid up in front, sirens blaring, in under three minutes. Two cops jumped out, a man and a woman, to find the robbers against the wall with Carlos covering them.

"Hi Rusty," said Carlos. "Hi Wilma."

"Hi Carlos. Looks like you shot some bad guys."

"Bullshit," shouted Esso. "That little girl shot us. You should throw her in jail."

"If she shot you," said Rusty, "you are fucking lucky. She can pick her spots and if she'd wanted you dead, you'd be on that floor right now."

"The medics are coming," said Wilma, cuffing the two robbers. "I'll take care of these guys. You better talk to Carlos."

"What's going on?" asked Carlos.

Rusty took him aside, along with the little girl.

"We've got a problem," he said. "Someone complained to Social Services about the little girl."

"That's no problem. Betty knows all about her. She comes over to check all the time, make sure she's all right."

"Betty's sick, and they brought in a hard-ass from Las Vegas to replace her. She's on her way over here now."

"Damn."

"She could take away the little girl and you could be up on charges. We were about to call you when you called us."

The little girl listened to all this and before they could stop her she darted out the back door. Carlos tried to go after her but Rusty stopped him.

"I don't think we should chase her," said Rusty, putting his hands on his friend's shoulders and looking him in the eyes. Carlos resisted, but then realized Rusty was right.

Carlos never saw her again. He was devastated.

He'd had the word out for months. How many little girls could shoot the filters off Marlboros or field-strip a Glock? The odd thing was, he just wanted to know she was safe. He hated the thought of her out there alone, and he wanted to be there for her.

One of his friends in Elko had gone through an ugly divorce and was on a lot of radical men's-rights sites. He was the one who found the story of Jupiter and Ted and the little girl with the gun at the rest stop in eastern Oregon.

Carlos wasn't short on computer skills. His wife had passed away ten years before with breast cancer and he'd had a lot of alone time since then.

So he checked out the two guys, Ted and Jupiter, the ones the little girl had shot. Online the two guys sounded like whiny bastards who couldn't take hard times. Yes divorce was hard. Yes a lot of guys had been screwed over royally by the courts. But these two just sounded like mean bastards out chasing some other guy's ex-wife. How stupid was that? The guy had to be paying them.

Carlos signed in to various radical men's groups and started posting about a fictional divorce that destroyed his life. Soon he was a regular along with Ted and Jupe. He logged on and found the latest scoop on the little girl story. Ted was pretty vocal on the websites, and word was he was in southern Idaho, chasing the woman, the man and the little girl. They'd found a way to track them

MIKE NEUN

and the dumb fucks even posted about it online. Carlos posted that he was coming up to Idaho anyway, did they need help?

Ted liked it. Free help. It would be like a posse, chasing down their targets. He invited Carlos to join them.

Carlos had been forced to close the gun shop during three lockdowns and he wasn't sure he wanted to ever open up again. He was free to follow up the lead. He chained all the doors, set the cameras and alarms, and drove north out of Elko up US 93 to Idaho.

CHAPTER 32

Tommy, Kirsten, Jo and Joyce drove straight through Ketchum and continued south to Twin Falls. They'd have three directions to go once they got there. Four if they doubled back, but that wasn't the plan. The obvious choice was to go east or west on I-84, which crossed the country and offered a lot of cover. Motels, small towns, truck stops and cities—there'd be a million places to hide.

Ted and Jupe wouldn't expect them to continue south because it was too empty. Northern Nevada had about two people per square mile, with lots of bare highway and very few towns. On the other hand, once they got further south there would be lots of choices. They gassed up in Twin Falls and hit a computer store. They traded in their phones and laptops for new gear and sim cards. The good news was Tommy could charge the new tech to Google as a business expense. They left a happy clerk and toted their iPhones, iPads and laptops to the truck. Then they drove out of Twin Falls to highway 93.

A half hour later, Ted, in the passenger seat of the Hummer, said, "Okay! We've got the signal back! Our guy is tracking their phones again. Turn right up here and go downtown. They're in Twin Falls."

"Good going, boys," said Holly. "I was beginning to lose faith in you two."

They followed the signals and ended up in a parking lot staring at Computer Connection.

"Fuck me," said Ted.

They got out and walked inside, Holly following with her pistol hidden in her jacket pocket. Behind the counter a young clerk was playing with an iPhone.

"Is that your phone?" asked Ted

"Nope. Just got it on a trade in."

"Don't tell me. One guy, two women and a little girl."

"That's them! They got all new stuff. Phones, tablets and laptops."

"Damn."

They trooped back to the Hummer.

"You boys better do some fast thinking," said Holly, menacing, from the back seat.

"If they get to the I-84 interchange," said Ted, "they can go any direction. Fuck!"

"Wait a minute," said Ted. "That other guy, Carlos? The one that's going to join us? He's coming up from Elko. If they go south they'll have to pass him and he can get word to us."

"Call him," said Jupe.

Ted dug out his cell phone, called, and explained the situation to Carlos.

"Got it," said Carlos. "If they come this way I'll let you know. Describe the truck."

"It's a Ram 1500, 4-door cab, dark green, with a faded black camper shell."

"Got it," said Carlos. "I'm coming north on 93 so I'm bound to see it if they drive south."

"Okay," said Holly, "That takes care of south. Now we just gotta choose east or west. They didn't go back north or we'd have seen them."

"They came from Seattle," said Jupe, "and they were running away. I don't think they'd go back in that direction. I'm thinking east."

"Works for me," said Ted, "what about you, Holly?"

"Sounds good. I think my love vibes are coming from that direction too."

"Love vibes?"

"You making fun of me?"

"No!" said Ted, quickly, thinking frantically how to get rid of this bitch from hell.

"Okay then," said Holly, "East it is."

Ten minutes later they turned east on I-84.

CHAPTER 33

Carlos drove slower now, headed north on highway 93, checking every truck he passed going the other way. Damn, there were a lot of pickups in Nevada. After an hour, he realized spotting it was going to be really hard. At the next exit he pulled off, swung across the highway, and parked, headed south. He got out, sat on the trunk, and watched the cars go by. Boring. But he wasn't far from Twin Falls so they should be coming soon.

He almost missed them. He had his battered cowboy hat pulled low because of the sun, and he was tired. But he heard a vehicle coming and looked up just in time. It was the truck.

He jumped into his dusty Almera and pulled out after them. Two hours later, just as he was about to fall asleep at the wheel, they finally stopped at a small truck stop, parked, and walked into a diner. Carlos wasn't sure how to handle things. He figured the best was to walk up to them in the diner, where there'd be people around and he wouldn't startle them.

He spotted them in a booth and walked over. Jo saw him first, leaped out and threw her arms around him. He grinned foolishly, and said, "Hi folks, I'm Carlos."

Kirsten said, "It looks like you're old friends with Jo here."

"Is that her name?"

"We don't know, so we just named her JoAnn. She seems to like it."

"Works for me."

He turned to Jo.

"Hi little girl. You okay?"

She nodded.

"These people been good to you?"

She nodded emphatically and Carlos smiled.

"That's wonderful news. I was really worried when you ran off, but I never knew where to look. I am really, really happy to see you're okay."

"How did you know Jo?" asked Tommy.

"She lived with me for over a year. Helped me with my shop."

"What kind of shop?"

"Guns. I sold weapons and outdoor gear, had a firing range out back. Did you know Jo is a crack shot?"

"We sure do. She saved us twice."

"She saved me too. It sure does surprise people when little girl here comes out firing. I tried to teach her never to do real harm. I hope she didn't kill anyone."

"No, but she sure scared the hell out of them."

"Yeah, she's good at that."

"Have a seat. We have a lot to talk about."

"We sure do," said Carlos. "You've got some real assholes chasing you."

"You know about them?" asked Joyce.

"That's how I found you. I convinced them I wanted to join in the hunt and I was on my way up to Twin Falls to meet them. I was going to be a spy! Infiltrate the gang of angry divorced guys and then if they caught up I was going to save little girl here. Carlos Gonzales rides again!"

"But you found us first?"

"Yeah. They wanted me to tip them off if I saw you headed south. I guess I forgot to do that."

"Where are they?"

"Going east on I-84. Hopefully they'll keep going. By the way, who are you people?"

Tommy, Kirsten and Joyce introduced themselves and filled him in on their adventures.

"There's one thing we're not sure of," said Tommy. "Who the hell is chasing us? And why?"

"You don't know?"

"We think Kirsten's ex-husband, Rick, is behind it but we don't know how. He's dead broke."

"Well," said Carlos, "it's Rick for sure, and those are two guys he found on a website for divorced guys. They're pretty radical women haters and he hired them."

"Shit," said Kirsten. "I tried to help him out! I gave him money and got him a job...."

"Is that the full story?" asked Carlos.

"No.... not really. I cheated on him and he was really pissed off. Then my divorce lawyer really stuck it to him. He's got a right to be mad, but I tried to make it up to him."

"How's he doing?"

"Really bad. He drinks too much, he's broke, he's got a shitty job..."

"And his ex-wife ran off with Tommy."

"It's not like that. Tommy and I are friends. Jo brought us together. We left because Rick and his dirtbag friend broke into our apartment."

"That's scary."

"Yeah," said Kirsten. "They were really drunk and had terrible things planned for us."

"How'd you get away?"

"Jo surprised them."

"She's good at that. She surprised me all the time down in Elko."

He looked at Jo.

"She can't talk, but she's one smart little girl. She saved my business and she saved my life."

"Wow. You'll have to tell us about that," said Joyce.

"Maybe later. It's a long story."

"How do you know Rick hired those guys?" asked Kirsten.

"I found Ted's stuff on the website. He said Rick hired him and Jupe to find his ex-wife. I think Ted has plans to turn it into a career. 'Hire us, we'll find the bitch.' Those were his words, not mine."

"But Rick is flat broke. How the hell can he hire two kidnappers?"

"It's obvious he found money somewhere. He's definitely the guy paying them," said Carlos.

"He's gone crazy," said Kirsten. Why can't Rick get over this?"

"Hard times bring out the worst in people," said Carlos.

They ate their lunches, and Jo snuggled between Joyce and Carlos, her family getting bigger and better all the time.

"Little girl," said Carlos, "can you talk yet?"

She shook her head no.

"I was so sad when you ran off but you probably saved both of us. That Social Services lady was going to take you away and press charges against me. You should've seen her face when she couldn't find you and was stuck with me playing innocent. It really wrecked her day."

Jo smiled.

"I sure missed you and I'm so happy you're in good hands,"

"Jo, how the hell did you get from Elko to Seattle?" asked Tommy.

Jo just shrugged her shoulders, like it was a long story. The others wondered too, and also wondered if they really wanted to know.

"We should get back on the road," said Kirsten. "You want to come with us, Carlos?"

"I'd like that. You folks don't mind?"

"Any friend of Jo's is a friend of ours. You want to lead the way? You know this country better than we do."

"Sounds good."

Joyce piped up.

"You want some company? I don't talk much but I can keep you awake."

"Sounds good," said Carlos, "In fact, if you could drive a bit I'm really tired."

They paid the bill, walked out of the diner, got into the Almera and Ram pickup and headed south.

"Oh shit," said Kirsten, "we haven't let Wendy and the Seattle people know what's going on."

"Damn. And they don't have our new contact numbers."

Kirsten was already digging out her new phone. She called and Wendy answered. Kirsten put it on speaker.

"Wendy, this is Kirsten."

"You've got a new number."

"Yeah, we had trouble again. Those hijackers almost caught us in Idaho. They were tracking us with our phones so we got new stuff."

"Holy cow. Are you okay? Is Jo okay?"

"Yeah, we got away and we're all fine, but we're on the run now. I guess our Ketchum plans are out the window."

"Oh hell, we don't care as long as you're safe. We'll sit tight here and you keep us posted on what's going on. All our best to Jo and if we can help in any way let us know."

"Thanks, Wendy, and you all stay safe too. We'll get through this somehow."

They said their good byes and hung up.

The blizzard caught them fifteen miles outside of Ely, and they barely made it into town. It was close to dusk when they drove in, with snow blowing hard. Ely was almost a ghost town, with boarded-up stores, restaurants and gas stations, but there was one motel sign, The Oceanview Motel, like a beacon in the darkness and blowing snow.

"The Oceanview?" said Carlos. "In Ely, Nevada? This has got to be a joke."

They pulled in and surprised the manager, an older lady who looked like one of the crones you see at cheap casinos, playing the slot machines for hours on end. She had a cigarette hanging out of the corner of her mouth and her voice was raspy.

"Welcome to the world-famous Oceanview Motel," she said.

"Seriously?" asked Kirsten. "The Ocean is five hundred miles from here."

"Hey, some California motel went out of business

and we got a good deal on the sign. The locals love it."

"I'm sure they do."

"And we get a lot of free advertising. We made the morning shows in San Francisco when we put it up."

"I love it too," said Tommy.

"How many people you got?"

"Five," said Kirsten, "so we'll need two rooms."

"Whoo boy, I don't know. We're pretty booked up.

Then she laughed.

"I've got 30 rooms and they're all empty. Pick any ones you want."

"We've got a problem," said Kirsten. "My ex-husband is following me and he's a mean bastard. If anyone asks, can you say you haven't seen us?"

"I had one of those husbands once," said the manager. "When I found out what he was, I was out of there like a shot. That's how I ended up in Ely. I knew he'd never think to look for me here. That was thirty years and two boyfriends ago."

"So you know the story. Can you cover for me?"

"Sure, honey, not a problem."

Tommy paid for the rooms and bumped it twenty bucks. The lady's eyes lit up.

"Hell, son, twenty more and I'll shoot the guy." she laughed.

"If I had twenty to spare I'd take you up on that," said Tommy. "Her ex-husband is an evil bastard, but that's the best I can do."

"Don't worry, son, I can take that down to the casino and run it into a fortune."

They laughed.

"My name's Maggie. If you need anything just give a

call, but I'm going to bed now so let it keep ringing."

"We'll be fine. You get your sleep and we'll see you in the morning."

They'd chosen a couple of rooms in back and they drove the truck and Carlos's car around to park. Best of all, the snow would cover their tracks.

Tommy and Carlos took one room and the ladies took the other. Everyone was dead tired and it didn't matter that the rooms were cheap and the beds lumpy. They slept the sleep of the innocent.

CHAPTER 34

The next morning they checked out.

"Did anyone ask for us?" asked Kirsten.

"Nope," said Maggie, "and I couldn't sleep so I took the shuttle bus down to the casino. I know this will surprise you but I didn't run that twenty bucks into a fortune. Damn slot machines must be rigged."

"Well, thank you for the rooms and better luck next time."

"No such thing as luck, or I'd own a casino in Vegas. If your mean bastard ex comes by, I'll deny ever seeing you. It's the least I can do."

Tommy gave her another five bucks and thanked her.

"Good money after bad, my boy, good money after bad. By the way, my here's my card. If you give me a number, I'll call and let you know if anyone comes around asking about you."

"That's really kind," said Kirsten. "If we make it back this way we'll stay again and buy you dinner. Is there a restaurant in town? We need some breakfast."

"Only the one in the Gold Rush Casino. It used to be a classy place, but it went bankrupt like the others.

Now it's shabby and cheap but the food's okay. Head south and you'll see it if you look quick. It's not the MGM Grand, if you know what I mean."

They thanked her again, and drove to the casino. It had seen better days, with threadbare carpets and the forlorn clang of a slot machine greeting them as they walked in. The restaurant was just off the main floor, with keno boards on the walls and old wooden tables surrounded by old wooden chairs. They picked a big table and sat down. At the counter a couple of dealers sat huddled over coffee, waiting for the morning shift. A blowzy blond waitress took their orders. Lots of coffee, eggs, bacon, hash browns, and more coffee.

"You guys sleep okay?" Tommy asked the ladies.

"I could've used three more hours," said Joyce, "I don't know if I've ever been that tired."

"Same here," said Kirsten, "I was out like a light."

"Tommy snores," said Carlos.

Joyce and Kirsten laughed.

"We know!" said Kirsten. "We told him and he doesn't believe us."

"You guys are making that up," Tommy said. "I sleep like a baby."

"A baby with a tuba," said Kirsten.

"Okay, okay," Tommy said, "maybe I do have a little snoring problem. The question is, what is our plan for today? The highway's been plowed so we can keep going but I have no idea where."

"I guess the choice is pretty simple," said Joyce. "We can either try to get lost in a big city or hide out in a tiny town. The trouble with tiny towns is that everybody knows everyone else's business and we're a strange-looking crew.

MIKE NEUN

"You're right there," said Carlos. "When I lived in Elko and a stranger came to town, we all knew in about fifteen minutes. On the other hand, big cities can be dangerous these days."

"The other thought," Tommy said, "is that we can keep moving. I think our danger increases if we settle down. Maybe a night or two in different places is the way to go."

"Works for me," said Kirsten. "Do you all mind being gypsies for awhile? Carlos, you and Joyce aren't even a part of this, so you could drop out if you want."

Carlos looked at Joyce.

"I don't know about you," he said, "but this beats hell out of staying home and not working."

"Same here," said Joyce, "but Tommy's going to end up being the sugar daddy. Can you support us all on your Google money? And do you want to? It's a lot to ask."

"I can do it," Tommy said, "and it would be worth it to have extra protection for Jo."

"Google money?" asked Carlos.

"Tommy has a job," said Kirsten. "Remember those? He works for Google and he's been bankrolling this run. That's the only reason we put up with his snoring and incredibly bad jokes."

"They're jealous," Tommy said to Carlos. "They know I'm just a couple open mics away from comedy stardom."

Carlos laughed.

"So you're Daddy Warbucks, taking care of all these ladies."

"Actually, I think of myself as a mighty warrior, protecting helpless females."

This time he did get a laugh. Bigger than he thought was absolutely necessary. And there was more rolling of the eyes.

"From what I can see," Carlos said, "Jo's the one protecting you."

"Well, there is that," Tommy said. "It's nice having the female Billy the Kid on our side."

He paused.

"You know, we're here planning our getaway and we're not asking the right person. Jo has been on the run all her life. She's the authority."

The others agreed.

"Jo," Tommy said, "should we try to hide someplace or keep moving?"

He held out his left hand. "Hide?"

He held out his right hand. "Keep moving?"

She pointed immediately to his right hand.

"Okay," Tommy said, "we're officially gypsies. I guess the next question is should we stay with the car and the truck, which is going to cost gas money, or just all pile into the truck? Carlos? What do you think?"

"You've got a point," he said. "I bet we could leave my car with the motel lady. If we paid her a few bucks I bet she'd watch it for me and Lord knows she's not pressed for parking."

The others agreed, and after breakfast they drove back to the motel. Maggie greeted them.

"Don't tell me. The splendor of Ely has overwhelmed you and you're going to move here for good."

"It is definitely tempting," said Kirsten. "That casino is what sold us. The bright lights, the big stars in the showroom, the huge fountain out front...."

"Yep, people come from all over the world," she said laughing and then coughing on cigarette smoke, "but I'm guessing you have something else in mind."

"You're right," said Carlos. "Would you mind if I left my car here for awhile? I'll pay for the parking."

"Oh I don't know," Maggie smiled, "Our lot is pretty full."

They looked out at the lot, totally empty, with sagebrush blowing in the snow.

"Yeah it is jammed, but I'll park it over in the corner."

"Oh hell yes. Better yet, if you let me drive it now and then you can leave it here for free. My car gave up the ghost a couple of months ago and I can't afford a new one."

"Done," said Carlos. "Just take good care of her. It's hard to find a classic like that these days."

"Classic my ass. There must be a million of those beaters out there."

"Yeah, but not in that beautiful brown color. It blends in with the desert."

"It is quite fetching. Trust me, I'll take care of her."

"If we don't get back," said Carlos, "The car is yours. I'll mail you the title and registration."

"Don't do that! I'd just sell it and put the money in the slots. I'm happy enough just driving it."

They shook on it and they piled into the truck. Jo and the gypsies were off, hitting the road to who knows where.

CHAPTER 35

Rick Bryson was out of a job. Hard to believe the owners would fire him because of one little break-in. The residents had gone ballistic when they found him and Shake, taped up, smelly, with a sledge hammer next to them and the door smashed. The note clinched it and the tenants had contacted the police, who were too short-handed to respond. Then they complained to the owners, but they were on some sort of camping trip in Colorado. Personally, Rick still thought they were hiding out from the tax man, but what did he know?

The owners came back to town a week later. Hard to believe, but they thought it was bad customer relations to have their manager breaking into apartments. They gave him forty-five minutes to clear out and he'd thrown all his stuff into the Toyota and driven out of town. He made it to North Bend, only a half hour out of Seattle. He booked a room at a Motel 6 for two nights, and logged onto the Internet with his laptop. Nothing. No word from Ted and Jupe. He drove to a 7-Eleven, got a six pack and a fifth of Jim Beam, drove back and drank until he fell asleep, still dressed, on the bed.

He woke up the next day around noon with a

monumental hangover and drove around until he found a bar that was open. It was called, fittingly, The North Bend Saloon. Inside it was blessedly dark, with a couple of regulars hunched over drinks at the bar. He sat a few stools away and ordered bourbon with a beer chaser. A few shots later he was feeling better, but the anger and humiliation would not go away. He pictured himself, lying on that floor, taped up, pissing himself, blind, terrified he'd fall asleep and lose the straw to his precious water. And then the outrage and disgust of the tenants who found them, the fear of the police, the loss of his job, the eviction, it was all too much. He ordered more shots. He got angrier.

More people came in, mostly working men, and a football game started on the big-screen TV. Rick, barely coherent, listened while the crowd in the bar cheered and groaned as the game went on. In time, he realized Seattle was playing somebody. The Browns? It didn't matter. All his anger surged through him. He stood up, waved his bottle and yelled, "Fuck the Seahawks! Go Browns! Kill the punter! Beat the shit out of those fucking Seahawks."

He realized it might not have been the smartest thing to yell in a bar full of Seattle fans. A couple of big guys got in his face. He swung his beer bottle and didn't remember much after that. What he did know is that he woke up in the parking lot, filthy, covered in blood, every piece of his body in pain, with a couple of loose teeth. He could barely get up. He staggered, doubled over, to the Toyota, got in, and managed to drive at ten miles-an-hour back to his motel.

The maid found him later that day, on the bed bruised and bloody, and called the manager.

"Sir," he said, "We need to call the police. You've been mugged."

"No. No police."

"Okay, but you need to see a doctor. You've been beaten up badly. I can drive to you a hospital."

"No, no hospital. Can you call a doctor to come here? I can pay."

"That's another thing. Our checkout was three hours ago. Are you going to stay longer?"

Tommy reached into his pocket and was relieved to find his wallet. Thank God. He pulled out a credit card.

"Can you book the room for a few days?"

"Yes sir. And I can call a doctor. I'll be back shortly."

The manager left. The maid, who looked to be Filipino, stood by the open door staring at him.

"You want to make some money?"

"No sir. I don't do that stuff."

"Not that. I need something to drink. I'll pay you thirty bucks to go get me two bottles of whiskey and two six packs of beer."

"Thirty dollars?"

"Yes. Here's half."

He handed her fifteen, then gave her money for the liquor, hoping she wouldn't run off with it.

"You get the booze and I'll pay you the other fifteen."

"Okay," she said, and left.

The doctor arrived three hours later to find him half drunk and still in the same clothes. He forced Rick to get undressed and take a long, hot shower. Then he tended to the wounds. Fortunately there were no broken bones, but there was heavy bruising all over his body. They must've spent some time kicking him in the parking lot. The doctor snitched up wounds on his forehead and cheek and patched up some bleeding scrapes on his elbows.

"I can give you pain killers," he said, "but if you take them you can't drink."

"I'll just drink," said Rick. "Don't bother with the pills."

Rick paid him, watched him leave, and poured more whiskey.

He'd never been on a blackout bender before, but he proved to be quite adept. Some days he sat in the room, drank, and watched TV. Other days he sampled the various bars in North Bend but wisely stayed away from The North Bend Saloon. He tried desperately to drown his sorrows and anger, but they kept coming back. So he stayed drunk.

Ten days later he woke up, again with a trainwreck hangover, and realized he was not alone. Beside him was a woman, bleached blond hair spread on the pillow, makeup smeared, a bit overweight, but not bad-looking. He vaguely remembered meeting her in a bar but not much after that. She opened her eyes, halfway, and said, "Who are you?"

"I'm Rick."

"Hi Rick. Do you have beer? I'm in pain."

He cracked open a Coors and they shared it, not talking.

Then they opened another, both of them feeling a tiny bit better.

"Did we fuck?" she asked.

"Hell if I know," he said. "Do I owe you money?"

"Naw, I'm not a working girl. But I think I'm an alcoholic. How about you?"

"I'm working on it. Want to go drinking?"

"Oh hell yes."

Two weeks later he woke up to find her gone. Maybe a mutual love of bourbon shooters was not the best basis for a lasting relationship. He drank a beer and took a long, hot shower. He came out, brewed instant motel coffee, turned on his laptop and checked the websites. A lot had been going on while he'd taken his brown-bottle vacation.

Ted had been reporting in. They'd almost caught Kirsten in Ketchum but she and the others had escaped. He and Jupe had followed, tracking Tommy's phone, but that had gone dead outside of Stanley and now they were flying blind because Tommy switched phones in Twin Falls.

Ted and Jupe had no way of knowing which way Kirsten and her little fucking computer geek had gone. They'd made a choice, east, and gone that way but hadn't found her or the pickup truck. They had a guy coming up 93 from the south, but he hadn't seen them. Could they have gone back west? Maybe I-84 back toward Portland or Seattle? It was possible.

Rick decided to join the hunt. He got on the various angry-guy websites and asked for help. He described the pickup truck and the people in it, including the little girl. He didn't mention the little girl was armed and dangerous. Who'd believe him? The good news was there were lots of disgruntled ex-husbands all over the west, and they promised to keep an eye out for a Ram 1500, dark green, with a camper shell.

Ted and Jupe had not told Rick about the psycho stalker who'd joined them. That was embarrassing. Here they were, hired guns on the prowl, and they were being bossed around by a small, crazy woman with a gun. That night she handcuffed them to bathroom pipes and then took the bed. Fucking humiliating. And what kind of woman carries handcuffs and a weapon? They'd heard about freaky ex-wives, but this was a whole new level of bad news. After a day going east, and a night of them sleeping on tile, Holly decided they'd been outfoxed. Kirsten and her little guy and little girl had not gone east. The other ex-husband, the one from Elko, said they hadn't gone south.

They must have gone west. Probably not back to Seattle but I-84 goes to Portland, so Holly decided, with no information whatsoever, that that's where they were headed. They turned around and drove back the way they came.

Rick, fighting his hangover with coffee and aspirin, decided to take an easy day at the motel and let others do the work. That afternoon, he got a text from someplace called Crystal Springs, Nevada. A disgruntled ex-husband had seen a pickup truck matching that description stopping for gas. He also saw a tall, black woman come out of the restroom with a girl and get into it before it headed south toward Las Vegas. Could that be the one?

Rick thanked him and wondered how the truck had gotten past the guy coming north. The guy in Crystal Springs said there'd been a blizzard a day ago and he might've missed the truck. It sounded possible. He called Ted and Jupe and they said they'd passed Twin Falls and would have to turn back to go south. This would be the second time to turn back and they were sick of it. Rick begged them to follow the new lead, not knowing they had no choice because of Holly in the back seat. He thought they were doing him a favor.

Rick wondered what to do. He decided to stand pat for awhile and see if Ted and Jupe got lucky. He was paying them, so why not? He drank instant coffee, ate aspirin, and settled in for his first sober night in four weeks. He lasted an hour and then decided one beer wouldn't hurt.

Ted, Jupe and Holly made it back to Twin Falls, gassed up, and turned south on.

CHAPTER 36

"We should paint the truck," said Carlos.

"Really?," Tommy said. "You think that'll help?"

"Who knows? But it would be smart to change colors and confuse people."

"You talking about a paint shop? One of those cheap ones?"

"No, I'm thinking of a do-it-yourself job, with spray cans. We can tape off the lights, tires, windows and trim with newspapers and garbage bags."

"I think it's a good idea," said Joyce, "anything we can do to throw them off the trail."

"Okay, let's do it. What color?"

"Maybe dark gray, like a primer coat. It'll look like it's being worked on. Taping it off is going to be the hardest part but with five of us I think we can do it."

They stopped in Alamo for rattle-can, primer-gray paint, tape and gloves. Alamo was nearly a ghost town, hard hit by the crash, and they found a deserted car wash. It had two stalls and was perfect for their purposes. The hose still worked so they washed and toweled off the truck, then taped off everything.

When all was ready, Carlos handed Jo the first can and she became paint sprayer in chief. He showed her how to shake the can and then spray back and forth to get an even coat. He held her up so she could get the high places and she thought it was great fun. Then he and Kirsten finished off the hood and roof. They left the camper shell a faded black and that worked fine. The paint dried quickly and they put on two more coats. Then they ripped off the tape, paper and garbage bags and checked out their new truck. It wasn't perfect, but what the hell.

"Little girl," said Carlos, "Did you know you're not a true teenager until you've done graffiti?"

Jo looked baffled.

"We've got a can left over. Come here and I'll show you."

He went over to a corner of the wall and scratched "Jo was here" in big letters with a rock.

"Okay," he said, "paint those letters and you'll be famous in Alamo."

"Is this a good idea?" asked Tommy, "teaching our girl to vandalize property?"

"Yeah," laughed Joyce. "It would be terrible to have her shoot four people, ride in two stolen cars and then get busted on a graffiti charge."

"Oh," said Tommy, abashed. "I guess if you look at it that way it's not a big deal. Go get 'em Jo."

Jo painted, and while her attempt wasn't easy to read, the others applauded. She was officially a teenage rebel.

They drove into the evening and reached Las Vegas at eight thirty. The Strip was just opening up and the gamblers were filtering back, but it was nothing like the crowds they'd hoped for. They found a Best Western motel downtown, parked out of sight of the street, and headed up to their rooms.

Carlos had clued them in to the ex-husband-women-hating websites and Kirsten and Tommy dummied up some fake identities and joined them all. Talk about depressing. These guys all had divorce horror stories and a lot of them rang true. Tommy decided not to marry Kirsten. Not even if she begged him. He was beginning to feel sorry for Rick until he found his graphic plans for revenge. They seemed rather severe for a one-night stand with a football player who didn't even block or tackle. Tommy was happy he hadn't gotten to know Rick, as his crazy-people radar was obviously faulty. The more he thought about his time with Holly, the more he realized she had been a bit outside the lines.

Kirsten shared all the angry-guy stuff they'd found with the others.

"Boy," Joyce said, "I didn't realize this was a movement."

"Me neither," said Tommy, "but these days everyone's outraged about something."

"I'm not," said Joyce. "I just want a little adventure, a road trip with friends, but I don't want to die."

"If you stick with us," said Carlos, "I'll do my best to protect you. Better yet, Jo will too."

Jo nodded, and that settled it. Again they slept with the ladies in one room the men in the other. They slept in late and ate breakfast at Circus Circus Casino in downtown Las Vegas. It was hard to believe it had been considered lavish years ago. Now it was a sad little casino with a few old age pensioners slipping nickels into the slots. The breakfast buffet was cheap and the food lukewarm, but they were hungry.

"Where should we go?" asked Joyce.

"I think we should keep it random," said Kirsten.

"We've been going south," said Carlos. "Want to switch and go northeast? Head up to Utah?"

"I do," said Joyce. "Utah has some of the best powder skiing in the country. Jo? You want to do some more skiing?"

Jo nodded enthusiastically and it was settled. They checked out, packed their gear and drove out of town on I-15 to Utah.

MIKE NEUN

CHAPTER 37

Holly slumped over the toilet, throwing up violently. They'd eaten a lot of road food and her last beef taco hadn't tasted right. She made them stop at a motel in Crystal Springs and barely got to the bathroom. Ted took the opportunity to grab her while Jupe took her gun and purse. He and Jupe shut the bathroom door and blocked it with a dresser, the bed, and every other piece of furniture in the room, but Holly was in no shape to break out. She was deathly ill and that night she slept on the tile floor. It felt wonderfully cool.

When she was finally able to dig herself out, Ted and Jupe were long gone and very, very happy. Three days of her was enough to rattle anyone.

Not only were they sick of Holly, they were also sick of the Hummer. On the other hand, they weren't sure if the paperwork was bogus. It would be a real downer to trade it in and get busted for car theft. So they were stuck with it and swore to make damn sure to check the back seats before they got in.

They then realized they had no idea how to find Kirsten and Tommy. They checked the websites but no dark-green Ram pickup with a camper shell had been reported. Could a truck disappear?

"This is going to piss you off," said Ted, "but you know our only hope?"

"Don't say it," said Jupe.

"Holly."

"I told you not to say that."

"I know."

"I want nothing to do with that woman. I'd rather walk through a biker bar in a pink jumpsuit."

"I'd pay big bucks to see that."

"I think she's a devil worshipper."

"Don't get carried away. She's just a run-of-the-mill husband-murdering, carjacking, psycho bitch from hell."

"Yeah. No sense getting worked up. You really think we've got to deal with her again?"

"No, I think she's our only link with those people and we should stay out of sight. Don't talk to her, do not get anywhere near her. But she could lead us to Tommy, and that will give us Kirsten."

"I know you're right, but it does piss me off. She might have super powers and get us with a death ray."

"Jupe, have you got some drugs I don't know about?"

"No. I just read too many comic books. Tell me your plan."

"Like I said, we park the Hummer out of sight and stake out that motel. If she leaves, we follow and hope she leads us to the computer jockey."

"I hate that fucking plan, but I can't think of anything better. Let's go find her, but don't come crying to me if we get blasted with cosmic particles."

On the way to the motel Ted messaged Rick and told him about Holly, the queen of the stalkers. If anything, it intensified their hatred of women. Rick promised to check the men's groups to see if anyone else had spotted the truck. In the meantime, they could stalk Holly and hope she would lead them to Tommy and Kirsten.

Holly, the subject of all this conjecture, was not pleased. She was weak from her bout with food poisoning, those bastards had stolen her money and credit cards, and worst of all, they'd taken her gun. All she had was her backpack with some clothes in it. It wasn't the first time she'd been dead broke in a strange town but it was still frightening. She had no one to call for help. Her first husband was in a shallow grave and it served him right, the bastard. She had no family and her second husband would run like hell if she called. No, there was no one. Or was there?

Tommy? Oh sure, she'd dumped him, but not hard. The truth was, life with him had been kind of boring. Also, Tommy was not a macho guy. He was small and quiet. But guys were funny, you could dump all over them and then get them back if you played it smart. A quiet life with a guy who made money would be a huge step up these days. Ted and Jupe had overlooked her cell phone because it was in her front pocket when she was heaving her guts out.

She checked, and she had an old number for Tommy. Please God, she thought, let it still work. Nope. So much for God. Somehow she didn't think He was on her side anyway.

Was Tommy on facebook or Twitter? She used the phone and searched for him. Bingo. She found him on Facebook and carefully composed a Messenger text.

Hi Tommy, Remember me? I still have bad feelings about how our relationship ended, and I hope you've moved on and life is good. I hate to say this, but I'm in trouble and I need help. Nothing big, but if you ever had any feelings for me I could sure use a small loan. I've been robbed, I'm in a strange town, and I have no one to turn to. Your ex-girlfriend, Holly.

She had until noon to check out and she hoped she could hustle the desk clerk for another hour or two. If Tommy didn't come through she was screwed.

CHAPTER 38

Carlos was driving when Tommy got the message. He showed it to the others.

"What do you think?" he asked.

"I think it depends on Holly. Is she a scam artist?" said Kirsten.

"I always thought she was a good person, but looking back there were things that should've bothered me. Then one day, out of the blue, she told me she'd found another guy. Broke my heart."

"Did you love her?"

"I don't know. We lived together for over a year and I could feel things going downhill. She could get really cold, not talk to me, walk away when I was trying to talk to her. Then, other times, she'd be really warm and loving. The cold days were happening more often."

"What did you do?"

"I tried to pay more attention, but the truth is, we didn't have much to talk about. She loved clothes, jewelry and styling hair and I loved computers. We didn't have much in common."

"Still," said Kirsten, "she's a woman alone in a strange town with no money. I wouldn't wish that on anyone."

"It sounds like a scam to me," said Carlos. "How do we know it's even her?"

"Good question," said Kirsten. "Maybe we should have her call and you can make sure."

"Okay," Tommy said, "I'll ask her to call on Messenger. No sense giving her my number."

She called almost immediately and Tommy put it on speaker.

"Tommy?" she said.

"Hi Holly. I just wanted to make sure this is really you."

"Can you tell by my voice?"

"I think so, but it's been a long time. If you could answer a couple of questions it would reassure me."

"Okay."

"First, where were we when you broke up with me?"

"Ooh, a sad one. Giovani's Pizza Palace. I told you I was leaving and you got up and walked out. That was the last time I saw you."

"What car did you drive when we first met?"

"I didn't have a car. I put all my money into the salon. Want me to tell you where that mole is on your thigh?"

"No, that won't be necessary," said Tommy, wincing. "I'm convinced. I can send you a little money, but not much. These are tough times. Will a couple hundred be okay?"

"That would be great. I can get home on that."

"How can I get it to you?"

"That's a tough one. They stole my I.D. and credit cards so if you send it to me I can't identify myself to pick it up."

"Damn, that makes it difficult. Are you in a hotel?"

"A motel."

"Where?"

"Crystal Springs."

Tommy damn near dropped the phone. What the hell was she doing in Nevada? Much less Crystal Springs? His companions were stunned too. What was going on?

"What the hell are you doing there?"

"You really want to know?"

"Yeah, I really do."

"I was stalking you."

This was beyond weird.

"You're not serious."

"Well, maybe stalking is the wrong word, but over the past few months I realized you were the best thing that ever happened to me and I made a huge mistake when I walked away. So I found you on the Internet."

"Nothing there would tell you where I am."

"Ah yes, but when I did a deep search I saw your name mentioned with some woman named Kirsten in a radical men's group. Do you know there are guys after her?"

"Yeah, I know."

"It scared me. So I decided to protect you."

"How would you do that?"

"I found out where those guys were and hooked up with them. Kind of an undercover cop. I've been with them the last couple of days, but then they found out I was your old girlfriend and they tied me up and robbed me. I just got loose a while ago."

Kirsten and the others were shaking their heads. It couldn't get any more strange.

"That is the craziest story I ever heard," Tommy said. "What kind of car were they driving?"

"It wasn't a car, it was a Hummer, and they hated it."

"What are their names?"

"One is Ted and the other is Jupe. Jupe is short for Jupiter."

"Where did you first meet up with them?"

Holly thought fast. They hadn't seen her in Stanley so she could pick any place along their route.

"Twin Falls, at the computer store."

"How were they tracking us?"

"At first they had your phone hacked and were following it. After you ditched the phones in Twin Falls they went on the Internet and asked all the men's groups to look out for your truck. Some guy saw you in Crystal Springs and said you were headed south. I don't think they know where you are now but they're guessing Las Vegas."

"Okay, Holly," here's the deal. "Give us the name of the motel and I'll do two things. I'll pay your room for another night and then figure out how to get you the cash."

"Oh thank you, Tommy. I had nowhere else to turn. Are you sure you don't want to bring it yourself? You can't be too far away and we could have a coffee or something. It'd be like old times."

Everyone was shaking their heads violently. No! Tommy agreed.

"Not a good idea, Holly. It would just open up old wounds."

"You got a new girlfriend? You hooked up with that Kirsten woman?"

Tommy wished.

"No, we're just friends."

"So there might be a tiny bit of hope for me?"

"No, Holly, that ship has sailed. I'll get the money to you and that'll be it. I've got to go now."

"Don't hang up..."

He hung up. She called back and he didn't answer. Soon she gave up.

CHAPTER 39

"Okay," Tommy said. "What do you believe? Joyce?"

"I believe she hooked up with Ted and Jupe and they almost caught us. I don't believe this is a labor of love, not a bit."

"Kirsten?"

"You have a mole on your thigh?"

"That has nothing to do with this."

"I don't know. Maybe we should check, make sure she's not lying," she said, giggling.

"Very funny. Come on, we've got to figure this out."

"Okay. I agree with Joyce," said Kirsten. "Her story is very strange, and that love thing? I don't buy that for a minute."

"Now hold on," said Tommy, "you're underrating the devastating effect I have on women."

"I don't think it's possible to underrate that," said Kirsten.

"Hey, you didn't know me in my glory days. I was a stud!"

"I believe you," said Joyce. "Even now I feel your wild sexual energy."

"It's a curse," said Tommy. "I try to keep it tamped down but sometimes it spills out."

"Something's spilling out," said Carlos, "but I don't think it's sexual energy."

"Are we done talking about super stud here?" asked Kirsten.

"I'm not," said Tommy. "This is a great conversation."

"But it's not solving our problem. I say get the money to her but don't get within five hundred miles. She is trouble."

"Carlos?" Tommy asked.

"Joyce and Kirsten said it all. Who knows? She might still be with Ted and Jupiter and the whole thing's a setup."

"Jo?" Tommy asked.

She pointed to the other three and nodded. It was unanimous.

"Okay, we're agreed. But we can't send a check because there's no way she could cash it. How do we send cash and make sure some clown at the motel desk doesn't steal it? Nothing's safe these days."

"A dead drop," said Carlos. "We have to stash the money somewhere near and then call and tell her where it is. We can watch from a long way off and make sure she gets it."

"Well shit," Tommy said. "We have to turn around and drive all the way back to Crystal Springs?"

"I can't think of anything else, can you?"

"Tommy," said Kirsten, "I admit I wish I could vote to ditch her but she's a woman in a strange town with no money and no one to turn to."

"If she's telling the truth."

"Right."

"If we can help her and never, ever come in contact, it's okay with me."

The others agreed. Then Tommy had another idea. Oh sure, it came with a possible prison sentence but life on the edge, right?

"Kirsten, when you checked her out, where was Holly living?"

"Her last address was in Los Gatos, why?"

"I might be able to hack in and get a copy of her driver's license. She can use it to get her other I.D."

"When they come to arrest you, do we get thrown in the slammer for aiding and abetting?"

"Hey, we already shot up an apartment and a rest stop, stole two vehicles and forged identities for Jo and the Hummer—one more little crime is not going to mean much."

"Don't forget the graffiti," said Joyce.

"Wow," said Carlos. "I feel like I've joined the mafia."

"Welcome to my world," said Joyce. "I thought what could go wrong? A little road trip with friends. Now I'm in a pickup truck with the godfather."

"The scary part is, I'm enjoying it," said Carlos.

"Don't encourage him," said Kirsten. "Next we'll be knocking over liquor stores."

They stopped for lunch at the Desert Café in Mesquite.

It had Wi-Fi and Tommy got on his laptop, broke through the DMV firewalls and downloaded Holly's driver's license onto a flash drive.

Luckily they didn't have to go all the way back to Las Vegas because I-15 cut into US 93 before then. They put the cash and flash drive into an envelope and circled Holly's motel looking for a good hiding place. They found a little park nearby and Tommy and Kirsten got out. Carlos drove the pickup four blocks down a side street while they walked into the park and taped the envelope under a bench. Then they called Holly and told her where it was. Kirsten and Tommy walked to the edge of the park and hid in some trees.

They waited.

It didn't take long. She came walking fast, almost running, and spotted the bench. She sat down, reached underneath and found the envelope. Kirsten and Tommy started edging away.

"Hello there!" said a soft voice behind them. They both spun around and there was Ted, smiling wickedly, holding an automatic. What the hell?

"How did you get here?" Kirsten asked.

"Jupiter and I figured the only way we were going to find you was by following Holly. You know that woman's a psycho, don't you?"

"I didn't know that," Tommy said lamely.

"Well trust me, she is. But she's real smart too and we figured you were her only hope. So we staked out the motel. When she came out, Jupe and I followed. Want to wave to him? He's over there on the other side of the park."

Tommy looked, and sure enough, there was Jupiter.

"What are you going to do now?" Kirsten asked.

"Jupe's going to get the Hummer, we're going to put you two in it and drive back to Seattle. Rick wants to talk to you real bad, and it'll be a nice payday for us."

"What about Holly?"

"What about her? She can wander the desert for all we care."

"She's not working with you?"

"Are you kidding? She is one scary lady. We're staying far, far away from that nut case."

"You hear that, Tommy?" said Kirsten.

"Don't say I told you so," said Tommy.

"I told you so," said Kirsten.

"Okay, Ted, you want us to go with you," said Tommy. "What if we don't want to go?"

"What if we want to beat the shit out of you because of that stuff you put on the Internet?"

"Hey, you have to admit it was pretty funny."

Apparently Ted wasn't prepared to admit that, because he caught Tommy with a sucker punch to the jaw. Tommy went down hard.

"Fucking wise ass," said Ted. "That shit cost us money."

"Leave him alone," said Kirsten through gritted teeth.

"Or what?"

"We will get you. Again."

"Not this time, bitch," and he jammed the gun into her midsection. She too went down hard, gasping.

The Hummer pulled up and Ted pulled them up and pushed them over to it.

"Hop in," he said. "Next stop, Seattle."

"No." said Tommy.

Ted clubbed him with the gun in the back of the neck and Tommy re-thought his options. He and Kirsten got into the Hummer.

"Where are the others?" asked Jupe.

CHASING EXES

"Damned if I know," said Ted. "I'll tie these two up and you drive. Make sure no one follows us."

Ted tied them up while Jupe drove the Hummer toward the highway. They could see little cuts on his face, the bandages on his nose and ear, and realized he might be a little grumpy.

"We go north?"

"Let me check," said Ted. He got on Google Maps. "Well, shit."

"What's up?"

"There are warnings posted. Normally we could take 375 north, but a couple of bridges are out. They're falling down all over the country. We've got to go south to Las Vegas and then head over to I-5."

"Las Vegas? Did you say Las Vegas?"

"I know what you're thinking," said Ted. "We've been on the road too long. You want to have some fun in Vegas?"

"Hell yes," said Jupe. "We can get a room, tie up these two, and go have a night on the town."

They turned south.

Nobody followed. Tommy was thinking wildly. Where the hell were the others? For that matter, where was Holly? Was she really a psycho bitch? Shouldn't I have seen that? In a year? He felt humble.

Joyce, Carlos and Jo waited. Tommy and Kirsten didn't come back. Carlos started the truck and drove very slowly over to the park. They got there in time to see Ted force Tommy and Kirsten into the Hummer and drive off.

"We've got to know which way they go on the highway," said Joyce.

"That's easy," said Carlos. "Their boss is Rick and

he's in Seattle. I say it's ten to one they turn north."

"We should still be sure."

"Okay, but we can't let them see us."

They drove toward the highway, careful to stay out of sight of the Hummer, and Jo pointed south excitedly. The Hummer was disappearing in the direction of Las Vegas.

"What the hell's going on?" said Joyce.

"I have no idea, but we have to follow them. We can't let them see us, but they must be going to Las Vegas. Everything about this trip is surreal."

Ted and Jupe got to Las Vegas as the sun was setting. They drove past the main turnoffs to a place Ted had been before, Deja Vu Showgirls strip club. Ted was a classy guy. They found a Holiday Inn nearby, took a room as far from the office as possible, and parked in front of it. When all was clear, they carried Tommy and Kirsten inside, let them use the bathroom with the door open, and then tied them securely to the bathroom pipes. Ted stooped down in front of them.

"Aren't you a lovely couple," he said. "I'd love to stay and talk, but Jupe and I are going to go have a few Jaegermeisters, and play with naked women. You better hope that works out, because if it doesn't, we're going to come home and play with you."

Casually, he put his hand on Kirsten's breast.

"Fuck you," she said, squirming, trying to get away.

"Get your hand off her!" yelled Tommy.

Ted backhanded him, banging Tommy's head against the drain pipe. It hurt a lot.

Ted got a washcloth, stuffed it in Tommy's mouth and tied it, He did the same with Kirsten.

"Can't have you yelling and bothering the neighbors. I hate to leave but it's party time."

Then softly, caressing Kirsten's cheek, he said, "Don't worry darling, it'll be your turn soon. Nighty night."

He stood turned out the light and shut the door. Tommy and Kirsten struggled hard against the ropes, but they were too tight. Eventually they gave up and spent a long, restless night.

MIKE NEUN

CHAPTER 40

Holly was puzzled by the thumb drive in the envelope with the money. Back at the motel she used the business computer to open it and found a file with her driver's license. Eureka! Bless you Tommy! She could print it out and use it to get new credit cards. Life was looking up, but the cards would take awhile.

She was not about to blow the two hundred dollars to get to Las Vegas, but that was the best place to sort things out. Two hundred was nothing. She had to get more cash.

She checked out, and headed over to the Shell station by the highway. An hour later she'd talked a trucker into taking her to Las Vegas. A pretty lady, a trucker, what could go wrong? He put his hand on her leg as soon as they got out of town. She'd learned years ago that in tough situations acting scared made it worse, fighting was useless, but a slide into complete insanity could be a girl's best friend.

"Oooh," she said, "the old hand on the leg trick. Smooth! You're looking for sex? A little fuck in the truck? No problem, but first I got to take my meds. Holly opened her purse, grabbed a pill canister she'd carried for years, flipped the lid and turning away shook some M&Ms into her mouth.

"I never remember how many to take, so I just guess," she said as she turned back to the truck driver.

"I got all these meds and I think it's four yellows, a blue and two whites, but I can never remember. You take meds?"

"No," he said, a little nervous. "No meds."

"The yellows are for something serious, like meningitis or HIV, and I know the blues are for the voices and I can't remember what the whites are for but the doc says I have to take them. You ever get voices?"

"No. No voices."

"No meds, no voices, you're a lucky guy."

"Yeah. Lucky. I'm driving a truck."

"I get these fucking voices and they tell me to do stuff and that's wrong, isn't it?"

"Yeah. I wouldn't listen to them."

"I know! My shrink told me the voices aren't real and I believe him but they sure seem real. It's very confusing. He put his hand on my leg too, just like you. Doctors aren't supposed to do that, are they?"

"No, that would be wrong. I was just being friendly."

"I don't think he was a nice doctor. He kept touching me and no one believed me. It got worse and then the voices told me to get the knife and I said, 'No way, I'm not getting no knife,' but the voices kept nagging me, over and over. A girl can only take so much. I told the police it wasn't my fault. You from the police? You working undercover?"

"No ma'am, I'm a truck driver, just driving you to Las Vegas. I don't want any trouble."

"Trouble? Am I in trouble again? The damn police just didn't understand it wasn't me it was the voices. There was a lot of blood. I hate that. I tried to clean it up and got it all over me. You ever tried to clean up blood?"

"No ma'am."

"It gets sticky. I hate it."

The guy was driving faster now.

"I forgot. You wanted sex, didn't you? Hand on the leg and all that?"

"I didn't mean anything," he said. "You just calm down and I'll get you where you want to go."

"You don't look good," said Holly. "Did you change? Weren't you younger when you picked me up? Are you some kind of shape shifter?"

"No ma'am, I'm the same guy and I'm just driving you to Vegas. We'll be there real soon."

"Shut up!!!" Holly yelled, and he damn near drove off the road.

"Not you!" she said. "It's those goddam voices, they won't fucking shut up! Don't worry, I can control them. Most of the time. I got these meds but sometimes I forget to take them. Did I take any pills?"

"You took some for meningitis or HIV."

"HIV? I don't have fucking HIV! What do you think I am, some kind of skank?"

"No ma'am, you just took some pills."

"No one calls me a skank! Shut up! Not you, the voices. You can talk, but none of that HIV shit. I'm having trouble enough dealing with the goddam nineteen stuff."

"Nineteen? Covid 19? You got the virus????"

"Virus? What virus? I had the flu once when I was a kid, but that was before they put me in the institution. I was nineteen! In an institution! Nineteen years old! With that old doctor putting his hands on me. Fucking shrinks. You're not a shrink are you?"

"No ma'am, I'm a truck driver. I just drive truck, mind my own business."

"No shit, I thought you were that doctor, putting moves on me. He sure was surprised when he saw the knife. Ha! The voices thought it was funny! They laughed and laughed."

"But the voices aren't real. You said that."

"Voices, what voices? You hear them too? They telling you to do bad things? Did I take my meds? Damned chlamydia and herpes. You get them at the same time and it fucks you up!"

Holly smiled to herself. She could keep this up for hours.

It was the longest drive the guy ever made. He dropped her off in downtown Las Vegas and was ungodly happy to see her get out of that truck. He drove to the next motel, parked, got a room and a bottle of gin from the minimart. Never again. No hitchhikers. Never, ever again.

MIKE NEUN

CHAPTER 41

Holly's first husband, the abusive rat bastard, had lived in Reno and he was cheap. So she'd gotten books on blackjack and soon she could do a rudimentary plus-or-minus card-counting system. In time she got deeper into it and even with a five-deck shoe, shuffled constantly, she had a little edge. She never won big and she exaggerated when she lost. She also dressed sexy so she attracted gamblers to the tables and the pit bosses liked that. She tipped the dealers well, and her small winnings went unnoticed. It had given her extra spending money.

Now she headed to the old casinos in downtown Las Vegas and bounced from one to the other, winning small but steadily. In twelve hours of play she parlayed the two hundred dollars into a thousand. Then she went looking for a partner.

She met the woman in the restaurant at the Aces Up Casino. The woman was by herself, a dealer who'd just gotten off shift. She looked to be about Holly's age, a little taller, brown hair, pretty face, nice figure, but with a certain hardness about her. Holly asked if she could join her.

"Are you gay?" asked the woman.

"No," said Holly, "just tired of gambling."

"Okay, have a chair."

Holly ordered a burger and a beer and asked her new friend if she wanted a beer.

"Sounds good, thanks."

Holly didn't say much. She'd learned years ago that when people want something they usually talk too much. Better to let the mark come to them.

They toasted with Coors and Holly learned her name was Susan.

"You a big gambler?" Susan asked.

"Not really. Just now and then."

"Smart. Too many people get hurt around here. Gambling's tough."

"Do you gamble?" asked Holly.

"Yeah. Most dealers do."

"You get hurt?"

"Sometimes."

"How about now, you okay?"

"Not really. I had to sell my car and the casino has a lot of my markers. I think I'm fucked."

"That sucks. What kind of car?"

"Mazda 3. I loved that car."

"Yeah. They're nice. How do you get around town?"

"Bus mostly. I'm saving up, staying away from the tables. Maybe I can buy my way out."

"You know where your car is?"

"Yeah, a guy bought it. He lives in town."

"You really want that car?"

"Sure. But there's no way."

"You love your job?"

"Oh hell no."

"Want to get your car, make some money and get out of Dodge?"

"You're talking crime, aren't you?"

"Yeah, I guess I am. But nothing major. Small stuff."

"I'll pass. I don't do crime."

"No problem. It was just a thought."

"I gotta go."

"Sorry if I made you nervous. I won't bother you again."

Susan left.

Holly wondered where she'd screwed up the pitch.

She had a thousand dollars, but that wasn't going to cut it. What she really needed was a laptop, a car, and enough money to continue her search for Tommy. She was obsessed now, more than before. He'd given her money, hadn't he? That must mean there was still a chance.

A laptop, a car, money—it was a lot to ask. She was mulling this over when she looked up and there stood Susan.

Holly smiled.

"I've been thinking it over," said Susan. "My life here sucks, I'm never going to get out from under, and the bosses are pressuring me. How big a crime are we talking about?"

"I was thinking car theft and a road trip, that's all."

"Where would we go?"

"Sit down and I'll explain. You can make changes if you want. I'm open to anything."

Susan sat down.

"Here's the deal," said Holly. "I'm in love with this guy and he's running away from me. I just want an hour with him, so I can present my case. If he says no, so be it. I'll move on."

"Wow, romance."

"Yeah, kinda."

"What do you need from me?"

"I need help getting a car and someone to share the driving. I'll supply money."

"Where are you going?"

"I'm not sure, but I'm guessing Seattle. You ever been there?"

"No, but I've heard good things. It would work for me. How much money do you have?"

"I've got a thousand bucks. If I play blackjack tonight and tomorrow I can bump that up."

"You a card counter?"

"Yeah, but I'm extremely careful and never win big. A little here, a little there, never enough to attract attention."

"Okay, so we steal a car, find your true love and end up in Seattle. But what then? If he says no we look for jobs and end up broke and homeless?"

"I honestly don't know. I can survive anything, but that might be too tough for you. We might find jobs, we might have to sell the car, we might have to hustle guys."

"Like hookers?"

"I draw the line there, but it's a thin one. I'm not above hanging out with a guy for some food and a roof. You know, like boyfriend-girlfriend with the girlfriend pretending."

"Hey, when times are tough you gotta do what you gotta do. I can get behind that."

"What do you think? Should we give it a shot?"

"I've got nothing to lose. Are you talking about stealing my Mazda back? If we did, I'd be the first one he'd suspect. He knows I love that car."

"Yeah, that's a shame. But there are a lot of Mazdas around. Maybe we could find one for sale and steal it."

"You know how to steal a car?"

"Well, yes. I've been through a couple of rough patches. If it's an older model I can work a slim jim and hotwire the ignition. Newer models are tougher. How old was your Mazda?"

"About five years. But if we find one with low mileage they're great cars."

"Okay, let's go online and check out the ads. You got a laptop?"

"It's in my locker, I'll go get it."

Susan got up to go. Then she paused and sat down again.

"I've got a better idea. If we steal a car from someone who really needs it, that would bother me."

"So?"

"What if we steal one from a raving jerk?"

Holly smiled. She was beginning to like Susan.

"You got one in mind?"

"I do. And the best part is no one would suspect me. He doesn't even work at this casino."

"I'll bite, who is it?"

"All of us dealers go to the same after-hours bars and we hear things. This guy is a pit boss on the Strip and word is he is a complete dick. Sexual assault, kinky stuff, the whole package. Women all over town hate his guts. Stealing from him wouldn't be stealing, it'd be more like payback."

"I like it," said Holly.

"Plus, he's got a nice car. Not a Mazda, but a new Honda SUV. It's that cool dark-red color and has all the extras. I wouldn't mind taking that."

"Sounds good to me. But the old methods won't work."

"So how to we steal it?"

"There are high-tech ways to steal the signal off his keyless remote but I don't know anyone who has that equipment. We'll have to go old school and steal the remote key.

"How?"

"I have to break into his house and steal it while he's sleeping. You can keep watch. If anyone comes you buzz my phone. I'll have it on vibrate. If anything bad happens to me in the house you run like hell and pretend you never heard of me."

"What about you?"

"I'll be screwed. But hey, I'm a thrill seeker. Want to give it a shot?"

"I'm scared. Have you done this before?"

"Yes, and I'm really small and sneaky."

"And you'll bail out at the first sign of trouble?"

"You bet your ass. I'm not stupid."

"Okay. I'm in."

"Seriously."

"Seriously. I have to get out of this town."

"You know where this guy lives?"

"I can find out. Lots of the girls have been to his house parties."

"Okay. Find out everything you can and we'll meet this afternoon. You know what shift he works?"

MIKE NEUN

"I'll find that out too."

They met that afternoon in the casino restaurant. Holly had mixed gambling with shopping and explained to Susan what she'd bought.

"I figure there's a chance someone could see us so it'd be best if we looked like teenage boys. I got black jeans, football jackets and baseball caps. It'll be late at night, so we'll be hard to see."

"Okay," said Susan. "I got his address and he lives alone. He parks the car in the garage."

"What time does he get off work?"

"One a.m. and he probably hits a bar or restaurant on the way home. I figured we could steal the car about four or four-thirty in the morning."

"That sounds good. I'll go to his house while he's at work and check for alarms. If he's got one I'll have to figure out a way to bypass it."

"You can do that?"

"If it's an older model. If it's new we'll have to find another way."

"And you can get into the door?"

"Sure. I picked a lot of locks as a kid."

"You did? What kind of kid does that?"

"The kind who wants to sneak in and out to see her boyfriend. It took practice but I got good at it. The alarm thing was a different deal. I had a friend who showed me stuff."

"You're a woman of many talents."

"I'll meet you in front of the casino later tonight, okay?"

Holly didn't tell Susan about the handgun. No way she was going to break into some guy's house without protection. She knew it changed the crime to a felony but that was way better than getting caught, so she bought one. She reviewed everything and felt she was prepared, so she went back to the blackjack tables, losing a little bit, winning a little bit more, staying under the radar.

CHAPTER 42

"What time is it?"

"Two thirty. Did you check for alarms?"

"Yeah, he's got an old one. I bypassed the contacts on the back door. Piece of cake. While I was there I broke in and cased the place. I know the layout of his bedroom so I can try to find his pants in the dark, but it'll be easier if he puts his stuff on the dresser. I'll take his phone too, so he won't be able to call the police."

"Fuck me. I'm dealing with a master criminal."

"Not really. This is small-time stuff. I don't do banks or anything."

"Oh good, a criminal with attainable goals."

"I know my limits."

"I think I exceeded mine hours ago," said Susan, wondering how the hell she'd gotten into this.

"Stay calm and trust me."

"I hope he didn't get lucky or drunk. If he doesn't come home soon we'll have to come back tomorrow."

"What's this guy's name?"

"Paul. Paul Gustafson. He's a big guy, likes to throw his weight around. His dealers hate his guts."

"Perfect. We couldn't steal from a better man."

They waited another half hour, hiding behind some shrubbery across the street and finally saw the SUV drive up. The house was a typical one-story ranch style, white with dark trim and an attached garage. The lawn and shrubs were neatly trimmed. They watched as the automatic garage door lifted, he drove in, parked and the door came down. They saw lights go on in the kitchen as he entered the house, then they went out as he crossed to his bedroom and those lights went on. They saw the glimmer of a TV. Holly and Susan sneaked around back and waited in the shadows behind the house. Finally everything went dark. They gave him another hour.

"We should go now," whispered Susan. "It's going to be dawn soon."

Holly took off her jacket and jeans and Susan saw she was all in black, with a hooded top. Cat burglar, just like the movies. Classy.

"Okay, let's do it," whispered Holly. "You locked and loaded?"

"What the fuck are you talking about?"

"Just joking. I always wanted to say that."

"Do I get to whisper, 'Go go go'?"

"Perfect. Lady SWAT team on the move."

Holly ghosted over to the back door and went to work on the locks. She could've left them open but he might've noticed, but she had sprayed them and the knob with WD-40. She'd fashioned a pick and tension spring years ago and always carried them hidden in the seam of her backpack. The second time was easier and soon she had the locks open. Susan couldn't hear a thing as Holly gently twisted the knob and entered the house.

Ten long minutes later, Holly appeared at the door holding up what Susan guessed was the keyless remote and his cell phone. Victory! Susan padded softly to her and they glided across the kitchen and through the door into the garage.

"You drive," whispered Holly. "The garage door switch is here by the kitchen door. I'll push it and jump in as the door goes up. We have to be quick and get out before he can wake up and realize what's happening."

The car beeped when Susan opened the doors. It couldn't be helped. She jumped in and Holly was about to press the garage door opener when the door to the kitchen slammed open and Paul Gustafson stood there in the dark with a flashlight and a gun trained on Susan.

"Freeze!" he yelled.

Susan froze, terrified.

Holly, in the shadows beside the door, did too. Then ever so slowly she eased lower and pulled out her new Sig Sauer P320.

"Okay God damn it," commanded Paul, "I've got a gun, come out with your hands up."

Susan whimpered and opened the door of the car. As she did, Holly, from the shadows beside him, jammed her gun into Gustafson's crotch.

"Put down the gun," she said in her lowest voice, "or I'll blow your dick off. Do it!"

Shocked, he lowered the flashlight, saw her gun and lowered his.

"Drop it on the floor. Now!"

He did.

"Susan, get his gun."

"Susan?" he exclaimed. "You're a fucking woman?"

"Yep, and proud of it you dirtbag."

Susan climbed out of the car and picked up his gun.

"Fuck you for scaring the shit out of me," she said, pointing it at him. "Get your hands way up high."

"Back up slowly," said Holly. "No quick moves or your little wee wee is going to disappear."

"Fuck! You're a woman too!"

"Right you are, dickhead. Now we're going to go into the house and figure this out. Susan, are you okay with that pistol?"

"I'm a single woman living in a town full of gamblers and meth heads. I can shoot the dick off a housefly."

"I don't know about you, Paul, but I'm impressed. Let's go talk."

They pushed him into the kitchen and sat at the table, Paul at one end and Holly and Susan at the other, guns trained on him.

"You bitches are in big trouble," he sneered. "Breaking and entering, car theft, weapons charges. You're looking at years in prison."

"Let me get this straight," said Holly. "You're sitting at a table with two guns trained on you, and you think we're in trouble? You've got to work on your logic skills. Now shut up and let us figure this out."

"You could turn yourself in."

"Oh sure, spend years in prison or shoot you, get out of town, and live happily ever after. Gee, tough choice."

Susan said, "He's seen us, and he knows my name."

"Sorry about that," said Holly. "It was the heat of the moment. Let me think a minute."

They sat in a frozen tableau while Holly thought.

"I think I have the answer," she said, finally. "Paul, I bet you're a big fan of porn."

MIKE NEUN

"No. No I'm not."

"Give me a fucking break. I bet your computer jumps to PornHub all by itself. Anyway, I think it's time to make a movie. Now I'm just spitballing here, so Susan, you jump in with any ideas. Let's go to the bedroom."

She made Paul lead the way.

"Okay, Paul, you're going to be the star. Take off your clothes."

"Fuck no!"

"We should make something real clear. There are only two ways to deal with this, because Susan and I are not going to prison. By the way, my name's Holly. So now, there is no way we can let you go. Got it?"

"Got it."

"So, choice number one. We kill you. Do you believe we could do that?

"Not a chance in hell."

"I've got your phone here. I want you to take it and Google Holly Carlson, Reno. I'll watch over your shoulder and shoot if you try anything else."

He Googled Holly Carlson, Reno.

"You see the first one that pops up? What does it say?"

"Holy shit. Police think you murdered your husband."

Susan turned pale.

"So I have a history. Read on."

"Fuck."

"And now, for your final Jeopardy question, if Holly Carlson, famous murder suspect, has the choice between a felony charge or blowing your ass all to hell, which one would she choose?

"Don't do it. Please."

"Sorry, wrong answer. You lose. Say goodnight, Paul."

"Please," he begged, "Don't shoot."

"You want to hear your other option?"

"Yes."

Holly took back the phone.

"We're going to make a movie and you're going to be the star. So what'll it be? Death or movie star? I'll give you three seconds to decide. Ready? Three....two...."

"Movie."

"Take off your clothes."

"Come on," he pleaded, "you can have my money, anything you want."

"What we want, Paul, is for you to take off your fucking clothes. I'm not going to ask again."

"Okay, okay. Don't shoot."

He took off his pants and shirt, socks and shoes.

"Boxers too," said Holly. "Susan, go get something frozen out of the refrigerator. Doesn't matter what."

Susan, baffled, went and came back with a bag of frozen corn.

"Give it to Paul."

Susan did.

"Okay, Paul, hold that to your private parts. Susan, you keep your gun on him, I'll be the cameraman."

"It's too cold," said Paul.

"Just another few seconds..... Okay, that should do it. Now throw the corn aside and stand tall. I want some teeny weenie dick pics. Guys always want people to think they're hung like Godzilla, let's prove 'em wrong."

Paul tried to cover up but it was too late, and his

hands flying to cover his shriveled dick made it look like he was ashamed. Perfect.

"Jesus, Paul," said Susan, "you gotta get to a gym. You're a fat bastard. No wonder all the girls are grossed out."

Paul tried to suck in his stomach but failed.

"Keep him covered," said Holly, and then she went through his closets and drawers, tossing stuff aside as she made a quick search. She found what she was looking for.

"Hey Paul, Susan told me you were kinky, liked S&M, and look what I found! It's like a sex store in here! Whips, cuffs, chains, ball gags, pincers....this is going to be a long movie."

They spent the next two hours videoing Paul being tied up, spanked, whipped, gagged, masked, and humiliated. Graphic stuff.

"Okay," said Holly. "That should do it. Now here's how we're going to play this. If you report any of this to the cops, if you report your car stolen, if you even tell a friend about what happened here tonight, all this video is going up on the Internet. We'll also email it to your bosses and all the dealers in your casino. You'll be a porn star!

Furthermore, if we get wind of you bullying any dealer, stripper, hooker or woman of any kind, not only will the video go out, I'm going to come back here and we're going to have a long talk. Then only one of us is going to leave. Do you understand?"

He was defeated. And still tied up with feathers sticking out of strange places.

"I understand," he mumbled.

"You're sure?"

"I'm sure. I won't report you and I won't talk."

"Okay. Now where's the title to your car?"

"In the desk."

Holly got it and had him sign where it said "Seller".

"Where's your spare car key?"

"In the bottom drawer, under the shirts."

Holly got it.

"And now, ta da, where's your money?"

"In my wallet."

"Any other money? Before you answer, I want you to think long and hard. We are going to search and if we find something you didn't tell us about we're going to use all the rest of that equipment in your closet. We'll make Fifty Shades of Gray look like a rom-com."

"No," he whimpered, "I'll tell you. There's a safe in the spare room, in the back of the closet."

He gave them the combination and they cleaned it out. Suddenly their money problems were solved. There had to be ten thousand in there, maybe more.

"Okay, Paul," said Holly, "Think of this as the world's mildest home invasion. No one gets hurt, no one's calling the police, and you can get on with your life. Just remember, we've got all this video and we've got friends in town. We will know if you fuck up and you will become a porn star. It's your chance to quit being a dickhead asshole."

Susan laughed.

"I like that phrase," she said, "it damn near combines all parts of his body."

"Okay, it'll take a while for you to undo all that crap, so we'll be long gone before you're done. Don't even think of chasing us because we'll have our fingers on the upload button. And now, on behalf of all the women you fucked over and abused, we say 'Fuck you, Paul, and the horse you rode in on. Good bye, you fucking weasel.'"

With that, they walked out the kitchen door into the garage, punched the opener, climbed into their new, legal Honda SUV, and drove out the driveway into the next chapter of their lives.

CHAPTER 43

Holly drove. Susan wavered between giddiness and shock.

"Was that stuff true? About you and your husband? Am I riding with a murderer?"

"A suspected murderer," said Holly, "and they never found a body so maybe there was no murder."

"I'm scared."

"Of me?"

"Yes."

"Let me tell you about my first husband, and then you tell me what you would've done."

Holly told Susan about the abuse in graphic detail.

"He did all that?"

"I'll swear to it and I have hospital records and scars. You want to see them?"

"No. I believe you. And he disappeared?"

"Yes. One night he disappeared."

"I don't want to know any more."

"I can drop you off anywhere," said Holly. "You don't have to come with me."

"Actually, I do. What's happening at the casino is worse than what I told you."

"You'll have to explain that."

"Maybe later. Are we going to Seattle?"

"I think so, and I think the best way is to head over to Bakersfield to 1-5 and go north. It's a freeway, with a straight shot to Seattle. If we get tired we can stop in Barstow and sleep and relax for a day. I'm exhausted, can you drive first?"

"Sure," said Susan. "I'm still buzzed. Taking down Paul was one of the highlights of my life. Too bad we can't stay in Las Vegas, we'd get medals."

They took turns driving until they got to Barstow and found a Red Roof Inn. They checked in, showered and climbed into the two beds. In no time they were asleep, worn out from their adventures.

They slept all day and woke up that evening. They walked to a nearby Applebee's and split fish and chips and a Caesar salad. Then they walked back to the motel. Susan opened her laptop, logged on, and turned it over to Holly, who surfed the get-those-bitches websites, looking for posts from Ted, Jupe and Rick. She found the ones that asked for help locating the pickup. She found a later one from Ted, gloating, "We found Rick's ex! Are we good or what???"

This didn't sound good for her true love, Tommy. He was with Rick's ex. If her hunch was right, they would be heading for Seattle. Time to go north, see if she could cut them off at the pass. They shut down the computer and took an easy night, then started driving north at the crack of dawn. Holly to the rescue. Tommy would be so pleased.

CHAPTER 44

Joyce, Carlos and Jo searched Las Vegas for the Hummer but never found it. It didn't occur to them to look in the Déjà Vu Showgirls parking lot. Finally they admitted defeat, got a room near the main freeway interchange, ate a quick meal and went to sleep.

And there, later that night, the kidnappers and their chasers slept twelve blocks from each other. Granted, Ted and Jupe didn't sleep much as they spent a large amount of Rick's money pounding down shots and getting lap dances.

The next morning Ted and Jupe woke up late and terribly hung over. They decided they had to at least start on their trip to Seattle. They let their prisoners use the bathroom and wash up with the door open, then checked to make sure it was all clear before loading them in the Hummer and tying them up again. On the way out of town they stopped for McMuffins and were on the road by eleven a.m.

Carlos, Joyce and Jo, their pursuers, did not spend the night at a titty bar, so they woke up much earlier. They assumed Ted and Jupiter would drive over to I-5 and go north, so they drove out at eight a.m., putting them in the odd position of chasing people who would be three hours behind them. Joyce was driving, trading off with Carlos every couple of hours to make sure they were alert. Carlos spent time on his laptop, checking the websites for any mention of the Hummer. Jo had her ear buds in, listening to boy bands. Carlos saw Ted's post about Rick's ex, but there was no mention of where they were. How hard could it be to find a Hummer? Then Joyce had an inspiration.

"They're using those hateful men's groups to get information, right?"

"Right."

"Why don't we use radical women's groups the same way? This is a perfect case of a man harassing his ex-wife, so there must be thousands of women out there willing to help."

"Do you know about those groups?"

"Oh hell yes. A friend of mine had some man problems a couple of years ago and got all kinds of assistance. I'm going to pull over so you can drive and I'll do some digging. We'll have help in no time."

Soon Carlos took over and Joyce surfed the websites.

She posted on the women's groups about her friend Kirsten's evil ex-husband who'd hired two guys to kidnap her. They were driving a black Hummer headed from Las Vegas to Seattle. Any sightings would be helpful. Carlos kept driving and three hours later Joyce got a sighting on highway 40 south of them. Someone had seen the Hummer at a truck stop getting gassed up. The descriptions matched Ted and Jupe and they were over a hundred and fifty miles behind. Chasing kidnappers was weird.

Carlos pulled off the freeway in Bakersfield and

pulled into a Denney's for a long, leisurely breakfast. They killed an hour and then drove over to wait at the on-ramp. Joyce saw it first.

"There! It's the Hummer. Don't pull out yet or they'll see us."

Carlos waited until the Hummer was out of sight.

"We'll stay back until we come to any place they might turn off, then I'll pull up. We don't want to lose them now."

They drove all afternoon, checking carefully at every off ramp to make sure they didn't pass the Hummer.

"Don't these guys ever get hungry?

"Maybe they're trying to get to Sacramento. All we can do is follow."

"The good news is that it's getting dark. No way they can tell whose headlights are behind them. We can close in."

South of Sacramento, the Hummer pulled off the highway into an EconoLodge. Ted checked in and pulled around back. No one was around, so they carried the prisoners inside and made themselves at home.

"I am fucking beat," said Ted.

"Me too," said Jupe, laughing, "those strippers wore me out."

"Them and the Jagermeisters."

"I think we set records."

"I want food, beer and a bed. In that order. This hangover's still killing me."

Carlos followed the Hummer and waited down the street while Ted checked in and pulled around back. Carlos, Jo and Joyce waited twenty minutes, then pulled up to the office and checked in. They got a room in front, took their bags inside, and Joyce and Jo stayed in the room while Carlos drove three blocks away, then parked and locked the truck. He walked back.

Jo kept watch at the front window and saw Jupe walk out to a 7-Eleven for beer and Pizza Hut for takeout. When the coast was clear, Joyce got pizza too, and the kidnappers, kidnappees and pursuers ate a hearty meal.

As they ate, Carlos and Joyce talked with Jo listening attentively.

"Can we rescue them now?" asked Joyce.

"I've been trying to think and I can't come up with a plan. There are people in other rooms and if shooting starts innocent bystanders are going to get hit."

"No way we can get the drop on them?"

"They could just threaten to shoot Tommy and Kirsten. Then what?"

"Well damn. I can't think of a way to get both of them out of the room, can you?"

"Nope. I'm thinking our best bet would be at a rest stop, somewhere deserted. Then maybe we can separate them."

"I feel helpless. I wish we could do something now."

"Me too, but our best bet is to rest up and be strong tomorrow."

And there, in an EconoLodge south of Sacramento, everyone went to sleep.

CHAPTER 45

Joyce, Carlos and Jo got up very early because they didn't want the kidnappers to get on the road before them. Joyce ran over to McDonalds for some take-away McMuffins and coffee while Carlos and Jo sneaked around back of the motel and hid in the trees to spy on the Hummer.

In a half hour they saw stirrings in the room and then saw Ted head to the same McDonalds and come back with a bag of

food. Ted and Jupe started loading stuff in the hummer, throwing bags in the back. They left the hatchback open and before Carlos could stop her, Jo threw on her backpack and darted from their hiding place. She ran across the parking lot and jumped in, burrowing under the backpacks and duffel bags. The last thing Carlos saw was her hand poking out, holding up her cell phone. Then she pulled it back and hid.

There was nothing he could do. Ted and the others could come out any minute.

"Damn," he mumbled to himself. Then he worked his way around to the front of the motel and into their room. Joyce was waiting.

"Where's Jo?"

"You're not going to believe this."

He told her what Jo had done.

"That settles it," said Joyce. "We have to rescue them as soon as possible."

"I agree, but I can't figure out what the hell Jo plans to do with that cell phone. She can't talk to us and we don't know how to track the phone."

"Did she think she could call us and let us listen in on the conversations in the Hummer?"

"Maybe, but it's a noisy beast."

"I've got a gun," said Joyce. "Do you?"

"Tommy's and Kirsten's are in the truck, I'll get one of them."

Just then, Joyce's phone rang. It was a call from Jo. Joyce answered in a whisper.

"Jo, are you okay?"

Nothing. Of course not. Jo couldn't talk and Joyce thought fast.

"If you're okay tap the microphone once."

One tap.

"Perfect! Okay, one tap for yes, two for no, got it?"

One tap.

"Have they left yet?"

Two taps.

"Okay, we're going to go to the truck and get ready. You stay quiet. When they leave, we'll follow but we'll stay back where they can't see us. Is your battery full?"

One tap.

"Okay, call back when they leave."

"A few minutes later, the phone rang."

"They're leaving?"

One tap.

"Okay, we'll follow. If they pull off the highway, call immediately, okay?"

One tap.

Carlos drove out to where they could see the entrance to the freeway. They saw the Hummer pull onto it and they gave it a head start and followed. Joyce thought of her quiet life of desperation in Ketchum and compared it to the craziness she was dealing with now. Then she thought, maybe this is like skiing down a black diamond run at top speed, knowing one false move could send her hurtling into the trees. Hell, she'd done that, so how could facing up to a couple of hired thugs be any scarier? She smiled.

"What are you smiling about?"

"Danger. It's all relative isn't it?"

"I suppose so, but I should've stuck to writing books."

Jo wriggled in amongst the bags, trying to find a comfortable position. She could hear bits of conversation from up front, but there was too much noise to make it all out. As near as she could tell, Tommy was in the back seat with Ted and Kirsten up front with Jupe driving. It was boring. She kept the sound off and played video games under the bags.

Up in front seat of the Hummer, Kirsten asked Jupe, "Why are you doing this?"

"For money. What else?"

"We saw your names in the hate-the-bitches websites so we figured you're against all women."

"Naw. Ted just put us in those things to get business. We figured if your guy paid us, others would too. I don't hate women."

"Bullshit. In La Grande you were going to rape me."

MIKE NEUN

As soon as she said it, Kirsten wanted to kick herself. How stupid was that? Putting that thought back in his head.

"Naw, back then I was just trying to scare you. Ted? Maybe he would've. There's a lot of anger in that boy. He got screwed royally in divorce court and really has a hard-on for women. He wanted me along because I look big and nasty. He figured one look at me and you'd be begging to give us your money."

"Why did you need our money? Hadn't Rick paid you?"

"Naw, he hooked up with us later, after he saw our post about the fuckup in La Grande. He got in touch and paid us to catch you and bring you back."

Jesus, thought Kristen, Rick was in the Twilight Zone. How could a man she'd loved turn into a psychotic bastard? She really knew how to pick 'em.

"But you don't hate women."

"Nope. I just don't give a shit. But I do hate you. You kicked me in the nuts and broke my nose. Then you posted that fucking motel video and made me look like a dumb shit."

"I'm sorry," she said, "but I was scared."

"You should be. Payback is a bitch."

Hoping to change the subject, she said, "Didn't your wife screw you in a divorce?"

"Nope. My wife died. The virus got her and our little girl. So fuck it. I just don't care anymore. I'll do anything to get by, including nailing some rich bitch who screwed her husband out of all his money."

Kirsten laughed.

"Rich bitch? Boy have you got that wrong. I'm as broke as you are."

"Bullshit. You got all of Rick's money and now you're hustling the little computer jockey. I figure you're loaded."

"You got it all wrong."

"Doesn't matter. We'll get you to Seattle, collect our money, and our job is done."

"We could pay you to let us go."

"Nope. Not a chance in hell. Ted and I are in the ex-wife business now. We got three more contracts lined up after this one."

"What if Rick does something horrible to me when you bring me back?"

"You got bigger worries than that. Ted has plans for you tonight."

"Plans?"

"Yeah. He realized it was stupid to blow money on those pole dancers in Vegas when we could have you for free."

"Have me?"

"Uh huh. He has the whole evening planned out. Lap dances, nudity, and then we'll take turns. I'm getting hard just thinking about it."

"You would do that to me?"

"Hell yes. You fucked me over."

Kirsten went quiet. Then she said, "Tommy will stop you."

Jupe burst out laughing.

"What's so funny?" Ted asked from the back seat.

"This bitch thinks Tommy's going to stop us from fun and games tonight."

Ted laughed too.

"Hell," he said. "Little Tommy will be lucky if he makes it through the day. He's a pain in the ass, we got no use for him. I say if we see a lake we tie a big rock to him and throw him in."

"Works for me," said Jupe. "Little bastard wrecked my Harley and told that kid to shoot me. I say we dump him and have fun with the lady tonight."

"You fuckers," said Tommy. "Murder and rape? You're looking at the gas chamber."

"If they catch us," said Ted. "I know one thing, you little piece of shit, you're not going to stop us so shut the fuck up."

"Jupe," said Kirsten, "I know Ted's a psychopath, but I don't think you are. How the hell can you buy into this?"

"Lady. I don't give a shit. God lost me when he took my wife and kid. Now I think you should shut the fuck up and let me drive. Got it?"

Kirsten shut up. She tried to loosen her hands, tied behind her back, but there was no hope. She wanted to cry, but swore she wouldn't. No crying, no begging, no matter what. And she would get these guys and Rick if it took the rest of her life.

Jo, in back, had heard bits and pieces of the conversation. She wondered what a lap dance was. She knew Kirsten and Tommy were in deep trouble.

A half hour later, Jo heard Jupe announce, "I gotta pee."

"Me too," said Ted. "too much coffee."

They slowed for the next rest stop and Jo called Joyce.

"Are they stopping?" asked Joyce.

One tap.

"Rest stop?"

One tap.

"Okay, have you got your pistol in your backpack?"
One tap.

"Here's the plan. Tap three times when they go to the toilets. We'll speed up and pull in. You try to get the drop on them and Carlos and I will too. Let's try to do this with no firing, okay?"

Pause. Then a reluctant one tap.

Jupe pulled into the rest stop and parked. They all got out of the Hummer and walked quickly to the toilets. Jo tapped three times. Carlos pulled the pickup quickly into the entrance and parked fifty yards away. He and Joyce got out with their pistols and ran quietly toward the restrooms. Twenty-three years in a gun shop and this was the first time he'd gotten close to actual combat.

Jo couldn't think of any way to get the drop on Ted and Jupiter without firing. Hard to yell, "Hands up!" when you can't talk. She was thinking fast as she dug for the Glock in her backpack and scrambled over the back seat and out the door. The Hummer was angled in, with the driver's side away from the toilets. She could hide behind it, but then what? If she got the drop on Ted coming around, Jupe could grab Kirsten and put a gun to her head. Standoff. There had to be a way to separate the four of them.

How would they come out? Probably with Tommy and Kirsten in front, Ted and Jupe behind them with guns hidden. Jo opened the back hatch and pulled bags and backpacks onto the ground. Then she ran to the far side of the Hummer and waited.

They came out as she'd thought, with Ted and Jupe behind Tommy and Kirsten.

"Oh oh," said Tommy.

"Oh oh what?" said Jupe.

"Looks like you've been robbed."

"What the fuck?" exclaimed Ted.

They shoved Tommy and Kirsten against the Hummer, eyes darting around looking for the culprit. Jo sneaked low around the front and as soon as she had a clear look she shot Ted's John Deere cap off his head. It wasn't a long shot, maybe ten feet. Ted froze. Jupiter spun around and came face to face with Carlos, fifteen feet behind him, gun aimed at his forehead. Joyce stood to the side in a shooter's stance, covering them too.

Jo put two more shots past Ted, one on either side of his head. He could hear them whiz past.

"God damn it," he yelled. "Not again!"

"Drop your guns," said Carlos. "She might get impatient, and I might too."

"Fuck." said Jupe. "Fuck, fuck, fuck, fuck."

Ted didn't bother talking. He dropped to the side, pulling his gun out and Carlos shot him. He was aiming for the chest, but hadn't expected Ted to drop. The bullet caught Ted in the arm, the one holding the handgun, and it went clattering to the sidewalk.

"Wow," said Kirsten. "Nice shot! Just like the movies!"

"Not really," said Carlos. "I was aiming for his chest."

"Oh."

Jupiter, sensing their distraction, tried to whirl and bring up his gun but Jo shot him in the calf and he kept spinning and went down hard. Tommy kicked his gun away.

Carlos picked up Ted's gun, Joyce got Jupiter's. Whatever happened, they weren't going to be short of weapons. Tommy wondered if they sold pistol racks for pickup trucks.

"On the ground," said Carlos. "Now."

Ted and Jupiter sat down, surrounded by five really pissed off people.

"I'm bleeding," moaned Ted, clutching his shoulder.

"Me too," said Jupe, clutching his calf.

"Good," said Kirsten. "I'm going to watch. I hope you bleed out, you fuckers."

Tommy decided he was never going to cross her.

"What do we do now?" asked Joyce.

"They were going to rape me and kill Tommy," said Kirsten.

"I say we shoot the bastards."

"We already have," said Carlos. "We just didn't kill them."

"Same problems," said Tommy.

He took them aside and explained to Carlos and Joyce.

"We've got a stolen Hummer, a stolen pickup, a kid with fake papers, no evidence of rape or murder, and if police come we lose Jo.

"Still," said Carlos, "We'd be doing society a favor."

"And me," said Kirsten. "You'd be doing me a really big favor. How about this? You all take off and leave me here with the biggest gun. It'd be worth going to prison to kill these fuckers."

"Me too," said Tommy. "I'm with Kirsten."

"What about Jo?" asked Joyce. "She'll never see you again. You want that?"

That stopped them.

"Fuck," said Kirsten.

"Well, we have to get out of here before some tourist comes along. Let's get them into the Hummer and tie them up. We can decide what to do."

"They're bleeding."

"Good," said Kirsten.

"We should tape up their wounds. If they bleed out we've got the same problems."

So the kidnappees kidnapped the kidnappers. They loaded them into the Hummer, tied them up and headed north. Tommy drove while Carlos did his best to bandage up the two hired thugs. Kirsten, Jo and Joyce followed in the pickup.

CHAPTER 46

Susan and Holly were unsure of the Hummer's location. Then Susan had a brainstorm.

"You know how those guys are using men's groups to track Tommy and Kirsten?"

"Yeah, we are too."

"What about women's groups?"

"What about them?"

"Why not get them to help us find the Hummer?"

"Seriously?"

"Sure. Your story's romantic—searching for a lost boyfriend, bad guys chasing him, true love trying to save him. We can leave out the part about you dumping him and the whole stalking scenario."

"Yeah, that could be confusing."

" I bet we'd get lots of help."

"And you can do that?"

"Oh hell yes."

Susan went online and found a bunch of women's sites.

"You're not going to believe this," she said.

"What"

"Someone beat us to it. There are posts in the women's sites about Ted and Jupe kidnapping Kirsten and asking help finding the Hummer."

"You mean we're not the only ones chasing those bastards?"

"Nope. And according to these women we're about two hours behind. There's a full-scale watch party going on up and down I-5. One report had the black Hummer south of Sacramento about three hours ago but the next one was strange. For some reason it's been joined by a dark-gray pickup truck and they're traveling together."

"That's just weird," said Holly.

"It does sound crazy," said Susan. Holly had filled her in on her adventures in Crystal Springs and she'd assumed the two hijackers had kidnapped Tommy and Kirsten and were driving north in the Hummer. The pickup truck with them made no sense at all. Oh well, Holly and Susan to the rescue.

"I'm hoping we can catch up and figure out what's going on. They have to stop somewhere. They can't drive straight through to Seattle."

"If we trade off driving and napping, we can maybe make up some time on them tonight. Drive longer than they do."

"Works for me."

The hours passed slowly. They talked.

"Where are you from?" asked Susan.

"California. Santa Monica. Both my mom and dad were actors."

"No shit? Have I seen them in anything?"

"Not unless you looked quick. They never got any big roles. I think the failure got to them because they split up when I was eleven. I stayed with my mom and she decided to start a new career as a drunk. She got really good at it and we became trailer trash."

"That's sad."

"What about you?"

"Ohio." said Susan. "I grew up in Columbus, married my college boyfriend, no kids, split up, got the house but lost it in the sub-prime crash. If anyone mentions balloon payments, I slap 'em. My ex couldn't pay his student loans and ended up living in his car. It's an American love story."

"Sorry about that. How'd you end up in Las Vegas?"

"I met a guy at a party and he was driving out to gamble. He asked if I wanted to go and it sounded better than waiting tables. He was a salesman and we had a pretty good trip. Once I got there I got into dealer's school and worked the tables for three years. That's when you found me.

"That's it? You were bored so you took off with me? You took a hell of a chance. I might've been a criminal!"

Susan laughed.

"Okay, there's stuff I didn't tell you. I didn't just gamble a little bit, I gambled a lot. Those casino guys owned me and they made Paul Gustafson look like a rookie. They took my house, car, bank account, everything, and I was pretty much working for free. I knew that next they'd be renting me out to high rollers."

"You got high rollers in that shithole?"

"Not really. In that place, anyone with ten grand was a whale. And you talk about sleazy people! Some of those guys would make you throw up. The thought of going up to their rooms was making me crazy."

"Hey, it looks like I came just in time. Will they send people after you?"

"I don't know. It's a dirtbag casino run by small-time crooks. I don't think they have the resources to chase

MIKE NEUN

someone like me."

"I hope you're right. We don't want to be dealing with goddam criminals," said Holly, laughing.

"Absolutely. We car-thieving, porno-producing home invaders don't want to deal with miscreants," said Susan, joining in.

"Miscreants? Where the hell did you come up with a word like that?"

"Probably CSI. You're not dealing with an intellectual lightweight."

"You know something?" said Holly, "I'm glad we did what we did to Paul."

"Me too. He was a legendary asshole, and that's saying a lot in Las Vegas. The competition is fierce."

"We should be poster girls for the women's movement. Wildly successful, got our own home invasion start-up, we produce movies, got a nice car, and we're headed for the great northwest. I'm surprised they haven't interviewed us for Cosmo."

They kept driving, talking about the men they'd known, the places they'd been, Holly's quest for true love. Mission Improbable.

They drove until almost midnight and from web reports they were closing in on the Hummer and the pickup, maybe just twenty or thirty miles behind. They talked about making their move that night but realized they were too tired and probably not thinking straight. They pulled off the freeway at a truck stop with a Quality Inn, checked in, showered and slept. They set their phone alarms for 6:30 a.m.

CHAPTER 47

Joyce drove the pickup, following the Hummer, with Jo and Kirsten beside her.

"What do you think of Carlos?" asked Joyce.

"I think he's a good guy," said Kirsten, "and Jo really likes him. I trust her judgment."

"Good idea. She was with him for a year. Jo? Is Carlos a nice man?"

Jo nodded and smiled.

"Why are you smiling, little girl?"

Jo pointed at Joyce, then held up her other index finger and brought them together.

"Ha! You think Carlos and I should hook up?"

Jo nodded.

"Tommy and I wondered about that," said Kirsten. "Are you two an item?"

"Well, no, but I've thought about it."

"Has he come on to you?"

Joyce smiled.

"No, I can't say that he has."

Kirsten paused. Then she smiled.

"Have you come on to him?"

"No, but the thought has crossed my mind."

"Alright! You go girl! You and Carlos, I think that would be a good thing."

"You don't think he's too old for me?"

"Nope. Never. If you find a good man, hang on to him. Don't sweat the details."

"I think so too. What do you think, Jo, would it be okay if Carlos and I got together?"

Jo nodded and smiled.

"How about you and Tommy?" asked Joyce. "Are you thinking about that?"

"A little, but I'm trying to be realistic. He's short, I'm tall, he's white, I'm black, he's got a psycho ex-girlfriend, I've got a psycho ex-husband.....there's a lot to deal with."

"So you're not going to jump his bones?"

"No, I'm not going to jump his bones. For once in my life I'm going to think things through. I'm the queen of bad relationships and I'm not crashing into another one."

"I can understand. Go slow, see what happens."

"Yes."

"Then jump his bones."

They laughed.

Up front, Tommy and Carlos were realizing how hard it was to deal with prisoners on the road. First they had to stop for bandages and antiseptic and do the best they could to treat the bullet wounds. Then, what do you do when two tied-up guys have to go to the toilet? No way Tommy or Carlos was going to unzip them and hold their dicks while they peed. So they had to find deserted rest stops and take them one at a time. It was time consuming and embarrassing. The ladies didn't help by laughing at their predicament.

That night they rented two rooms at a Howard Johnson's and gathered in one of them with Ted and Jupiter tied up on the floor against the wall.

"We can't keep traveling like this," said Carlos. "It's too much work."

They all agreed.

"And we can't kill them in cold blood because none of us can do it," said Kirsten. "Where's Charles Bronson when you need him?"

"Charles Bronson?"

"I love old movies."

"And," continued Carlos, "we can't get police involved because we're driving stolen cars and we'd lose Jo."

"And," said Kirsten, "There's no way we're letting them go."

"This is hard," said Carlos. "No wonder I wasn't a criminal, it's too damn much work."

"The wilderness." said Joyce.

They stopped.

"The wilderness?" Tommy asked.

"That's where we put them. We drive them forty or fifty miles into the mountains and let them work their way out. They'll be slow because Jupiter has that leg wound, so that would take a week or more."

"We could make it longer," said Carlos, excited, "if we take their shoes. We could have two or three weeks to disappear."

They were animated now. The Hummer would be good in the back country, and they were almost to Redding. North of that was a huge expanse of wilderness. Perfect! Oddly, Ted and Jupiter did not look enthused.

"What do you say, boys," asked Tommy, "you up for a little backpacking? A little barefoot trek through the forest?"

"Just let us go," said Ted. "We won't bother you ever again. You have my word."

"Oh sure," said Kirsten, "and we can take that to the bank. I trust you about as far as I can throw that Hummer. No, I think you guys are in for an adventure."

"We'll get you for this," snarled Jupiter.

"Jupe," said Kirsten, "Isn't it time you figured out you're in the wrong business? As strong-arm guys, you two suck. If I were Rick I'd fire you and hire professionals."

"You just got lucky."

"We got lucky, what, three times? Seriously, you've got to get into another line of work. Maybe this wilderness trek will give you time to think."

"Fuck you, bitch," said Ted, "we will get you. Count on it."

"That just added fifteen miles onto your hike. Want to try for thirty?"

Ted shut up.

CHAPTER 48

The next morning they packed up their prisoners, got take-out breakfast and hit the road by seven. In Redding they stopped at an outdoor store and got maps of Shasta-Trinity National Forest. They drove north to an old logging road that cut miles up into the forest.

They drove a half mile up the dirt road, found a clearing and pulled the pickup into it. If someone found it, they'd assume it belonged to hikers. Then they all climbed into the Hummer and set out. The road hadn't been used in a long time and was overgrown with weeds and bushes. The Hummer didn't have the ruggedness of its military predecessor, but they plunged on, clocking the miles on the odometer. It took them almost five hours to make seventy miles and that had to be it or they wouldn't make it back out before dark. They stepped out of the Hummer and stood, taking it all in.

"Wow," said Joyce, "it's beautiful up here."

"This area escaped the fires," said Carlos, taking in the vast forest views around them. "Thank God the rains finally came or we'd be looking at devastation."

"I wish we could camp out a few days. This is my idea of heaven—trees, lakes, streams, mountains—it's just glorious."

"Makes you wonder if we're actually punishing

those two criminals, leaving them in a place like this," said Kirsten.

"The good news," said Carlos, "is they won't have tents, sleeping bags, boots, food, or water. The wilderness can eat you up if you're not prepared."

"I'm rooting for the wilderness," said Kirsten.

They hoisted Ted and Jupe out of the back seat, which wasn't easy. Jupe, especially, was a load but the five of them managed to drag him out. Kirsten took great pleasure in removing their boots and throwing them into the Hummer.

"Dammit," said Ted, "That's just cruel."

"No," said Kirsten, "Cruel would be taking your clothes too. Want to play that game?"

"No," mumbled Ted. "You're going to untie us aren't you?"

"Nope," said Carlos. "It'll give us more time if you have to do that yourselves. Think of it as a test of teamwork. Okay boys, I'd wish you luck, but I really don't want that. I hope your wounds get infected and you die."

"What about food? Water? You can't leave us up here to starve!"

"The hell we can't," said Kirsten. "I hope you fuckers die slow, lingering deaths and I'm just sorry I won't get to see it."

"I just had a thought," said Tommy. "Aren't there bears up here?"

"Could be," said Joyce. "That would be natural justice, wouldn't it? Mother Nature's death penalty for kidnapping and attempted rape."

"Leave us a gun," begged Jupiter. "You can't leave us to the bears."

"Wanna bet?" said Carlos.

"Wolves," said Joyce. "I hear they've got wolves up here too."

"Did you know bears and wolves can smell blood? I just hope those wounds don't open up."

"Wow. I'd hate to be in your shoes," said Kirsten. "Oh wait, you guys don't have shoes. I forgot. Happy trails, you bastards."

They climbed into the Hummer, and as they drove back down the trail Kirsten rolled down her window and yelled, "Here bears! Fresh meat! Come and get it!"

"I'm starting to worry about you," said Tommy. "You're enjoying this a little too much."

"After what they did, fuck 'em," she replied.

Again, Tommy decided to never piss her off.

"You poke the dragon, you get the bears," mused Joyce.

"Nice mixed metaphor," laughed Tommy.

"Personally," said Carlos, "I'm rooting for the wolves. I think they take longer."

"I just wish I could be ruthless," said Tommy. "Shooting them made so much more sense. We'd have solved that problem forever."

"I like knowing you all couldn't do that," said Joyce. "Maybe in the heat of the moment it would be different, but shooting a guy who's tied up is awfully cold."

They made it out of the forest as the sun was setting, picking up the truck on the way. This brought another discussion.

"You know we don't need two vehicles," said Tommy.

"You're right about that," said Kirsten, "and the Hummer is too conspicuous. We should ditch it."

Everyone agreed. They drove to Weed, exited the freeway and found a Walmart. They parked the Hummer, put the key on the seat and left the doors open. If that wasn't an invitation, they didn't know what was. With luck, someone would steal it and any pursuers would then have to choose which vehicle to follow. Win-win.

They climbed into the pickup and drove on to Yreka, where they found a Travelodge and got two rooms in back, parking the truck in the shadows. It had been a long day. Jo wanted to sleep between Kirsten and Tommy, like they had in the apartment, so Carlos and Joyce took the other room. Carlos hoped it wouldn't be awkward. He was twenty years older than Joyce, he'd never been a lady's man and he'd never thought of himself as good-looking. He also didn't know how she felt about Mexicans. He'd been born in the U.S. but he sure didn't look like he came over on the Mayflower. He would give her privacy and that would be that.

They finally climbed into the two beds and lay there, talking quietly. He knew Joyce's story from conversations about Ketchum. All she knew about him was that he owned a gun shop and had taken care of Jo for a year. He wasn't a talkative guy.

"How'd you end up in a place like Elko?" she asked.

"Easy. I had a scholarship at Berkeley, studied English and Creative Writing. A gun shop in Elko was the obvious career choice."

She laughed.

"Makes perfect sense to me, but maybe you'd better walk me through it."

"Okay. After I graduated I was going to write the great American novel."

"I bet your parents loved that."

"My parents were gone."

"I'm sorry. Bad comment on my part."

"No it wasn't. How would you know? They were driving up from New Mexico to see me graduate and dad fell asleep at the wheel. They hit an overpass and died instantly."

"That is so sad."

"They were really proud of me. No one in our family had finished high school, much less college. I didn't tell them an English degree usually led to a career in the service industry."

"How did the writing work out?

"Badly. I gave it a good shot, wrote three books and sent them all out. Publishers weren't interested. I gave copies to friends and they read them but there were no rave reviews. I got the message."

"Do you still have them?"

"What, the friends or the books?"

"Either."

"I've still got the manuscripts. My friends drifted off to other things and not many people pass through Elko. I'm in contact with some of them on Facebook."

"So you were a failed novelist. Were you still in Berkeley?"

"Yeah. And I was dead broke, working odd jobs, barely scraping by. I tried to write a fourth book, but I hit the wall halfway through. I think deep down I knew it wasn't good and I wasn't going to save it."

"It sounds like a low point."

"It was definitely that. I couldn't afford graduate school, corporate recruiters weren't knocking down

MIKE NEUN

my door, and I didn't have an advanced degree so I couldn't teach."

"What happened?"

"My uncle passed away. I didn't know him that well, but he was the one who owned the gun store in Elko. He'd been in Special Forces and was one tough dude. He ran the store til he died and he left it to me. I think it was his idea of a joke."

"A joke?"

"Sure. Most guys who run gun shops are ex-military. I was a pot-smoking Berkley liberal with a college deferment. The closest I ever came to combat was watching a couple of drunks duke it out in North Beach. I loved hanging out with stoners and musicians in blues bars, so me running a gun store was like Sheldon Cooper taking up Mixed Martial Arts. Also, I was Mexican and had no desire to sell weapons to a bunch of rednecks in Elko, Nevada."

"You're Mexican?"

He laughed.

"I prefer the term, 'Beaner'".

She laughed.

"What'd you do?"

"I drove down there and figured I'd sell the shop, take the money and get back into school. Have you ever tried to sell a gun shop in Elko, Nevada?"

"Not really."

"It was awful. I couldn't even get pennies on the dollar so I thought, the hell with it, I'll run it for a couple of years, sell off everything and get out. Twenty-three years later I was still there."

"So you got to like guns?"

"Not really. I know a lot about them, and I know all kinds of people came into that store. Some were good, some bad, and some were batshit crazy."

"How'd you handle the crazies? Did you sell them guns?"

"Not if I could help it. I told them the feds were cracking down and I had to jump through all the legal hoops—background checks, waiting periods, and crazy stuff I made up. Sometimes it worked."

"What if it didn't?"

"I told them about gun shows. They would've found out anyway."

"And you never learned to like guns?"

"I liked the workmanship, I liked fiddling with the mechanisms, but they're too damn loud. If I want noise I turn up the Red Hot Chili Peppers or Nirvana. I had a range out back so I fired lots of weapons, mostly out of boredom, and I can shoot pretty well, but Jo makes me look like a rookie. I've never seen anyone take to it like she did. That little girl brightened up my shop, won us money on bets and sold more guns than I did. When she left, all the fun went out of the business."

"You must love being back with her."

"I sure do. She's a great kid."

"I like her too."

"I can see that. And she likes you. She's a good judge of character so you must be a nice person."

"I don't know if I'd go that far," Joyce smiled. "Did you ever get married?"

"Yeah, but she died ten years ago."

"Again, I'm sorry to hear that."

"How about you?"

MIKE NEUN

"Yeah, I was married but it didn't work. I've been single for awhile."

"Life isn't fair."

"It sure isn't."

"We should get some sleep."

"Okay. Good night, Carlos."

"Good night, Joyce."

In the middle of the night Carlos, half asleep, felt her slide into bed with him. He moved over to make room. They didn't talk. They held each other, and slowly, like the quiet people they were, they made love. Then they slept.

CHAPTER 49

While Tommy and the gang had been ditching Ted and Jupiter in the wilderness, Holly and Susan pressed on to Yreka. They'd driven fast, hoping to catch a glimpse of the Hummer and the pickup, and whizzed past the logging road where both vehicles had turned off, putting them too in the strange position of chasing people who were now behind them. They took turns checking the websites but there were no reports of either vehicle. They had vanished! How could that be?

They got to Yreka in the early evening and realized something was wrong. They decided to stop for dinner and keep checking the websites. Surely the radical women networks would pick up a sighting. They were about to pay the check when finally a message came up. Someone had spotted the Hummer in a Walmart parking lot in Weed. Damn, that was a half hour back down the freeway! Also, where was the pickup truck? Holly felt like she was being pranked. Susan calmed her down and pointed out that if the vehicles were together, they could just wait for them. Why go back down south if their targets were going to come up north anyway?

They decided to get coffee, drive out to the freeway, and watch for either the Hummer or the pickup. They could also keep checking the Internet. After two hours they were ready to tear their hair so they called it quits.

"How do cops do this shit?" asked Susan. "On TV they pull all-night stakeouts, pee in pop bottles, live on donuts. One more hour of this and I'd be ready for the rubber room."

"Me too. This is fucking stupid. Let's go rent a room and get a hot shower and a good night's sleep."

"Sounds good. We can keep checking the Internet. I like that part, where we've got a whole network of spies working for us. Let them do the watching."

"Agreed."

They rented a room in a Red Roof Inn and spent the evening watching chick flicks on TV.

"You ever fall in love like that?" asked Susan.

"You mean where you meet the guy, think he's a pain in the ass, then find out he's Ryan Gosling?"

"Yeah. Mostly when I meet a guy who's a pain in the ass, I find out he's Darth Vader."

"Absolutely."

"How about Tommy? Was he a pain in the ass when you met him?"

"Naw, he was a computer geek and he was small."

"That's a turnoff for me. I like 'em tall and with some muscles."

"Well you'd have passed on Tommy. But he was shy and kind of cute, and brains? That guy was a wizard. You know how Google laid off thousands when the crash came?"

"Yeah, the Thursday Night Massacre. It was famous."

"Well they kept Tommy. That's how smart he was."

"That's impressive. How'd you hook up?"

"He came in for a haircut. I took one look and thought, nope, not my type. We didn't even talk that much during the haircut, but something about him got me. I asked him to lunch the next day."

"Now we're talking chick flick! We could get Tom Cruise to play him, he's small."

"I'd go for that. Do I get to play me? I wouldn't mind boinking Tom Cruise."

"Boinking? I haven't heard that in years."

"Boinking Tommy Price," said Holly. "Perfect name for my chick flick. Starring Tom Cruise and Holly Carlson."

"Nice of you to give him top billing."

"Yeah, I'll have to talk to my agent about that."

"Tom Cruise, Tommy Price, it's meant to be!"

"For sure!"

"So you hooked up with Tommy?"

"Yeah, and it was a good career move because I wasn't making much money as a stylist."

"What was he like?"

"Just like you'd expect. Geeky. Spent most of his time on the computer."

"How about in bed?"

"You know? I still am not sure if he was a virgin. He certainly didn't know his way around a woman's body. I had to teach him. Do this, no, don't do that, slower, all that stuff."

"Maybe it's better that way. You get to train him."

"Could be. After a while he could get me off."

"Could you get him off?"

"You're joking. He was a newbie. By the time I got my clothes off he was halfway there. I didn't even have to try."

"Did he have a little dick?"

"Yeah, kind of. But I'm a little girl, so those guys with monster junk don't excite me. I'm not into pain.

I wished his was a bit bigger, but not much, and I could still get off. He got really good with his tongue too. That was the best."

"Well you sound like a dumb shit for leaving him."

"I was. This other guy came along, more handsome, taller, outgoing, and I ran off with him. Bad move."

"Why?"

"He was the abusive guy, the one who disappeared."

"Wow. Way to trade down. You think Tommy will take you back?"

"I don't know. He didn't sound enthused when we talked on the phone. But I have to try. You okay with this? Chasing him all over the place?"

"It's better than dealing cards with cheesy crooks trying to rent me out to low rollers. I like the adventure."

"I like having you with me on it. A girl needs someone to talk to."

"Same here."

As they drifted off to sleep, Holly couldn't help wishing she were a better person. She still had nightmares about her first husband, the things he'd done to her and what she'd done to him. That had been kind of messy. Then too, there were episodes of thievery and violence that didn't reflect well on her character. She decided these were things that Susan and Tommy didn't really need to know about.

CHASING EXES

Susan drifted off thinking that she'd found a friend, but one who didn't have a firm lock on mental stability. She was determined to keep her guard up and never, ever piss off Holly. Outside, it started raining.

MIKE NEUN

CHAPTER 50

"Do we still want to go to Utah?" asked Kirsten. They had slept in, worn out from the wilderness activities of the day before, and were eating a noon breakfast at Tony's Diner at the north end of Yreka. They were happy to be rid of Ted and Jupiter, unaware of Holly and Susan, and back down to one vehicle—the pickup truck.

"It was a random choice," said Tommy, "so we could go anywhere now."

Carlos and Joyce were quietly eating their scrambled eggs and toast, trying not to look at each other and trying not to smile. Jo, having slept between Kirsten and Tommy, now sat between Carlos and Joyce, balancing out the affection protocols.

"Did either of you mention Utah when Ted and Jupiter had you captured?"

"No, but anything we can do to disguise our destinations would be smart if you ask me," said Kirsten.

"I'd like to get off I-5," said Carlos. How about backtracking to Weed and catching highway 97 north? I like the idea of leaving I-5 and once we get to Klamath

Falls we can take our pick of three directions. I bet the scenery's better too."

They liked that idea. After breakfast they packed up and got into the pickup to drive back south to Weed.

"I wonder if anyone stole the Hummer," said Carlos.

"I hope so," said Kirsten. "If Jupiter and Ted ever get out of the wilderness they'll have to choose which vehicle to track."

"Good," said Tommy, "anything to confuse them."

"We need a name," said Joyce.

"For what?"

"Our group. We're kind of a team now, the five of us, so we should have a name."

Kirsten laughed.

"Like The Five Amigos?"

"The Five People Who Don't Know What the Hell They're Doing?" chimed in Kirsten.

It got to be a game, and new team titles kept coming up as they drove. Joyce chimed in.

"Jo and the Joettes?"

Jo nodded vigorously at that one, obviously her favorite.

They made it to Weed and turned off I-5 to US 97 north, trading drivers to keep everyone fresh.

"I would like to go skiing," said Joyce. "I miss Ketchum and the other resorts should be open now."

Jo nodded enthusiastically at that. She loved skiing, even though she'd just done it for a short time.

"Carlos," asked Tommy, "Are you a skier?"

"Nope. Hard to believe isn't it, when you think of all the famous Mexican skiers. Don't people break legs a lot?"

MIKE NEUN

"Not anymore," said Joyce, "the bindings are better and the skis are shorter. They're a lot more forgiving than they were in the old days."

"By old days," said Carlos, "are you talking about when I was a kid?"

"Not that old," said Joyce, smiling, "I don't think they even had skis when you were a kid."

"The good news," said Tommy, "is you're sitting next to a world-class instructor. She knows her stuff."

"I'm happy to give it a shot," said Carlos. "It's always smart to take up a new sport when you're fifty-six."

"Okay," said Kirsten, "How about Bend, Oregon? I know friends who skied there and they liked it a lot."

"Works for me," said Tommy. "I hear the snow's better than it is around Seattle. Also, the town's not as small as Ketchum so it might be easier for us to get lost there."

Jo and the Joettes set off to do some skiing.

CHAPTER 51

While Jo and the Joettes had been sleeping in that morning, exhausted from their wilderness excursion, Holly and Susan woke up early, refreshed, ready to continue the chase. They logged on to Susan's laptop. Bingo! Someone had seen the Hummer going north on I-5 out of Weed. They threw on their clothes, tossed their stuff in the car, and drove over to the freeway to watch for it.

After twenty minutes, Susan spoke up.

"Another fucking stakeout. If I ever decide to join the police force just shoot me, okay?"

"I can't think of any better way to do this, can you?" asked Holly.

"No, but I reserve the right to piss and moan. It's good practice in case I ever get married. Have you ever noticed..."

"There!" shouted Holly, and she started up the SUV. Sure enough, the Hummer was cruising up the highway and they let it get a head start before she pulled out behind.

"We don't want them to spot us," said Holly. "Warn me if there's a turnoff coming and I'll close the gap. We don't want to lose them now."

"What's our plan?" asked Susan.

"I guess we wait for them to stop and figure out some way to rescue Tommy. Then I profess my undying love, he realizes I'm the girl of his dreams, and we ride off into the sunset.

"Piece of cake," said Susan. "You think that'll work?"

"It would work a lot better if I got naked. I could get him to do anything when I was naked."

"You don't think that would be a little obvious?"

"We can't sweat the small stuff, Susan. This is true love. On the other hand, he does get embarrassed easily."

"Don't you?"

"Girl, I've been naked in a lot worse situations than this. I might even function better."

"What's the next best plan?"

"I guess close to naked would do it. Can you think of any excuse for me to be in a bikini?"

"Oh sure. I bet there are lots of chicks driving up I-5 in bikinis. You'll fit right in."

"You're no help at all. I'm going to have to go with the skimpiest halter top I can find and really short cutoff jeans. He was always a sucker for jeans shorts. He thought they looked sexy as hell."

"You got that stuff?"

"Oh hell yes. I came prepared. We'll do a quick driver switch and I'll change clothes."

Holly pulled off on the shoulder and they ran around, switching sides. Susan pulled back on the freeway as Holly reached back for her bag. In no time, Holly was down to panties and bra, and debating on whether to ditch the bra. It was at that point they passed a semi, and the driver, looking down, got a good view of most of Holly. He tooted his horn and gave her a fist pump. Holly immediately undid the bra and waved it out the window. The driver leaned on the horn and flashed his lights. He'd have a great story for the next truck stop.

Susan pulled away from the truck and Holly pulled on the shorts and halter top.

"What do you think?" she asked. "Too obvious?"

"Not if you're auditioning at Hooters."

"That's the message I'm hoping to convey. For Tommy, sex was the pot of gold at the end of the rainbow. I don't think he had a lot of women in his life."

"Well, that outfit should wake him up. We got any turnoffs coming up?"

Holly checked the map.

"The next one is Hornbrook. Doesn't look like much there, just a gas station. What did people do before Google maps?"

"They had these paper things...."

"I know that, but you couldn't zoom in and see gas stations and stuff. I call that progress. I think we're getting close so step on it and we'll see what they do."

Susan speeded up until they caught sight of the Hummer. It took the Hornbrook exit. They watched as it drove under the underpass and back up onto the freeway going south.

"What the fuck?" exclaimed Holly.

"This is weird. Should we keep following?"

"I can't think of anything else, can you?"

"Nope."

"What the hell are they doing?" asked Holly. "Why drive up a freeway and then turn around and drive back?"

"If you ask me, it fits in. This whole adventure has been an exercise in weirdness. Why stop now?"

They drove awhile, letting the Hummer get out of sight until the next exit.

"Okay," Susan said. "What are we going to do when we catch them? Do you have a plan? Ted and Jupe might not be dazzled by your outfit."

"Ah, but they are scared of me."

"That makes sense. So am I."

"Susan! You're my partner in crime, I would never hurt you."

"I hope not. So what's your plan?"

"Have you still got Gustafson's pistol?"

"I do. You want me to go in, gun blazing?"

"No, I want you to have it in your hand, in your purse, while I handle Ted and Jupe. I've got my gun too, so you're backup."

"Should I take off my bra? Keep them distracted?"

"Up to you. We could both take off our tops and really give them a show."

"If it keeps us from getting killed, I'm all for it."

"Let's just go with what we've got. No sense making a spectacle of ourselves," said the woman who'd just waved her bra at a trucker.

The Hummer pulled off the freeway in south Yreka, and eased into the parking lot of an IHop.

"Got 'em," shouted Holly. "You ready?"

"Locked and loaded," said Susan.

"Go go go!" yelled Holly, and jumped out of the SUV with Susan right behind. They were almost to the Hummer when three teenage boys got out. One of them saw Holly and gave an enthusiastic, "Okay! That's what I'm talking about!"

Obviously he'd watched too many football players on TV.

Susan felt like she was standing beside Halle Berry. Invisible. Next time she was going the Hooters route too.

"Who the hell are you guys?" demanded Holly.

"I'm Bill," said one, "this is Ted, and you look like an excellent adventure."

"High marks for comebacks, but who the hell are you?"

"Those actually are our names. This other guy is Bruce. Who the hell are you?"

"None of your business. Where'd you get the Hummer?"

"None of your business."

Holly turned to Susan.

"You think there are two black Hummers like that in this zip code? What are the odds?"

"About a zillion to one."

"Okay, let's call the cops," said Holly, bluffing. She had a record in three states. No way she would ever call the cops.

"Wait a minute, lady," said Bill. "We can explain."

"Get to it."

"It's not like we stole the Hummer. We found it at the Walmart. It had the doors open and the keys inside. We waited a long time to see if anyone was coming, but nobody did."

"How long did you wait, like thirty seconds?"

"No! Almost an hour. We didn't want to get banged up for car theft."

"And nobody came."

"Nope, nobody. So we just took it for a ride. If it's yours, you can have it. We don't want any trouble."

Holly thought.

MIKE NEUN

"Okay," she said. "Here's the deal. People are looking for that thing and they're not nice guys. My advice is to park it over there and get the hell out of here. You don't want to be around if they show up."

"They're bad dudes?"

"You ever been around gangbangers?"

"Lady, look at us. We're not exactly Hell's Angels."

"Well, these guys are. Got the picture?"

"Got it. We'll do as you say."

"Okay," said Holly, "and stop looking at my tits."

Susan burst out laughing. The boys, abashed, climbed into the Hummer and drove it to the back of the parking lot. Then they got out and ran.

Holly turned and walked back to the SUV.

"Fuck," she said. "Fuck, fuck, fuck and double fuck. I thought we'd found Tommy."

"You're not going to believe this," said Susan.

"I'm not going to believe what?" asked Holly.

"I just saw the pickup truck."

"You're joking."

"Nope. While you were flashing your tits at those boys..."

"I wasn't flashing my tits."

"Bullshit. You were having all kinds of fun teasing them. I worry for Tommy. I don't think you're a one-man woman."

"You may be right. It was fun. I bet it brightened up their day."

"Between the boys and the trucker, you're leaving a trail of happy guys on I-5."

"Stop! You just said you saw the pickup."

"I did. I happened to glance over to the freeway, and

I think it was the same truck. It was kind of gray and dirty but it's got that same camper shell in back."

"There must be a ton of those around here. This could be another wild goose chase."

"Let's think it out. Why did they ditch the Hummer?"

"I don't know. Those two bozos kidnapped Tommy and Kirsten and took off in it, didn't they?"

"Yes."

"And now the Hummer is empty?"

"Yes."

"You think they hijacked the truck and ditched the Hummer?"

"I don't have a clue what's going on, but we know that pickup is all we got. What do you think?"

"I guess we follow it. With our luck it'll be filled with horny teenagers."

"If it is, it's my turn to flash my tits. You can't have all the fun."

Holly laughed, and they got back in the SUV and drove south, following a dusty, primer-gray pickup.

MIKE NEUN

CHAPTER 52

Ted and Jupe were tired, wounded, sore, mosquito-bitten and pissed off. They were also smarter than Tommy and the others had figured. Instead of trying to hike seventy miles and live off the land, they'd found a large clearing and dug a pit with dirt piled around it. With twigs, branches and dried leaves they built a campfire and lit it with Jupe's Bic. When it was blazing, they put wet leaves over it and soon smoke was pouring up into the sky. A forest ranger saw the smoke and flew into panic mode. Fires had decimated California and a new one could be a disaster. He got out the warning, a spotter plane flew over, and soon a helicopter came to rescue the two stranded outlaws. Oh sure, they had trouble explaining themselves. They said they'd hiked up, camped five miles further in and then been scared off by bears, not even time to grab their boots. Not bad for flagrant lies, but Ted and Jupe were pros.

Tommy and his crew hadn't robbed them, so they had money and I.D. The chopper took them back to Redding, they booked a motel room and slept fourteen hours. They were awakened by the police, telling them their Hummer had been found in an IHop parking lot in Yreka. They found a trucker headed north. Instead of a survival trek in the woods, Ted and Jupiter had cut it to a few hours, and the next afternoon they had their Hummer back. It proved good guys don't have a lock on resourcefulness.

The bad news was they didn't have phones or computers so they couldn't check the Internet. They asked around and found a video game parlor. By ten a.m. they'd posted notices on all the men-who-hate-women sites, asking for help finding the pickup truck with a camper shell somewhere in northern California. They got about 30 sightings, with more coming in. Did everyone in California drive pickups? But one guy had seen a gray pickup stopped for gas on I-97 and gotten a look at the people inside.

CHAPTER 53

Jo and the Joettes were headed up I-97 in the pickup. Kirsten was on the computer, typing.

"What are you doing?" asked Tommy.

"Messaging Wendy."

"How are they? Still eager to leave Seattle?"

"Yeah, and they're happy to hear Jo is safe and that we are too. I told them about Rick and how he sent guys after us. It really upset them."

"I hope they don't do anything silly."

"I told them we had everything under control, but I'm wondering if they can check to see if Rick is still at Sherwood Apartments."

"Are they going to?"

"They're sending Charlie and Pat to see about renting an apartment. If Rick answers, we'll know he's there."

"Are you worried about him?"

"Oh hell yes. He's gone off the rails and somehow he's paying Ted and Jupe."

"Okay, let's see what they find."

A half hour later Wendy texted Kirsten. Rick was gone. The new manager said he got the job two weeks ago. Apparently Rick got fired as soon as the owners got back.

"Well damn," said Tommy. "We might have Rick on our trail. Should we get rid of the truck? Get some other wheels?"

"I hate to do it," said Carlos. "I've come to like this truck, but I don't think re-painting it is going to do the job. You think we could trade it for something?"

"That would take time," said Kirsten, "and I like the idea of staying on the road."

"You know what we could do," said Carlos, "is change the profile. Get rid of the shell."

"What about all our stuff back there?"

"For the moment we could just pick up a tarp and cover it up. Maybe later we could find a hard cover.

"That sounds good," said Tommy. "Lets buy a tarp, then ditch the camper cover. Too bad we can't sell it, but that would leave a trail."

"Yeah, and it's not worth much anyway. If we use a tarp we're going to have to load and unload everything at night, but there are five of us so it's no big deal."

They gassed up in Klamath Falls and got a cheap tarp and rope at a Target store. They drove for an hour and found a dirt trail and drove a couple hundred yards in. They unbolted the camper cover and took it off, feeling kind of sad. It was nice to have a place to lock up their stuff, but there was no other choice and they replaced it with the tarp. They tied it down and the truck looked entirely different. They shoved the cover back into the underbrush and Jo tugged Tommy's sleeve. She pointed at herself and then the back of the pickup.

"You want to ride outside?"

"She nodded."

"I don't know if that's legal. Or safe."

"Oh hell," said Carlos, "Farm workers do it all the time."

"You were a farm worker?"

"Dad was when I was a little kid. We traveled all over California following the harvests."

"She shouldn't be alone back there," said Tommy. "You want to ride with her?"

"Sure. It'll be a blast from the past. Come on little girl, let's catch some open air."

They bundled up in parkas and and slid under the tarp. They sat on sleeping bags and leaned on their back packs against the cab, their heads barely showing.

"Okay," said Tommy, "if it gets too cold just beat on the cab and I'll pull off so you can get back inside. You guys okay?"

Jo nodded happily. It was another adventure. Carlos smiled.

Joyce, Kirsten and Tommy got back in the cab and Tommy turned around to get onto the highway.

They waited for a red Honda SUV to pass and pulled onto the road behind it. There were a million SUVs out there, and they didn't give it a thought.

CHAPTER 54

"Keep driving," said Susan, "and don't turn around."

"Why?" asked Holly. "What's up?"

"We just passed a fucking pickup truck, that's what's up."

"What the hell? Is it the same one?"

"It's the same make and model but it didn't have a camper shell. Do you think they took it off?"

"Can you see inside?"

"Not really. Slow down and I'll look."

Holly slowed and the pickup gained on them.

"There are three people in the front seat, a little guy driving, a dark-skinned woman and a kid. It's them!"

"Fuck me! How did we end up in front of them? Don't they know how stalking works? I'm supposed to be following him for Christ's sake!"

"I guess he didn't read the instructions. What do you want to do?"

"We could do the old breakdown at the side of the road routine. Helpless women, show a little leg."

"Uh uh, don't go switching to leg. It's my turn to do titties."

"Don't you think that'll be a bit obvious?"

"Seriously? You're worried about obvious?"

"We have to speed up, get enough time to stage a breakdown. How close are they?"

"Maybe a quarter mile now. Oh, what the fuck?"

"What now?"

"I do not fucking believe this!"

"What? What's going on?"

"You know what's behind them? A fucking Hummer. A fucking black Hummer!"

"No way. Is God up there playing jokes on us? Who the hell could be in that Hummer?"

"I don't even want to mention their names," said Susan.

CHAPTER 55

Carlos and Jo had seen the Hummer too and quickly scrunched down under the tarp. They pounded on the cab of the pickup. Tommy checked the rear view mirror.

"Fuck me," he said.

"Not in front of Joyce," said Kirsten.

"I'm serious," said Tommy. "Look behind us."

The two women looked back, and there was the Hummer, closing fast.

Ted and Jupe had stopped at a Walmart to buy handguns. It was easy, because the country was still lawless and people wanted protection. No background checks, no waiting period.

Jupe couldn't wait to use his so he leaned out and fired a couple shots from his Smith and Wesson Model 29 Magnum. Dirty Harry would've been so proud. They were taking no chances and no little squirt of a girl was going to take them out with a pop gun this time.

In the pickup, Joyce grabbed for her pistol.

"Wait," said Kirsten. "If we get into a gun fight, Jo and Carlos are unprotected back there."

"I don't want to get kidnapped again," said Tommy. "Can we outrun them?"

"Too late. They could shoot us before we get out of range."

"Shit."

Jupe fired again, the bullet starring the back window of the pickup, too high to hit them but glass chips sprayed in.

"Holy fuck!" said Tommy. "I'm pulling over."

He signaled, pulled off to the side and stopped on the shoulder. Ted and Jupe pulled up behind them. Tommy, Kirsten and Joyce sat and waited. This wasn't good. Ted and Jupe got out of the Hummer, and walked carefully up to the truck, Jupiter limping, Ted with a bandaged shoulder, one on each side, guns at their sides away from any passing traffic. They eased up past the pickup bed, wary of sharpshooter Jo and her pistol. They got to the back of the cab and Ted rapped his gun butt on the back side window.

"Everybody out," he yelled. "Hands where we can see them."

From under the tarpaulin, two arms snaked out holding automatics, one on each side of the truck. They pressed the muzzles of the pistols hard into the necks of Ted and Jupiter. Carlos said in a loud, deadly voice, "Don't move. Don't even think about moving or we blow you away."

"Fuck!" yelled Jupiter. "Not again!!!"

"Drop your fucking guns. Now!"

Jupe dropped his weapon, but Ted was pissed off. He started to lift his and spin around. Carlos moved his gun to the side and fired close to his head, deafening him. He dropped his gun and grabbed his ear.

"Fuck me!" cursed Ted. "Fuck! I think you broke my ear drum!"

"Good. Next time I'll blow off your head."

"Next time," said Jupiter sullenly, "we're bringing rocket launchers."

"Not going to be any next time you son of a bitch," said Carlos. "Get down on the ground, both of you, hands behind your heads."

Tommy, Kirsten and Joyce got out of the pickup and looked down on Ted and Jupe. They picked up the two weapons. The truck had officially become an arsenal.

"You guys never give up, do you?"

"Fuck." said Jupe.

"And your guns are getting bigger. What the hell are these?"

"Jupiter's got a Smith and Wesson Magnum," said Carlos. "Ted's got a Ruger SR40c. They could bring down elephants with those things."

"I've never seen so many guns," said Kirsten. "This is just fucking ridiculous."

"How the hell did you guys get out of the wilderness?" asked Joyce.

"Fuck you. We're not telling."

They made Ted get up and walk around to the passenger side of the truck and lie down beside Jupiter.

Just then the red Honda SUV pulled up and stopped across the highway. Everyone watched as two women got out.

"Tommy?" yelled one. "Are you okay? We heard shots!"

Tommy stood astonished as Holly ran to him across the highway.

"Holly?" he chirped wonderingly. "What the hell are you doing here?"

He couldn't help noticing her outfit. Subtle.

"We came to save you. We read on the Internet that those guys kidnapped you so Susan and I rode to the rescue."

"That's really nice of you, but I think we've got things under control."

Holly looked down.

"Hi Ted, Hi Jupe," she said. "Long time no see."

"Oh fuck me," said Ted. "It's the psycho."

"No shit," said Jupiter. "We're doomed."

"Now boys," said Holly, "That's no way to talk. We're old travel buddies. But you did lock me in a bathroom and rob me blind when I was deathly sick. That was mean!"

"We're fucked," said Jupe.

"Tommy," said Holly, "could you give me one of those guns and a little time with these boys. I'd like to teach them the error of their ways."

"Don't do it," yelled Jupiter, "she'll kill us."

"Actually," said Kirsten, "that would solve a lot of problems."

"Let's slow down a bit," said Carlos. "First, let's figure out who everyone is. I'm confused."

"Me too," said Susan, "Who are all these people?"

"I'll do the honors," said Tommy. "That's Ted and Jupe on the ground. They're hired thugs trying to kidnap Kirsten and kill me. This is Kirsten here beside me, and beside her is Jo, our little girl who doesn't talk."

"She doesn't talk?" asked Holly. "No shit, is she the pistol wizard?"

"She is that," said Carlos.

"It's an honor to meet you," said Holly, bowing.

Jo smiled and bowed back.

"Okay," said Tommy, "and next to her is Joyce, our ski bum friend from Ketchum and beside her is Carlos, our friend who owns a gun shop in Elko. And this, everybody, is Holly, my old girlfriend who dumped me for another guy."

"Now that's kind of harsh," Holly said.

"But true."

"Well, yes, but we should talk about it."

"And next to Holly is who?"

"I'm Susan. I'm Holly's friend from Las Vegas and I've got two questions. Why do these gangsters keep coming after you and how the hell did a black lady get named 'Kirsten'?"

"To answer the first one, my ex-husband hired them. It's a bad divorce thing," said Kirsten.

Holly turned to her.

"I'm so sorry to hear that darlin'. Those nasty divorces can get real dangerous. I know that from experience."

"My ex has gone off the deep end. I think when you hire hit men it's a sign you're overreacting."

"Guys are so irrational," said Holly, the queen of clear thinking.

"Yes. This is the third time we caught them."

"You should call the police."

"If the police come we could lose Jo. We thought we had these guys stranded in the wilderness."

"I hate to interrupt," said Susan, "but no one answered my second question. About the name?"

"It's a long story," said Kirsten, "and I think we have more important stuff to deal with."

"Okay, but I can't wait to hear it."

Carlos spoke up.

"We're on a public highway with two guys face down in the dirt. People might get curious."

"Let's tie them up, load them into the truck and decide what to do," said Tommy.

CHAPTER 56

They tied Ted's hands behind him, loaded him in, and tied his feet. Then they did Jupe.

"It's time for a council of war," said Tommy. "We've got to put an end to this craziness."

"Makes sense," said Holly, "and then you and I can talk."

"About what?"

"About getting back together, dummy. I didn't come all this way for nothing."

"Holly, you dumped me. I've moved on and I'm not going back."

"Well that sucks."

"You could always show him your tits," said Susan, laughing.

"You stay out of this. Tommy, don't you remember the good times? The fun in bed? I could make you real happy."

"I think she's throwing herself at you," said Kirsten. "You must be a major stud!"

Tommy was embarrassed.

"Holly," he said, "you were right to leave. We don't belong together and it's just not going to happen."

"Well shit," said Holly, "this could end my career as a stalker."

"I doubt it," said Susan. "From what I've seen you'll be back on his trail tomorrow."

"Could be," said Holly. "I'm nothing if not persistent. What are you guys going to do with the Brothers Grim over there?"

"Last time," said Carlos, "we ditched them seventy miles from civilization and hoped bears and wolves would get them. We don't know how they got out so fast. It should've taken weeks."

"It was such a good plan," said Kirsten.

"I'm assuming you don't want to kill them and dig graves," said Holly. "You all look way too uptight for that. My other go-to solution is blackmail."

"It worked in Las Vegas," said Susan, "did you know Holly is a big-time pornographer?"

"Why am I not surprised?" said Kirsten dryly.

Susan told them what they'd done to the pit boss.

"We can show you the movie," she said, "but it's not that sexy. The guy was overweight and kind of gross."

"I think we'll pass," said Kirsten. "Would it work on these two?"

"I doubt it," said Tommy. "These guys are proud of being assholes. In their circles it's a badge of honor."

"Give me a minute with the boys," said Holly. "I may have an idea."

Holly walked over to the truck, climbed in the front seat and kneeled on it to talk to Jupe and Ted tied up in back.

"I'm thinking of going to San Francisco. You guys ever been?"

"Yeah, we've been to San Francisco. But we're sure as hell not going any place with you."

She continued as though Ted hadn't spoken.

"I love it down there. Cable cars, San Francisco Bay, great restaurants. When all this is over, you want to head down there?"

"Are you fucking crazy? Not a chance in hell."

"Well damn, I thought it would be a fun trip. Me and two studly guys. We could let bygones be bygones, kiss and make up."

"Lady, you are the stuff of nightmares. Get the fuck out of here."

"Oh wait, I get it!" she slapped her head. "Why didn't I see this before? You guys are a couple! That never even occurred to me. No wonder we didn't connect!"

"Fuck you!" said Jupe. "We're not a couple and we're not going anywhere with you. You're a fucking nut case."

"I'm crazy, you're gay, no big deal. Your secret is safe with me and we could still take the trip. You'll love San Francisco and they'll love you! Rough trade is big down there."

"Goddam it bitch, get out of the fucking truck!"

"You could get married! Can I give away the bride? Will you both be in dresses? This is so exciting!"

"Will you fucking shut up about that fag shit? We're not gay!"

"Seriously? You're with each other all time. I figure you solved that divorce thing by going AC/DC."

"Fuck you," snarled Jupe.

"I don't know," she said. "When we were traveling together I had the feeling you liked being handcuffed together. Spend the nights rubbing up against each other..."

"Fuck you bitch," sneered Ted, "You're pulling something and it's not going to work. Everyone knows Jupe and I are straight as hell and fucking proud of it. San Francisco my ass."

"Did you see Jupiter perk up when you mentioned your ass?

That's a dead giveaway."

"Nice try, bitch," said Jupe. "It's not going to fly. You want to find out? Just untie us and spend a little time in the back seat."

Holly jumped out and walked back to the others.

"We have a winner!" She crowed, and outlined her plan.

With Ted and Jupiter tied up in the back seat, Tommy drove while Kirsten and Jo kept an eye on them.

Behind them, Joyce drove the Hummer. She liked sitting tall in this monster SUV with Carlos riding shotgun. Maybe things were looking up.

Holly and Susan brought up the rear in the Honda.

"I love a parade," said Susan.

"I can't believe Tommy dumped me." said Holly.

"Payback is a bitch."

Up in the pickup, Tommy said, "I don't want Holly and Susan with us. Holly is truly scary."

"It took you this long to figure that out?" said Kirsten. "Jo and I knew it about three minutes in, didn't we?"

Jo nodded vigorously.

"How can we get her to leave us alone?"

"Want to leave her in the wilderness? Blackmail her? Shoot her?"

"I vote for all three," said Tommy.

"You know," said Kirsten, "it must be kind of an ego trip, having your own stalker."

"It's not," said Tommy. "It's creepy. What do you think of her friend, Susan?"

"She seems okay," said Kirsten. "Kind of fun, really. I wonder what she's doing with a crazy woman like Holly?"

"I just want them both to leave," said Tommy.

CHAPTER 57

Rick was angry and had the mother of all hangovers. Nothing new there. Ted and Jupe had gone silent and he wondered what that was all about. Where the hell were they? Oh well, maybe it was better if he found Kirsten himself. He was still a little shaky from his monumental drinking spree, he owed Ted and Jupe a fair amount of money and he had no job. On the positive side, he still had money in the bank. For the first time in a long time he wasn't dead broke.

In the websites he found sightings of the pickup truck, the Hummer, and for some reason a Honda SUV. Somehow they'd all connected, mostly in Northern California and southern Oregon. Now there were sightings on US-97.

He looked at a map. From where he was in North Bend, Washington, he could drive south to Yakima and pick up 97. All he could hope for was more sightings while he was on the road and that the used Toyota would not conk out on him. He thought mournfully of the BMW he drove when he and Kirsten were kicking ass in the business world.

He stopped for lunch in Ellensburg and checked

the Internet again. Things were getting really weird. A divorced Oregon guy had posted seeing all three vehicles on highway 97 going north. They were still south of Bend, Oregon, and Rick knew that's where he had to go. He stopped at a 7-Eleven to pick up a six pack of Rainier. One or two beers wouldn't hurt.

He listened to a golden oldie station on the radio and got nostalgic. He drove on and sunk deeper into self-pity. He popped the third beer. Driving made him thirsty.

He passed through Bend, Oregon, and kept his eyes open as he turned down 97.

MIKE NEUN

CHAPTER 58

n Chemult, Kirsten found a small drug store and Holly bought what she needed. Then they stopped at Applebees for lunch. Tommy and Carlos took turns watching Ted and Jupiter in the pickup and after lunch Holly walked out with takeaway burgers for the prisoners. She fed the burgers to them and their three-vehicle caravan set out north again.

A half hour later Tommy looked back and Ted and Jupe were out cold in the back seat. Apparently Holly was an expert in knockout medications and again Tommy realized she was beyond dangerous.

They looked for another unused side road. In time they found a two-lane dirt trail and drove until they found a deserted clearing in the woods and parked. With a huge effort they dragged the limp bodies of Ted and Jupiter out of the truck. Kirsten took Jo down the path out of sight and the rest of them went to work. The hard part was getting the clothes off the two comatose big men. Holly and Susan couldn't help noticing Ted was a hunk. Jupe? He was definitely big, fat, and kind of hairy. But hey, he was a guy and they were horny. Too bad Ted and Jupe were rapists and murderers. It seemed like all guys had little flaws like that.

Then they put flowers in the guys' hair and had great fun posing them in all sorts of gay positions while they took cell phone photos. Brokeback Mountain rides again. Oh sure, their eyes were closed, but you could chalk that up to ecstasy. The bandages on Ted's shoulder and Jupe's nose and calf looked a little strange too. Tommy thought he could photoshop them out. Then they got the two men dressed—again really difficult—loaded them up and tied them hand and foot. They drove back to the highway and Jupe and Ted never knew what happened.

That night they stopped at the Timbercrest Inn in LaPine and rented two rooms. They pushed Ted and Jupiter into one while Joyce and Jo took the other. Once settled in, Tommy spent time working on the photos and then Holly took over. She was the director of this production and the two thugs were genuinely afraid of her. It made sense to have her take charge.

The two kidnappers sat on the floor, backs against the wall, hands tied behind them, feet tied in front of them.

"Hi boys," said Holly, squatting in front of them, "have a good trip so far?"

"Fuck you," said Ted, ever eloquent.

"Remember how you slept really hard after lunch?"

They now looked suspicious.

"I have to admit we roofied you. And then we did despicable things. Want to see the pictures?"

Ted and Jupe looked at each other. What the hell was going on?

Holly held up Tommy's iPad and scrolled through pictures of them naked, on top of each other, heads buried in crotches, heads buried in butts, flowers in their hair, panties and bras draped over them, and so on. Lots of pictures.

"Son of a bitch!" snarled Ted. "That's bullshit!"

"Of course it is, and one press of the upload button will make you two famous. All the guys on the get-the-bitches websites will see these, and I'm guessing it'll blow holes in your credibility. You'll be the Adam and Steve of the angry men movement!"

"We'll deny it. We'll tell everyone you drugged us!"

"Oh sure, that'll work. It always does. Face it, you're about to become gay porn stars."

"You haven't posted them yet?"

"No. But we've each got them on our phones. It anything happens to any one of us, those photos go viral. You get the idea?"

"This is blackmail!"

"You're just mad because you didn't think of it. You concentrated on kidnapping, rape, murder, and forgot all about blackmail. Don't you just hate that?"

"We're not paying," said Jupe.

"Oh hell, we don't want your money! We want you gone. Out of our lives. What do you think? You want us to make you famous, or you want to get the hell out and never come back?"

Ted and Jupe tried to brazen it out, but Holly kept scrolling through the pictures. Deflated, they could see horrible things in their future. Also, they were having a tough time looking at each other. Fuck! Their heads had been in each other's crotches, their dicks in places they never should've been. Manly friendship might not survive that kind of humiliation.

"Okay, you win."

"You'll disappear? Never contact Rick again, never bother any of us, ever?"

"Okay, and you won't post the pictures?"

"Nope."

"There's one more thing," said Tommy. "You know I'm a hacker. I will check the websites and if I hear of you guys chasing any ex-wives ever again, I will upload those photos and make them go viral. Is that clear?"

Ted and Jupe nodded.

"Okay, here's the deal. The Hummer is out front. We hid a tracking device in it. We're going to keep your weapons but we want you gone. As long as you keep driving away from us, you are safe. If we see you turn back, those videos are going online. Got it?"

"We got it," said Ted sullenly.

"Better tell them about the other thing," said Carlos.

"What other thing?" said Jupe.

"Yeah, what other thing?" said Tommy.

"Rick isn't the only one who can hire people. I ran a gun store for twenty-three years and I met a lot of ex-military guys—Navy SEALs, Marines, Special Forces, CIA spooks. So Joyce and I put up a bounty on you two bastards. It's not much, but a lot of those guys are strapped for cash and we got some takers. You'll never see them coming. Let's see how you like being hunted, you fuckers. I figure if you leave now you might get a head start."

"Bullshit," said Ted, "we don't believe you"

"Good," said Carlos. "It'll make their job easier."

Ted and Jupiter considered that. Tommy and Carlos untied them and everyone covered them as they walked to the Hummer and climbed in. They drove out and headed for the highway.

"Where'd you find enough money to put a bounty on them?"

asked Tommy.

"I didn't, but they don't know that," said Carlos. "They'll be hearing bumps in the night. Where'd you find a tracking device?"

"We didn't," said Tommy, "but they don't know that. They can go crazy looking for it and in the meantime I'll be tracking their phones.

"Tommy!" said Holly, "Aren't you the sneaky devil! If I'd known that I would've never left you. What a team we could be."

"In your dreams," he said. "We don't belong together, we never did, and we never will."

"Come on, Tommy, tell us how you really feel," laughed Susan.

"I get it," said Holly, "but you're making a big mistake."

"Holly, I've watched you terrify hardened criminals. I think this is the best decision I ever made."

"I don't know about the rest of you," said Kirsten, "but all this excitement has worn me out. I'm ready for bed."

"We need another room for Holly and Susan," said Tommy.

"I could sleep with you," said Holly.

"You never quit! But that's not going to happen. Ever."

"Can't blame a girl," she said. "Okay, Susan, we've been kicked out. Let's get our own room and some beers to drown our sorrows. I just lost two gay friends and got dumped by my true love. It hasn't been a good night."

They left to rent another room.

"Tommy," said Kirsten, "I didn't realize what a chick magnet you are. That little woman traveled hundreds of miles just to be with you."

"It would be more impressive if she weren't a nut case," said Tommy.

"I've got the solution!" piped up Carlos. "We fix Holly up with Rick!"

"That is fucking brilliant," said Tommy.

They laughed and talked about how it would solve all their problems. Then Carlos went next door to Joyce and sent Jo back to bunk with Tommy and Kirsten.

"Do you think Joyce and Carlos have a thing going?" asked Kirsten.

Tommy stopped.

"I hadn't even thought of that. But they do seem happy, don't they?"

"They do. I think it would be great for both of them."

"I do too. Do you think he's too old for her?"

"Maybe, but these are hard times and it helps to have someone along for the ride. I hope they're paired up."

"Me too," said Tommy, realizing that pairing up had occurred to him too. But then he had an awful thought. Both his girlfriends had cheated on him and run off with other men. Kirsten had cheated on her husband. Some people would see a pattern there. He pushed down the thought and climbed into bed in jeans and tee shirt. Jo snuggled between them and eventually they fell asleep. It had been a long, stressful day.

They slept late and didn't leave Klamath Falls until after lunch. There was no hurry, and that evening their two-vehicle caravan was back on the road, headed north.

CHAPTER 59

Rick stopped for a bottle of Smirnoff in Bend. He'd drunk the beer and he wasn't feeling any buzz at all. The emotions were getting too much for him and liquor always helped level him out. At least that's what he told himself, but after a few more miles, drinking and driving, he was sobbing. He didn't realize he was driving way too fast and weaving all over the road. He didn't even notice when his Toyota crossed the middle line and plunged into the forest. He crashed head-on into a tree and a heavy limb burst through the windshield.

If he'd done it ten minutes later, he might've hit Jo and the Joettes in the pickup. As it was, they came upon the scene of the accident and pulled over to the shoulder, with Holly and Susan pulling in behind them. Steam poured out of the radiator, the horn was blowing, the front end was crushed against the tree and the windshield was bashed in.

"Call the cops!" yelled Tommy as he leaped from the truck and ran to the wreck with Kirsten and the others close behind. Carlos pulled out his phone and dialed 911, reporting the accident, wondering if any cops would come.

Tommy and Kirsten got there first and tried to pull open the driver's door but it was jammed. They ran around to the passenger side and got that door open. The air bags in the old car had not gone off, and the drunk had only been saved by the seat belt. His face was torn by flying glass and covered in blood. Tommy got the belt unfastened and yelled, "Should we move him?"

"I smell gas," said Joyce, "we've got to get him out. Do you smell liquor too?"

"Yeah. There's a bottle of vodka on the floor. He's a fucking drunk driver. I'm going to pull him out."

Fear gave him strength, and Tommy struggled to pull the driver across the transmission hump. Other arms reached in and helped him get the guy out. They carried him back toward the highway and laid him on the shoulder.

"Holy shit!" exclaimed Kirsten. "It's Rick."

"Your ex-husband?" asked Joyce.

"Yes. Is he alive?"

"He's breathing, but he's unconscious and I see a lot of cuts. You see any major bleeding or broken bones?"

"Not really, but I'm no medic. Any of you guys had medical experience?"

Everyone shook their heads.

"I guess we wait for the ambulance," Tommy said. "Should we hide the bottle?"

"No," said Carlos. "Don't tamper with the evidence."

"Good thinking. And they'll test his blood anyway."

They heard sirens, and for once the police and medical people answered the call. Maybe times were changing. The paramedics loaded Rick, unconscious, into the ambulance and took off with siren screaming.

The police got everyone's statements but it was obviously a single-car accident with liquor involved.

"Where did they take him?" Carlos asked the cop in charge.

"Bend. It's the closest hospital. The medics didn't find any major injuries but he's pretty banged up."

He turned to Kirsten.

"What was your ex-husband doing out here?"

"I have no idea," said Kirsten, "but he's been acting crazy for months."

"Bad divorce?"

"Yeah. And he lost his job. He was really depressed."

"We've seen a lot of that. Did he threaten you?"

Kirsten didn't want to talk about Rick hiring Ted and Jupe to kidnap her. That would get complicated.

"Yeah. I left Seattle to get away from him."

"Is this your daughter?"

Oh oh. She hoped Tommy's paperwork held up.

"No, she's Tommy's daughter. She's living with him because his ex-wife can't take care of her."

"Yeah," Holly chimed in, ever helpful, "his ex-wife is psycho."

Susan turned away, trying desperately not to laugh. Jo sidled up to Tommy and hugged him, helping him keep a straight face. The policeman looked oddly at Holly.

"Psycho?"

"She has problems," said Tommy. "She's in good hands."

The cop nodded and turned to Kirsten.

"Do you want to visit your ex-husband in the hospital?"

She looked to Tommy for help.

"We're headed that way anyway," said Tommy, "so maybe we should talk it over. We'll decide before we get to Bend."

"Okay," said the cop. "I guess we're done here. Drive carefully."

"We certainly will," said Tommy.

The police got in their patrol car and drove off. Tommy and the others got in the truck. Holly and Susan got in the SUV. They pulled onto the highway and drove slowly north.

"His ex-wife is psycho?" asked Susan, laughing.

"Serves him right, the bastard."

CHAPTER 60

Ted and Jupiter thought about going back to La Grande to lie low, but there was nothing for them there. Ted's ex-wife had his house, and Jupe had been crashing in a friend's doublewide. He didn't think his friend was eager to have him back. Also, too many people knew that's where they were from. La Grande was out.

The other problem was cash. Most of the money Rick had paid them was gone. The situation wasn't good.

"Where should we go?" asked Jupe.

"I was thinking about Seattle. I've got friends there and maybe we can hide out."

"I guess our ex-wife chasing business is out the window." said Jupe.

"I don't want those pictures getting out, and all they'd have to do is check the websites to know we're back in it. Fuck. It really was a good idea."

"I don't know," said Jupe. "I didn't like working for Rick. He's a fucking loser."

"Well, there is that. What do you think about that bounty thing? Was that guy bullshitting us?"

"I'm pretty sure of it, but it wouldn't hurt to go quiet for a while, just in case. Those military guys are lethal."

"Okay, and we should get rid of this fucking Hummer. We could do a quick sale and live off the money. Give us time to regroup."

"Works for me. I might find some motorcycle work. Lots of bikes in Seattle. Let's do it."

"Okay," said Ted. He'd grown used to Jupiter's company. The pictures had been awkward, but they'd decided they'd been drugged and anything that happened in that condition didn't count. Lord knows they weren't gay, so it was just a matter of keeping those photos off the Internet and hoping there weren't a bunch of trained killers after them.

They also spent time looking for the tracking device but couldn't find anything.

CHAPTER 61

It was Susan's turn to drive the Honda and they followed the pickup truck to Bend.

"I'm beginning to think Tommy doesn't like me anymore," said Holly.

"I'll bet what tipped you off is when he said, 'I don't like you anymore.'"

"There was that. Also, any idiot can see he's fawning all over that Kirsten chick."

"I sure don't understand that. Just because she's about a ten-plus on the babe scale."

"She is a fine-looking woman. And she seems nice too. That's not fair," said Holly.

"It sure isn't. I've been losing guys to women like that all my life. I don't think they should be allowed out in public. Maybe the Muslims have it right. Cover us all in black and let the guys play Russian roulette."

"Not sure I'd go that far."

"Me neither. I was just joking. But that Kirsten woman is really a fine hunk of femininity," said Susan.

"You're starting to sound a little gay there girl. You're not going over to the dark side are you?"

"No, I'm still looking for a guy, but these days the pickings are slim. I was even thinking Ted and Jupe didn't look all that bad."

"I got dibs on Ted."

"Too late," said Susan, "I already picked him. But Jupiter would do if you didn't mind fat bikers with bad tattoos, gunshot wounds and broken noses."

"And both of them have some character flaws."

"True. If they weren't rapists and murderers they could've been boyfriend material."

"Picky picky."

"You're right," said Susan, "I'm sure we could've reformed them."

"Dream on. I've tried that reform-the-outlaw shit and it is not the way to go. That's why I tried to get back with Tommy. I've had it with bad boys."

"You're never going to tell me what happened to your first husband are you."

"You're testing our friendship, Susan."

"Forget I asked. Just remember, if I ever get on your nerves just tell me to leave. You don't have to take drastic measures."

"As long as you don't get physically abusive, you're safe."

"Good to know. We'll be there soon."

MIKE NEUN

CHAPTER 62

Tommy drove the pickup. Joyce was busy on her laptop looking for places to live in Bend, but Kirsten had an idea.

"Did we tell you about the boathouse people?"

"No. Don't you mean 'boat people'? Have you been in contact with refugees?"

"No. Boathouse people. In Seattle, Jo introduced us to this group of older people who meet in a boathouse and we became friends. Remember us talking to Wendy? She's their leader and you'd like them. Anyway, they've been trying to get out of town and join us, but we put them off because of our troubles."

"Ah, but now we've got the problems solved."

"Yes. Tommy and Jo, what do you think, should we invite Wendy and the gang to join us in Bend?"

"Sounds great," said Tommy.

Jo nodded enthusiastically.

"Okay. So instead of renting a house, maybe we need something bigger. There are seven of them."

Carlos and Joyce looked at each other. The surprises just kept coming.

Joyce switched her search from houses to small ski lodges. She found one out toward Mount Bachelor and it was empty. Joyce sensed desperation. She called the real estate company and asked for a tour the next day.

Kirsten called Wendy.

"We've got some good news," she said. "our hijacker problems are over and Rick's in the hospital."

"Seriously? What'd you do to Rick?"

"Nothing. He was testing his drunk-driving skills and it didn't work out."

"Well too bad for him and good for you."

"Do you still want to leave Seattle?"

"We do. It's dangerous and not getting any better."

"That's too bad," said Kirsten, "How do you feel about Bend, Oregon?"

"I've got you on speaker and everyone here is nodding. We've all been there and we like it."

"Perfect. We've got a lead on a small lodge that'll hold everyone."

"That sounds perfect. But first, tell us how you dealt with the hijackers."

Kirsten told them the whole story about Ted and Jupe and could hear the others laughing as she related the gay porn video and the bounty on their heads.

"Where are those guys now?" asked Wendy.

"They headed west. I hate to say it but Tommy's tracking them and it looks like they're driving towards Seattle.

"Thanks a lot. Just what we needed. Two more gangbangers in Seattle."

"All the more reason for you to come to Bend."

"They still in the Hummer?" asked Charlie.

"Yeah. But they'll probably sell it. They don't have any money."

"They don't know anything about us do they?"

"No, we never mentioned you guys, so even if they go to Seattle they won't know about you. Now for the important question. Do any of you ski?"

Wendy looked around. The other six nodded and smiled.

"Hell," she said, "We lived our lives in Seattle so of course we ski. And it's not that fancy-pants dry snow you get in Bend. We can ski slush, rain, crust and ice. On the other hand, we're old, so maybe Bend would be a step up."

"How long will it take you to get here?"

"Probably three or four days, maybe more. We want to get a bigger vehicle so we can ride together."

"Sounds good. We'll see you here."

CHAPTER 63

Tommy spotted a Holiday Inn and they stopped at the office. They got three rooms, drove around and parked. When they brought their stuff in, Tommy realized all motel rooms were starting to look the same. Someone was making a fortune selling beige paint to motels.

At dinner that night, drinking microbrew beer and feasting on ribs at Bert's Broiler, Tommy spoke to Kirsten.

"What do you think? Do you want to go see Rick?"

"No," she said. "I can't think of anything I want to say to him."

"Maybe you could get him to quit harassing you."

"You think? I've been trying to do that for two years. Can you come up with anything that would get him off my back?"

"Not really. It's probably a lost cause."

She looked at the others.

"Do any of you have ideas?"

"We could all go with you," said Joyce. "Maybe we could intimidate him with numbers."

"If that doesn't work, we can drug him and get nasty pictures," said Holly.

"You're turning into a one-trick pony," said Susan.

"Hey, it's worked twice already. Nobody's complaining."

"How about you, Carlos? Any ideas?"

"Not really. He seems so obsessed and broken I don't know how you'd get him to change."

"We could bring in some strippers, take his mind off his troubles," said Holly, whose solution to every problem seemed to center on sex.

"I think that would last about as long as they were there. Then he'd go back to being a vengeful bastard."

Joyce spoke up.

"I had a stalker once, when I was the young queen of the skiers. He followed me around, called all the time, trolled me on Twitter. It got really old."

"What did you do?"

"I stalked him back."

They all laughed.

"Seriously. We mountain girls aren't easily intimidated. I got all my friends and we followed him around, took pictures wherever he went, called him at all hours and trolled him on Twitter and Facebook. Soon other people in town heard about it and all the ski bums joined in.

"What happened?"

"He couldn't take it. One night he slinked out of town and we never saw him again."

"Damn," said Carlos. "That has possibilities."

"It does, doesn't it?" said Kirsten. "But Rick's already at rock bottom. He could get suicidal."

"Problem solved," said Holly, always the optimist.

"I don't think I'd want that on my conscience," said Kirsten.

"You still got one of those? I traded mine in long ago for self-preservation."

"Let's keep thinking," said Kirsten. "There's no hurry. I called the hospital and a nurse told me Rick had two cracked ribs and a concussion, along with a bunch of cuts and bruises. They'll keep him there at least a week and then the cops want him for drunk driving. He could end up in jail."

"Hey," said Tommy, "that works. It's hard to stalk an ex-wife from a jail cell."

The next morning they drove out to see the lodge. It was a sprawling log structure, perfect for the mountains, with twelve units, a lobby with a stone fireplace, a rustic dining room and a well-equipped kitchen. Best of all it was just a short drive to Mount Bachelor and the real estate lady told them some of the chair lifts were open and tickets were cheap. Joyce knew all the real estate ins and outs and they rented the lodge for three months. They drove back to the Holiday Inn, packed up, checked out, and moved into their new home.

They spent time getting Carlos some ski gear, but Holly and Susan declined. They did, however, check out the bar scene and found it to their liking. Tommy and the others drove over to Mount Bachelor and it was glorious under deep blue skies. Oh sure, the locals warned them there were other days with high winds or dense fog but they didn't let that dampen their spirits. The lifts were running, lines were short, and soon they'd be up on the mountain.

CHAPTER 64

The boathouse people had a problem.

They wanted to ride together but none of their cars could hold them all. They decided to sell all three and buy something big. Even though theirs were pristine old-people cars, they didn't get much money for them. They pooled it and checked the Internet for SUVs or vans.

Charlie was the first to spot the Hummer for sale. He showed the ad to Walter.

"How about this?" he said, smiling slyly.

"Hold it. You thinking what I'm thinking?"

"Bet your ass. It sounds very, very familiar. Should we check it out?"

Ted and Jupiter had driven to Seattle and rented the cheapest mobile home they could find. It was way in the back of a ratty trailer park down by the airport and had an old blue tarp over the roof held down by tires. On those rare Seattle days when it wasn't raining, they left all the windows open but the awful smell of the previous tenant—a cat lady—lingered. On the positive side, it was set away from the other trailers and they rarely saw their neighbors.

Desperate for money, Ted immediately put the Hummer up for sale. Cheap. Anything to afford better accommodations. They were about to lower the price when two old guys answered the ad and arrived in a taxi. Ted, in jeans, work boots and a Kid Rock sweat shirt, stood out front waiting for them.

"You here about the Hummer?" he asked.

"Yes sir. Is that it?"

"Yeah. It runs good, has about 80,000 miles on it, and the tires are okay. Want to look?"

He led them to the beast-on-wheels and opened the doors. The old guys had a bit of trouble getting in. It was a high step but they made it and looked around.

"You ever drive anything like this?" asked Ted.

"I drove the real ones," said Charlie, "In Iraq. This is kind of a Hummer wannabe, doesn't even have the tire inflation set up. Out in the desert you could deflate the tires from inside the cab and get a better grip on the sand. Then you'd get back on pavement, push a button, and inflate them back up. It was a hell of a system."

"Oh man, you were over there?"

"I was. Did a couple of tours. We had had to beef up the armor ourselves. FTA."

Ted hadn't been in the army, but he quickly figured out the initials.

"So you can drive this?"

"Oh hell yes. I just hope it doesn't bring back memories."

"Want to take a test drive?"

"Sure."

Ted climbed into the back seat and Charlie eased out of the trailer park. Obviously he knew his way around the

MIKE NEUN

big SUV and after a few blocks he said, "It seems okay. You still asking the same price?"

"I'm willing to talk."

"I bet you are. Gas is expensive and these things gobble it up."

He drove back to the trailer park and checked the engine, tires, the electronics, and had Ted drive it a few yards away so he could eyeball the alignment. Then he made an offer. Ted countered and soon they agreed on a number. It far less than it would've been before the financial crash, but it was the best Ted was going to get.

They were about to settle up when Jupiter came limping out of the mobile home scratching and yawning. He still had bandages on his nose and ear. Ted introduced them.

"This is Jupiter," he said.

"I can see where you got the name," said Walter.

"Yeah. I've always been a big guy. Hope you like the Hummer."

"I hope so too," said Charlie.

They signed the papers, Charlie paid, and the two old guys drove away.

"I'm happy to see it go," Jupiter said. "That damn thing was cursed."

"It sure was. I hope that paperwork holds up."

A block away, Charlie stopped the Hummer.

"Walter," he said, "what do you think?"

"I think we found the sons of bitches who shot at our friends and kidnapped them."

"I'm sure of it. This is the only Hummer for sale in three states and how many huge guys named Jupiter are walking around with broken noses?"

"What should we do?"

"Kirsten and Tommy think they've got them neutralized, but I don't think a bunch of gay porn and an empty threat is going to keep those guys down. They've got that thug mentality and sooner or later they're going to kill someone."

"They're dangerous," agreed Walter.

"Unless we stop them," said Charlie.

"Us? Two geezers?"

"I know. Crazy idea."

"Call the police?"

"What would we say? 'These guys assaulted our friends and we want you to arrest them?' I don't see that working out."

"No, maybe not."

"Guess it's up to us."

"In the movies," said Walter, laughing, "we'd go in full frontal and take them out in hand-to-hand combat."

"Two sixty-five-year-old vigilantes beat the shit out of of big, young thugs. I don't think that scene computes."

"You killed people in your time," said Walter soberly.

"Yeah, in war. How about you? Were you ever in the military?"

"Nope. Worked forty years at Albertson's, did all my fighting with food suppliers. It was brutal."

Charlie laughed.

"What can we do?" asked Walter.

"I guess we take them out, but we probably shouldn't tell the others."

"How? Guns? Explosives?"

"I'm thinking beer."

CHAPTER 65

Ted and Jupe were surprised a few hours later when the Hummer drove back up the dirt driveway and the two old guys got out carrying six packs.

"Hi boys," said Charlie.

"Everything okay?" asked Ted

"Better than okay. This Hummer is just fine. We went on a beer run and thought we'd come by and thank you. I don't suppose you guys drink Heinekens do you?"

"We've been known to tip a few," said Jupe, smiling, "and it is cocktail hour."

"Well, we've got some cold ones and we're willing to share."

"Sounds good," said Ted.

They sat on logs outside the rusted mobile home and Walter opened four beers and passed them out. The sun was setting and it was a nice time of the evening.

"Tell us about Iraq," said Ted.

"Not much to tell," said Charlie. "It was hotter than hell, it was an awful war and we lost a lot of good people."

"That sucks."

"Yes it does."

"What kind of unit were you in?" asked Jupe.

"Well, it was kind of a Special Ops thing. We worked behind enemy lines. I'd tell you about it, but then I'd have to kill you," Charlie smiled.

Ted and Jupe chuckled and swallowed more beer.

"Seriously?" asked Jupe. "You were like Special Forces?"

"Yeah, but our group didn't have a name." said Charlie. "It was top secret stuff."

"Awesome."

"Yeah. There were some murderous bastards over there and sometimes we used devious means to take them out. War can get really ugly."

"Wow," said Jupe, "I bet you've got some wild stories."

"Maybe. You wouldn't believe the crazy shit that went on over there."

"You sure you can't tell us a story or two?"

"I don't know," Charlie said, "Maybe I can tell a little bit."

"Really? Isn't it still top secret?" asked Ted.

"Yeah, it is. And it's going to stay top secret."

"Damn right. You can trust us."

"I don't have to. You're never going to tell anyone."

"How do you know?"

"I know because in five minutes you're going to be dead."

It took a few seconds for that to register. Then Ted spoke up.

"Dream on, old man. We can take you two apart in about thirty seconds."

"You sure about that? You don't look too good."

Ted and Jupe were growing pale, with beads of sweat on their foreheads. Jupe tried to stand up, but couldn't.

He was cramping up and suddenly in terrible pain.

Shocked, he said, "What the hell?"

"What'd you do?" snarled Ted, feeling the same agony rip through his body.

"Something our friends couldn't do because they're nice people. I admire that. I hope they take over the world from all of the assholes we have now. In the meantime, we not-so-nice people have got to have their backs."

"Who the hell are you?"

"Just a guy. We were all just guys and they turned us into stone-cold killers. I lost a lot of my humanity. You did too, but you just did it out of meanness. It's like gunslingers. You're always going to find someone faster, colder, more ruthless, and that's what's happening here. You guys are pissant thugs, I'm an old pro. Welcome to the big leagues."

Ted tried again to rise, but the pain was too great. Jupe toppled off his log onto the ground, hugging himself and moaning.

"We worked behind enemy lines," continued Charlie calmly, "and we couldn't use all that bang-bang stuff. No grenades, automatic weapons, none of that shit. So I got pretty good with knives, poisons, traps of different kinds."

Ted rolled to the ground, his face contorted in pain.

"You doing this for the bounty?" he managed to ask.

"Nope. I'm doing this because it needs to be done. You never should've shot at our friends, or kidnapped them, or threatened rape and murder. It just pisses people off. I know it pissed me off and I know you're going to hurt someone else down the line unless you're stopped. The good news is that thallium is perfect for this sort of thing. It's colorless, odorless, and goes well with beer.

'Death in a Bottle' we used to call it. We took out some really bad people with thallium and I just gave you guys a massive dose."

Ted and Jupe lay there writhing in pain.

"You killed us," moaned Jupe.

"Yeah, I guess we did. Isn't that a bitch? Can't even yell, can you? And you know what? You guys thought you were scary bastards but I've seen a lot worse. This is more like pest removal."

It wasn't a pretty sight. The two big men spasmed a few more moments, then grew quiet. Charlie and Walter sat and stared.

"Fuck me," whispered Walter. "They're dead, aren't they?"

"Yep. Problem solved."

Charlie and Walter emptied the rest of the beer bottles, rinsed out the poisoned ones, wiped them down for prints, and spread them around on the ground. It was dark now and it would probably be a day or two before neighbors figured out Ted and Jupe weren't just passed out in front of their trailer.

"While we're here we better get that bill-of-sale for the Hummer," said Charlie. "It's got our names on it."

"And they won't be needing the money," said Walter.

"It'd be a shame to leave it," said Charlie.

They found the papers and money in the old trailer and then Charlie and Walter got back in the Hummer and drove away.

"You okay?" asked Charlie.

"I think I'm going to throw up," said Walter.

"Wait a couple of minutes. We want to get out of the neighborhood."

Walter opened the window and breathed deeply.

"That helps. I might be okay now. I was terrified I was going to get the bottles mixed up."

"So was I. Welcome to black ops."

"Fuck. That was the scariest thing I've ever done."

"We will never, ever, talk about this again, okay?"

"Fine with me. I don't see it coming up in conversation. Do you have nightmares?"

"All the time. If you get them, call me and I'll bring over some beer."

Walter blanched.

"Fuck me. I'll never drink beer again. Better make it scotch, lots of scotch."

CHAPTER 66

The next morning the boathouse people packed up, climbed—some with extra effort—into the Hummer, and drove out of Seattle. "Hotel California" played on the stereo. Rock and roll!

Wendy called Kirsten.

"We're on our way," she said. "We just left Seattle."

"Happy trails. We'll see you here."

They hung up and Kirsten turned to the others.

"I just had a great thought," she said.

"Let's hear it," said Tommy.

"Okay," she said, "Seven older people are going to drive from Seattle to Bend on highways that could be dangerous."

"Yes."

"Remember those cops in Yakima? Could we pay them to give Wendy and the gang a police escort?"

"Damn, that is fucking brilliant!"

"I accept your adulation, but I think you should make the call."

Tommy called the Yakima number.

"Hello?" said Chuck.

"Hi Chuck, this is Tommy, the guy you escorted out of Yakima. Remember me?"

"Sure. Did you make it to Idaho?"

"It's a long story but tell me, are you and Roy still strapped for cash?"

"We sure are. Our families are just hanging on."

"Would you like a job? Maybe two days of escorting some people from Seattle to Bend?"

"Oh hell yes! You'll pay us?"

"For sure. Payment on delivery. How much do you want?"

Chuck thought about it, and named a price.

"I was thinking more," said Tommy. "They're old and there'll be a lot of rest stops."

"You are a lifesaver, man. God bless you."

"I'll tell them you're coming."

"Okay. We're on our way."

Kirsten called Wendy back.

"Wendy? This is Kirsten. We've got a present for you."

"What's that?"

"You know the highways can be dangerous, don't you?"

"Yes, we've been worried about that."

"Well, we met a couple of Yakima cops on our trip out of Seattle and they're going to escort you to Bend."

"That is wonderful!" exclaimed Wendy, but then she paused.

"They're not doing it out of the goodness of their hearts are they?"

"No, but Tommy is going to pay for it."

"Not a chance. We'll take care of it."

"We could split it."

"Not on your life. It's worth every penny to us and we can't thank you enough."

"Here's the number. His name is Chuck and you can arrange where to meet. By the way, Jo says hi and can't wait for you to get here."

"Tell her we love her and we're on our way. Bye bye."

Wendy turned to the others in the Hummer and told them about the police escort. Walter looked at Charlie and smiled, knowing the most dangerous man in the state was probably inside the vehicle.

CHAPTER 67

The next day Wendy called and said they should be there late that afternoon. Kirsten gave her directions to the lodge, and realized they would soon have fourteen people.

"Damn," she said, "I think Jo has started a cult."

Tommy spent the day catching up on work. Jo played video games, Holly and Susan went shopping. Neither of them had any interest in skiing, and deep down Tommy hoped they'd get bored and move on. The others felt the same. They all projected bad vibes and Holly remained blissfully unaware.

At five p.m. they heard a shout from the front window. Joyce was pointing down the road. They rushed to the window and saw the goddam black Hummer chugging up the driveway. They rushed to get their weapons and by the time the Hummer pulled to a stop they were on the porch, fully armed.

"Don't shoot!" yelled Wendy. "We come in peace."

The passenger door opened and she stepped out.

"Holy shit!" exclaimed Kirsten. "Where'd you get that thing?"

"Put down those guns!" Wendy said. "You're scaring the hell out of our friends."

Sheepishly, they put down their guns. Jo ran to Wendy and gave her a big hug. The others got out tentatively and again Kirsten repeated, "Where'd you get that Hummer?"

"We bought it," said Walter, smiling innocently. "Got a hell of a deal too. Why? Do you have a fear of Hummers?"

"Hell yes," said Tommy. "I still have nightmares."

"We should've warned you," said Charlie. "After you told us about your adventures we realized a Hummer would be the perfect vehicle for our trip."

"You didn't get it from two guys named Ted and Jupe, did you?"

"No way," he said, "That would be stupid, dealing with dangerous criminals like that. We bought it from a little old lady in Bellevue. She just drove it to the store for beer."

Walter turned pale at the mention of beer.

"Where's your police escort?" asked Kirsten.

"They're coming. They stopped to get gas for the trip back."

As everyone introduced themselves, the two cops drove up, and Tommy took them aside.

"Did you get paid?" he asked.

"Oh yes, with a nice tip. Thank you for lining up the job."

"I'm glad it worked out. If you guys ever want to bring your families to Bend we've got extra rooms."

"That's great, Tommy, and we may take you up on it."

The policemen drove out early the next morning. Everyone skied that day except Holly and Susan, who again went shopping.

That night at dinner, Kirsten spoke up.

"I think I should go visit Rick. Give it one last try to calm him down."

"I'd say the odds against that are about a gazillion to one," said Tommy.

"I know, but I have to try."

The others held a council of war and came up with a better plan.

The hospital wasn't used to fourteen people visiting one patient, but Kirsten asked very nicely and explained some of the older people were Rick's relatives. A nurse led them to his room and they filed in with Kirsten leading the way. He frowned when he saw her and that turned to bewilderment when the room filled with people.

Rick had one wrist handcuffed to the bed.

"Hi, Rick," said Kirsten. "The nurses say you're feeling better."

"I'd feel a lot better if we could talk alone."

"That's not going to happen. These are my friends and they want to talk to you."

"Hi Rick," said Tommy. "You still in pain?"

"Mostly my ribs. They hurt when I laugh."

"That won't be a problem. Are you still mad at Kirsten?"

"Yeah, I am. My life is shit and it's all her fault."

"Are you still out to get her?"

"You bet your ass. As soon as I get out of here I'm will make her pay."

"That's too bad. I was hoping you'd wised up. In that case, everyone here has something to say to you. I'll start. If anything happens to Kirsten, ever, I'm coming for you."

"Big deal. I can whip your ass."

"Maybe, but I'm not the guy you knew in Seattle. I will surprise you, and that's a promise."

Rick was unimpressed.

Carlos stepped up next.

"Hi Rick. I own a gun store and firing range and I have access to over two hundred weapons. Do not mess with our friend."

Rick didn't have much to say to that.

They went down the line. Fourteen people, all swearing to protect Kirsten and do him in if anything happened to her. Charlie, at sixty-five years old, was especially impressive.

"Son," he said, "I served two tours in Iraq and one in Afghanistan. I've seen stuff you've never dreamed of. Nightmare stuff. And if you do anything to Kirsten, you'll never see me coming. Now look me in the eye."

Rick did.

"Do you believe me?"

"Yes."

Then he leaned over and whispered in Rick's ear.

"Ted and Jupiter are dead. Murdered. I watched them die and it wasn't pretty. Don't ever fuck with us again."

Rick paled. Stunned. Then he looked up but the old man was gone.

The next couple of people were a blur, but even some of the old ladies were scary.

"Son," said Wendy. "I am too old to care. Jail doesn't scare me and nobody notices an old woman. If you hurt Kirsten, I will come at you out of nowhere. You can take that to the bank."

Holly was scary too.

MIKE NEUN

"Hi, Rick," she smiled. Then she got close to his ear and whispered, "I look harmless but I'm not. I'd ask my first husband to back that up, but the police can't find him. He was an abusive, mean son of a bitch, and one day he just vanished. I did that. I made him disappear and I can do you too. If you don't believe me, Google 'Holly Carlson, Reno'. Read it and weep. Don't even think of fucking with Kirsten."

Rick blanched. Who were these people?

Last was Jo. She handed him a note. He opened the note.

"I'm just a little girl, but I lived years on the streets and I'm sneaky and fearless. Remember those holes in your pants? Next time I will shoot higher. That's a promise. Never, ever mess with Kirsten again."

She took back the note and walked out. Just like that, they were gone.

Later on, Tommy asked Kirsten about the note.

"Is there something I don't know? Did Jo learn how to write?"

"No, I wrote it for her. I tried to make it look like a child's handwriting."

"How'd you know what to say?"

"I just made stuff up until we thought it was really scary."

"I wouldn't want to cross Jo. I'm glad she's on our side."

"Me too."

CHAPTER 68

Rick lay there in stunned silence. He'd just been threatened by fourteen people, some of whom were insanely scary bastards. He lay awake that night, re-thinking his choices. He decided he didn't need revenge after all. He decided to get as far away from these people as he could.

In their room that same night, Holly and Susan were making decisions too.

"I don't like snow and I don't like being cold," said Holly.

"Same here," said Susan. "I want to be somewhere with bikinis and sun lotion. I don't like pickup trucks and gun racks. Oregon sucks."

"So we agree. Let's blow this pop stand."

"Absolutely."

"One other thing," said Holly. "What did you think of Rick?"

"I thought he cleaned up okay. Once those cuts heal, you dress him up, keep him sober, and he'd be a minor stud. He's no Matt Damon, but he beats the shit out of most of the guys I saw in Vegas."

"Same here. Are you thinking what I'm thinking?"

"Boy toy?"

"Definite boy toy. We could have some fun with that dude. How do you feel about threesomes?"

"To tell the truth, I've always wondered about that. Have you tried them?"

"Sister, I tried things you've never dreamed of," said Holly.

"Well, I'm happy to give it a shot. How long do you think it'll take us to wear him down to a quivering mass of protoplasm?"

"I'm thinking he'll be begging for mercy in two or three days, but we can let him rest up and go again."

"Boy toy," said Susan. "You think he'll go for it?"

"I'm guessing we could get him to levitate off that hospital bed if we do it right."

"What if he turns crazy? You think we can handle that?"

"Sister, he hasn't even seen crazy. If it pulls that shit I'll show him crazy that'll give him night terrors."

"And this'll be a short-term thing?"

"Oh hell yes, just for the trip. We'll dump his ass as soon as we get where we're going. Use him and lose him I say."

"You know, he must have some money if he was paying Ted and Jupe."

"Susan! You have a nasty mind! Are you saying we should use Rick as a sex toy and then rip him off? Leave him in a strange town with no money or I.D. just because his hit men did that to me? Just because he's a raving lunatic son of a bitch who tried to fuck up our friends?"

"It'll look good in our Cosmo feature. 'Feminist Home Invader Gay Porn Producers Destroy Crazed Ex-Husband.'"

"I wish I were gay. You'd be the girl of my dreams."

"One last thing," said Susan. "Are you sure you're over Tommy?"

"Yeah. I'm sure. And I'm sure I hate tall, drop-dead gorgeous women. They really fuck up romance for the rest of us."

"But we've found the cure for that, right?"

"Right. Boy toy."

CHAPTER 69

The next morning the gang went skiing. Susan and Holly said they were going to do more shopping. In a way, they were going shopping.

They waited for the others to leave, then loaded their stuff into the Honda and drove to the hospital. At the front desk, they asked the nurse how Rick was doing. She said if it weren't for the police they could release him but he would need a few more days in bed. Holly and Susan looked at each other. That could be arranged.

"It's a shame he's in trouble," said Holly. "We've known him for years and he's always been such a nice guy."

"Really?" said the nurse.

"Oh yes, but the divorce just blindsided him. I've never seen him drink like that. All the people in church were shocked."

"Church?"

"Oh yes, Rick was an usher. Never missed a Sunday."

Holly thought that was laying it on a bit thick, but the nurse seemed to be buying it.

"Do you think he'll go to jail?" asked Holly.

"Maybe."

"Well darn it. I wish we could just make this all disappear. What would happen if he sort of escaped?"

"I don't know. The police are understaffed and there's so much crime out there. I doubt if they have the manpower to chase a drunk driver who banged into a tree."

"He's such a good guy," said Holly. "Do you suppose you could take a break in about fifteen minutes? Maybe a long one in the lunch room?"

"I am kind of hungry," she said.

"We'll be real quiet, and when you get back, can you act surprised and wait as long as you can before you call the cops?

"I can do that. But I've got a little girl at home and we're really hurting. You don't suppose you could help out a single mother, could you?"

Ah, a woman after her own heart. Holly smiled.

"We could do that."

"Oh wait, he's handcuffed to the bed!"

"I'm sure we'll think of something."

Holly slipped the nurse a hundred bucks and they walked to Rick's room. He was surprised to see them.

"What are you two doing here?" he asked. "More threats?"

"We're here to make you an offer you can't refuse," said Holly. "How do you feel about threesomes?"

Rick laughed. "This is a gag isn't it? Kirsten put you up to it?"

"Nope. We're headed to someplace warm and we haven't had sex in months. Do you think you can handle two women?"

"This is a prank. I know it is." He called out, "Kirsten,

MIKE NEUN

you can come out now!"

Nobody came out.

"They're all skiing," said Susan. "Maybe we need to prove we're serious."

With that, they both lifted their sweaters and laughing, flashed their boobs.

Rick sat up, groaned and clutched his ribs with one hand, the other one clanked on the handcuffs.

"I'm all yours, ladies, but as you can see there's a problem."

Holly reached into her backpack for her lock picks.

"Handcuffs are easy," she said, and three minutes later he was free and seated in a wheel chair being pushed out the front door. They helped him, groaning, into the SUV and drove out of the parking lot.

"Where are we headed?" he asked.

"South," said Susan. "Someplace warm with a casino and a pool, but not Las Vegas."

"What do you do?"

"I'm a dealer."

"Can you teach me?"

"My boy," said Holly, "you won't believe the things we're going to teach you."

They laughed and headed south on US 97.

The nurse gave them plenty of time, then called the police. It took them a half hour to get there and they didn't seem too upset. Drunk driving had become the national sport.

CHAPTER 70

After skiing, everyone drove back to the lodge and noticed Holly and Susan hadn't returned. Oh well, they might've found a bar in town.

"I'm going to check on Rick," said Kirsten. "I'll be happier when he's out of that hospital and either in jail or out of town. But I don't know how he'll get anywhere without a car."

She called the hospital and as she talked to the receptionist she started smiling, then laughing.

"What?" said Tommy. "What'd they tell you?"

"Apparently two women in a red Honda SUV came and broke Rick out of the hospital. They told the nurse they were headed someplace warm and sunny. As they drove away, one of the women waved a bra out the window. They all seemed very happy."

"I never thought I could feel sorry for Rick," said Tommy, "but I think he just stepped down the rabbit hole."

"I thought he'd gone psycho but he's just a rookie compared to Holly," said Kirsten. "Poor Rick."

"Did you actually say that? Poor Rick?"

"Okay!" said Charlie, lifting his beer, "A toast! To stalkers!"

"To stalkers!" everyone cheered, and they drank.

That night, as Tommy and Kirsten lay in bed with Jo, Kirsten asked, "Why have you never put a move on me?"

"Because computer geeks don't put moves on women. Hell, we don't even have moves."

"Are you afraid?"

"Of course. I could give lectures on rejection, I'm not into psychic pain and I've been dumped twice."

"What if I put a move on you?"

"I'd assume I was already asleep and dreaming."

"Jo, would you mind if I kissed Tommy?"

Jo smiled happily and gave her a thumbs up. Kirsten climbed over and kissed him. It wasn't the most graceful kiss in the world, but it rocked Tommy. He wrapped his arms around her and she folded her body into his. Then they felt a weight and realized Jo was on top of them. It was a group hug, maybe the greatest of all.

Holly had a threesome, he had a threesome, and deep in his heart he knew his was better.

The end.

EPILOGUE

There's an Indian casino outside of San Diego that reopened with little fanfare after the third wave. If you go to the pool, you're likely to see two women in bikinis happily sipping fruity cocktails with little umbrellas. The staff likes the ladies because they tip big and laugh a lot. It's common knowledge that one of them is a card counter but the pit bosses let it slide because the two of them are very good at attracting high rollers. They party hard. The tables do well. The high rollers tip well. Everybody wins.

Five miles away, in San Diego's old dockyard slums, you might come upon a wild-eyed homeless man with long, matted hair, broken and blackened teeth, layers of stinking clothes, and brain cells destroyed by cheap wine. Sometimes, as he staggers through the alleys, he thinks back on the women in his life and his face contorts in drunken anger.

"Bitches," Crazy Rick mumbles, "all of them bitches. Take them down....."

Made in the USA
Coppell, TX
13 May 2021